PRINTED IN THE UNITED STATES OF AMERICA

Publisher, OSAAT Entertainment

Reprint 2nd Edition Copyright ©2023. Fiction
First Print, Published ©2012

Contact the Author Visit: oebooks.blogspot.com
Email: rycjoebooks@gmail.com

Copyright ©2023 RYCJ, Lock Box.
Cover Design & Layout by Rhonda Y.C. Johnson

Library of Congress Control Number: 2023922413

ISBN: 978-1-940994-24-6

Printed in the United States of America

Paranormal Mystery

Part One

1

When the nurse looked down at us and offered what on first glimpse appeared to be a paranormal apparition, we honestly thought these people were playing a twisted sick joke on us.

"I'm sorry Mr. and Mrs. Cummins, but that is your baby daughter and you cannot leave her here. You will be leaving this hospital with her!"

I didn't even have to look down at Tigga, who happened to be my darling wife of a few years. We met at a beauty pageant. She was one of the contestants. A contestant who won, let's just squeeze in here. She was crowned *the* Most Beautiful Sex Goddess on Mother Earth. That's right. I married the prettiest woman on God's natural green earth. Long shapely legs, nice round soft toned behind, hourglass waistline, swan neck, and strawberry lips …I… Curtis T. Cummins, married the woman in every man's dream. This woman had a face that melted all the scantrons trying to vote for other contestants. I know. I saw it with my own two eyes, as I slid my ballot in her box and flicked my bic setting the other boxes on fire. Wasn't much of a contest after that. Tigga won fair and square.

So, she owed me one…and ultimately paid me well when I offered her my hand. I carried her over a threshold, into our beautiful new home, and nicknamed her Princess right away. She didn't care for the nickname, and really, after we got to know each other a little better, I didn't care for the name as much either. She fit the abrasive nickname her parents called her—Tigga. What an ugly name.

Didn't stop me from taking my new trophy any-where jealousy was in high abundance though, just to tick people off, and make myself that much bigger.

Back East, out West, down South, and so many trips up North our weekend getaways often included rounds to the moon. Yes, we were some luxury travelers back then. We hit that moon each and every weekend. So many times that...well...that well this happened.

Still, I wanted to shake green snot out of that nurse's stodgy nasally nauseating tone, and just may have had not my lovely Tigga been lying in bed, million dollar hair-do flowing over both sides of the pillow—*it's really how much it did cost to sew Indonesia thoroughbred hair into her head*—with her eyes rolled back, and violently shaking and screaming, "Oh God No! Oh God No! It can't be. It's no way that could have come out of me! I wasn't fucking pregnant!"

My wife was really frazzled, as you might under-stand. She was under the impression that a woman, and a man, had to have a conscience meeting of the minds to get pregnant. I know this doesn't sound right, but this was a new day we were in, where literature on matters like this wasn't as wide spread like the olden days in the 2000s. Most couples went to *the banks* when they wanted to con-ceive. That's what I mean by a conscience meeting of the minds. The couple would talk about it, agree upon it, and then find a bank that collected the best specimens. It used to cost up in the ten's of thousands of dollars for this pro-cedure, but not no more. Now people could get shot up with that baby juice for free. In fact, there was a big scare going around for a while. Because not many were inter-ested in dealing with them little creatures; changing BA-hinds that weren't self-cleaning or self-fed and whatnot... that baby banks almost closed down and went into extinc-tion. Except some wise-ass got the bright idea to inject people in hospitals with this stuff. Yeah, it was really scary there for a while. People were afraid to get sick and go to the hospital. No one wanted to return home with the accidental injection in them and have to deal with that accident for 20-years to life.

So this was why we were legitimately confused about this pregnancy. At the very least there should have been at least a few months gestation; you know...a swelling of the abdomen, something that would warn us she was knocked up. We were in total shock about this situation...rushing to the hospital for what we expected to be and in and out outpatient visit, to end up having to check in. We would've never guessed all those blasts to the moon could've landed her in this provocative position—poor wailing Tigga spread eagle and feet strapped in stirrups—without prior notice.

Yeah, Tigga looked a darling mess. I honestly didn't want to claim her either. Truth be told, I really wanted to collect my coat and hat and be gone from the entire ordeal. After all, I had my meal. In fact, the very next week I was scheduled to judge another beauty pageant—the hottest of pageants of all the pageants ever held...one that no judge like myself wanted to miss—Most Beautiful Fuck Goddess of All Mother Earth.

And excuse the slanderous term *fuck*. Honest to God I didn't pick it. Someone else did. And yeah, I agree. These panels had gotten way out of hand, but it wasn't up to me to change the times. This was just how it was. If people were more consumed with the exterior and posterior of matters, and all things that brought immediate gratification, such as the way one looked, and *fucked*, then who was I to complain?

Over and over, and very repeatedly it was explained how no one gives a *flem-flam bim-bam fuck about tomorrow. It's all about today, right now*, which Tigga knocked up and laying up the way she was, and me still being the filthy rich handsome stud I was, I had every intention of throwing her out with last pageant's scud-duds. I wanted me another one of them hot *fucking* thoroughbreds.

Except I did the unmanly thing no man or woman were doing in this time. I kicked the masculine trait and brought Tigga and this holy catastrophe home.

I laid our little screw up on the bed and unwrapped it out of all the hospital bedding, gauze, curtains, towels, shams, and pillowcases I tried concealing her in, and had a good look at our misdeed gone horribly wrong.

Man this kid was super ugly, but I asked Tigga anyways, wondering when she would finally get around to inspecting our moon-work, "So, whadda ya' think, darling?"

Tigga was still in no shape to speak. She had shut down after the child came out, refusing to look. Already she had her *'Young Forever'* glamour magazine out and open, blocking my view of her rapidly deteriorating face.

Trying to lighten the mood I asked, "you think if I had hooked it a bit to the left, maybe she'd have one less eye?"

"One less eye!?!" Tigga yelped, hurling the *'Young Forever'* glamour magazine she'd been reading across the room. Leaving the chair she was lounged in she rushed over to the bed to see what I was seeing.

"Let me see what in the hell you done F'd up now," she fumed. I guess she didn't believe me. Our brand new ostensibly awry deed actually had two ears, one nose, no mouth, and three eyes.

"Lord have mercy! I'm suing the fucking hospital," Tigga swore to after examining this otherwise perfectly still child. "Ain't no way they're getting away with this shit. I bet them damn clamps they pulled it out with done this!"

"But Tigga, honey, sweetie pie, baby doll," I said, trying all the lines that went over well when we were making them lavish trips over and beyond the moon. "I'm sure the hospital did the best they could," I wimpishly added. "Maybe if you hadn't been cursed with so much beauty, hording it all for yourself, you could've spread a little of your innerlings and perhaps shared your beauty."

—BAP! Tigga bapped the rectitude out of me.

"How dare you accuse me of having anything to do with creating that...that...ugh!"

Tigga couldn't even think of a name to call our little monster, and it wasn't solely because her lips were pinched so tight her mouth looked tangled up behind barbed wire. She had been doing all right getting out the first part of what she had to say. It was that earthquake her face was experiencing that kept her from being able to give our little three-eyed monster an uglier name. Honest to goodness I thought Tigga was going to soon start exhaling fire. She was already exhaling spit that touched my skin like nails.

"Curtis T. Cummins, you know damn good and Frankenstein well that spreading my innerlings had nothing to do with whatever that is lying there! That thing came from somewhere else, and you of all evils have the nerve to blame me when you were the one who let that witch doctor put that thing on us!"

I moved my face away from Tigga to deflect them nails pinging me. Them pointy tacks hurt. Had I known she was this sensitive about her beauty being called into question, and had breath sharp as nails, I would've bic'd her ballot box first. Come to think on it, she really wasn't all that anyway. At least not up against all the other beauties I could've selected from. Plus, I hated her retooling my name like that, dragging it out like scraping mud off her tongue.

But I couldn't think of nothing else to say. The ugly deed had been done. I had no choice but to see this thing through. Yes, I was that curious. Like the boy child who wants to see what happens when he pulls a skunk's tail, or sticks a rod in a cat's rear, or as in this case, I wanted to see a monster grow, especially since this thing was mentioned to have been made by my sperm.

It's something like sitting in a theatre, watching a real scary movie, not that I was frightened of much, unless you count my nagging worry about what Tigga might do to our little monster, or me, but I, like a boy, wanted to see what would happen. And not what that vengeful woman I married might make happen, but I guess what I'm getting at here is, I wanted to see what this thing we created would do to Tigga, who I started depreciating from the day we married. She was a vengeful soul I wanted to see bent, and this thing I was sure could do it. Yeah some things about women never change.

A few days later Tigga came up on a plan. *See, I knew she would.* "Damn! I think I've got it," she said springing up in bed early one morning. "I'll give her a makeover," was the answer she found to solve the riddle.

In less time than it took to bat an eye she had run over to her dresser, yanked open the top drawer and grabbed a handful of bedspread size colorful scarves. In the next blink she had out her sewing kit and had licked the tip of a thread, fed it through the eye of a needle, and got to angrily sewing more scarves together.

I watched her arms going, up and down, back and forth, but couldn't see around her, to see what she was doing to our little three-eyed monster.

"Umm hmm...umm hmm," Tigga hummed, looking from my vantage point like she was kneading dough. The whole time she worked the child made not a sound. Off course too, it probably was because the child had no mouth, which reminds me, I haven't the faintest idea how the child ate, or what all might've been in that one diaper she left out of the hospital wrapped in. I never saw Tigga go near the child the entire three days she laid in that baby bed. And I know I never went near to the basinet. I hated even peeking over there. The first, and the last time I did, the child was staring straight up at the ceiling, looking out of all three eyes. It was super surreal.

"Now how's that," I heard Tigga sigh at last, standing back, proud of her designer handiwork.

I peeked down at the child lying in the basinet, almost too afraid to look long, and thought about all the refund policies I had come across over the years. Really. That's what came to mind; and stayed there. I wanted so badly to return this child. What kind of life could she possibly have? Even if we loved her with everything we had, the world was a cold cruel place. People can sigh all they want about what I was thinking, but listen to the sighs when this child grows up and asks one of them for a job, or a date, or when she merely walks up and asks anyone anything. That's right. Let a three-eyed person walk up to you and then just listen at your sigh.

"She looks wonderful," I told Tigga. Like what else could I say? Tigga had moved her arms in that frantic pace for a long time. She would've hemmed me up too had I answered any other way. Plus Tigga did know all about fixing up a look. Her talent stemmed from her pageant work; her winning my affections being proof of her dramatic skills. Anyone can attest to this, even doctors who had her pinned in them stirrups, *foot to ass*, pulling our monster out.

This wasn't what Tigga looked like when we first walked in. When we first got to the hospital all of them doctors and nurses dropped their stethoscopes and charts to admire the most beautiful woman of Mother Earth waltzing into their facility. I may have not mentioned this before, but Tigga was some kind of popular. Everyone knew who she was and came to her side the moment they saw her doubled over in pain. No one, to include either of us, knew why she was in this demonic pain, and consequently wanted to do all in our power to rid her of it. Naturally we assumed her illness had to do with a beauty flu, something only really beautiful girls get. But then her stomach got to swelling some kind of awfully grotesque huge, and the next thing we knew, doctors were pulling *that thing* out.

At any rate I started to add, 'just like you, honey,' to let Tigga know she'd done a wonderful job disguising all that was wrong with the kid, but decided to leave that part out. Had I added that ending it likely would've been my most famous last words. That child looked nothing like neither one of us, and we by the third day looked pretty damn unpalatable.

From the brief glimpse I'd gotten, after Tigga's beauty work, I couldn't see nothing but an itty-bitty nose. Tigga had wrapped the child so well I got to thinking how we might be able to pass her off to our parents, or some-one in the family, or anyone actually, as a Christmas pres-ent. That's how good Tigga was; and how cute she had our little monster looking, dolled up in the Elfin Santa hat and gear, with the colorful scarves wrapped around her neck so many times that nothing but her nose showed.

Tigga had just turned, putting away her sewing kit, when I thought I caught something move out the corner of my eye; the left eye... my weakest eye. The one I don't see as well out of as my right eye. I was about to move closer, using my right eye this time to see better, when Tigga sud-denly flew around me, rushing up to the basinet.

"Who—" and Tigga quickly darted looks both ways and all around us.

I knew just what she was about to say, because I wanted to know too. *Who yanked the Christmassy hat off our little monster's head and face!?!*

Tigga stared at it, shooting an accusatory glance at me, and then back at the kid again. She repeated the sequence of looks a half dozen times, surely knowing it wasn't me. She, in fact, was closer to the basinet, than me.

Carefully this time, and I watched, Tigga replaced the hat she doctored up and put it back on the kid's head. Perhaps the kid had turned its head, or moved in some sort of way that made the hat come off. It wouldn't explain how the hat had gotten to the opposite end of the basinet, somewhere down by the child's feet, but then this was no time for playing around with second and third guesses.

Amazingly, and sure as Heaven preceded Earth, the kid reach up and yank the hat off—AGAIN! We both saw this happen... with OUR OWN eyes!

The child hadn't even learned how to sit up, much less lift her head, and yet it had the dexterity to reach up and pull that hat right off its head...and face. The hat ended up back down to where it was before. It was like Abracadabra, and that hat may as well have never been made.

"I swear Curtis B. Cummins," Tigga spat, interchanging my middle name for the times when she called me a bastard. "I'ma kill you!" she screamed. "Look at what *the fuck* you've done did!" she shouted, spewing more nails rapidly down my throat.

I'm looking around. I'd been standing in one place since I walked into the room, too damn afraid to move. "I didn't do it," I garbled in a whiny fruity voice. "How could I have done it standing way over here!?!"

"I'm not talking about that! I'm saying look at what you done created!"

2

Exactly 24 hours later and Tigga was on the horn talking with her long-time friend, and face-lift physician. Now when Tigga was on the horn with the woman, *and Folana was her name*, it wasn't safe to mention what I'm about to disclose here.

Back in the wise-age Tigga could have been dethroned had anyone caught wind of her relationship with Folana. Beauty-queens were supposed to be born beautiful, not turned into stark raving beauties in the way Folana made women goddesses. It was like how athletes back in the day were ripped for taking steroids.

At any rate, Folana had skills to turn ugly ducklings into Princess Diana's. All the ugly duckling needed was 1.555.2-6 million dollars to get the job done. And yeah, money wasn't what it used to be either. Counting money got lurid crazy. To calculate, most people bought these elaborate gaming apps and deposited them into their bank accounts to keep tabs on their loot, or just plain made the figures up. The only way to tell the difference between the stanking filthy rich and the stinky well off, was by looking at who was the most skilled...you know, those who could do the things Folana could.

Point being, Folana could turn ducklings of all sorts into Gold Bars if that's who they wanted to be.

In fact, lots of people changed their identities this way, on both sides of the law too. It was a sign of the times...great times, and they all dealt with Folana to make most of this happen. The woman, if you haven't already added it up, was a NUquazillionaire. She was stanking stupid snotty filthy rich.

This was who Tigga got in touch with—good 'ole times Folana, who told her to bring the child in the next day. She typically needed a year's notice, sometimes up to a decade's notice, but for Tigga, and what she described, Folana was free the next day.

We packed the kid up, who we still hadn't named, and drove it over to Elkinsville where Folana would perform the surgery. She worked out of her home, every bit clinic legit and surgical sterile, though one could hardly tell from the outside. The building resembled a straight up residence... albeit for the filthy rich. Tall coliseum pillars, stained glass windows, gargantuan shrubbery and plants... the place looked like a haunted house...or maybe an insane asylum for the morbidly crazy. Tigga said Folana owned over a dozen of these structures.

"Baaaaa..." we heard coming from the back seat as we pulled up to Folana's morbid pad. The noise sounded like a wounded sheep, a noise we heard coming out of the child before, why neither of us bothered to look back. In just the few days this child had been home with us, we heard and saw many strange things. Both of us looked like we packed—heavily—enough baggage beneath our eyes from staying wide awake at night. Now, I'm not exactly sure why Tigga's bags were so loaded, but *I*, for damn sure, didn't want all them eyes I saw on that kid watching me while I was trying to sleep! That got creepy real quick. I hadn't gotten a straight hours' sleep since the child was born. Count it up, cause I sure did. That was about seven eyes that stayed open around the clock.

Tigga looked like she was coming up on her millennium birthday, instead of the 33 years she had thus far, *according to her story*, been alive. Bags hung so heavy beneath her eyes it looked like she had dumped a drawer full of silverware in two of her hobo bags and sewn them beneath both of her eyeballs. Looked like two floppy tits laying on her cheeks, each boob trying to ignore the other. And that wasn't all. Her hair was white as snow. And she lost nearly 20 pounds, when she didn't have 20 pounds to lose. She looked like a wilted banana trying to stand upright on banged up stilettos. I felt bad for her, and didn't even want to look in the mirror to see what I looked like. Tigga said I looked pretty bad myself, which I'm sure she was right, cause if I looked anywhere near to how I felt, then I looked like shit.

"Baaaaa..." that noise went again, just as, thank God we had arrived at Folana's morbid house-hospital.

"Cover her face," Tigga warned as I opened the back door to retrieve the child.

I hesitated outside the car for a second, something like wending up a good stream of air to stabilize my bearings. I did this every time I had to touch the child, or even get near it. Sometimes she'd haul off and hit one of us. I don't know how the child was doing it, because although we would see the arm raise, and swing, the blow actually felt like it was packing a man's punch. Thank the Lord she never hit one of us in the face or anything, but still, it was unnerving enough given how this kid *(at a few days old mind you)* had been throwing the towels and blankets Tigga started throwing over it, on the floor, and swinging at us like she was Babe Ruth trying to win a World Series ring.

And this wasn't all. Occasionally it would somehow move the basinet to the other side of the room. And Lord, if we tried to close the door, to keep *it* separated from our world while we guessed on getting ourselves out of this thing, that kid would go the *fuck off*. And I do mean go the *Fuck O-F-F*! The 'baaaaa's' would get so loud it sounded like thunder hitting the house. Once the banging got so bad that walls caved in and crumbled; namely the wall that separated our room from the kid's room. Every day I expected the house to lift up off its foundation, and maybe grow legs...and arms, and storm on down the road, mowing down anything that got in its way.

Amazingly, I since learned in those few days, the child was most calm when I wended up this air, took a deep breath, and held it gently in my arms. That's what I did getting her to the car and laying her in the back seat, except I did keep the blanket away from her face. I just didn't look down was how I handled that part. But now Tigga for some reason wanted me to cover its face, which I was hesitant to do, knowing this kid clearly did not want to be covered.

"But why," I turned to ask Tigga. "You've already warned Folana on what she looks like, right?"

"Just do it," Tigga hissed, nudging me in the back while trying to steal a peep over my shoulder to see what the child was doing. "Someone could be in her office. We don't want the whole world seeing your screw-up!"

That was another thing. No one but those doctors, and that nurse who shoved the kid on us knew about its existence. And they only knew about it at the day old stage...not five days old swinging at us, moving furniture, crashing and crushing walls, and tearing things off its face.

The way hospital records accounted for this madness, was documenting that we had us a perfectly normal healthy baby girl; manifested on the birth certificate they handed us while shoving us towards the door. But none of our family knew about this birth. We never got up the gall to call them and tell them. We didn't tell no one, and for whatever reason, the doctors, and that nurse didn't bother to sell Tigga's predicament to tabloids. Paparazzi would've torn up our doorstep, followed us all the way here, and no telling what all else they could've done. But that's interesting, now that I think of it. Wonder what was keeping the hospital so silent about this thing?

I wanted to, but was too afraid to do as Tigga requested. I just positioned my body so that Tigga couldn't see the child's face as I retrieved her from the car. Gratefully she was already at Folana's door ringing the bell when I turned around.

Dr. Folana Gladwell opened the door, smiling. She obviously was expecting us, as in standing by the door watching us fussing over getting the kid out of the car. Kind of creepy if you ask me.

"She's a tiny little thing," she remarked, apparently noticing the size of the bundle I kept close to my chest. "Was she a preemie?"

Tigga looked back, saw me standing with my back braced against the door, and snarled. "I don't know what that thing is, but trust whatever it is you can fix it!"

Honestly, I was petrified. By the fangs Tigga started growing, and the tiny sack of needles I clutched, suddenly stabbing me in the chest, I had no substantial expectations about how this visit might end. But for the first time in my history living above soil, I prayed. I prayed hard for 'ole good times Folana. She was about to piss off little Regan Hannibal.

3

Beyond this point, and the entire facelift procedure, I am hard pressed to elaborate on details. From my scant blurry memory I think I recall Folana moving towards me, braced against the door. I know I saw her peek over to take a look at what I held in my arms. I vividly recall that first gasp. But for some reason things got blurry after that.

If I'm to fill in this portion of the visit based on what I'm seeing and feeling now, I would say that Folana handled things a lot better than expected, or rather, the child handled the visit a lot better than my worst fears.

Folana was a tall gorgeous woman herself. Rather than a doctor, she looked more like a VP, or at least a TV VP, like she belonged in a corporate setting, and not dressed in scrubs working from a small drabby medical office. Like Tigga, she too had that long swan neck and the polished sharp features like most women in their twenties...you know, the edgy jaw lines, big white bright eyes, buttery-soft marker felt tipped drawn lips, and a nose that hadn't begun to round off just yet.

At some point the three of us made it to her office, where the surgery took place. Somehow an exchange was made where Folana ended up with the child. This might have been the point when I really blacked out, or at least the part where I became disoriented, amazed by my distant recall of Folana swaying back and forth with the kid in this rocking fashion. That child only allowed me to cuddle her like that, which true had only been once or twice. Any other time and we could expect one of them mean hooks.

But no hands whipped around and walloped Folana upside the head, or any other body parts. Folana even nuzzled the child with the tip of her nose, directly in the child's face. Still no complaints. Nothing. None of that *'baa baa baaaaa'* noise came out of the child either.

Then I saw it. Another moment clearly marked in my memory bank. I saw Folana's right hand come out from somewhere behind her, holding what I estimated to be a ten inch syringe, the needle was something like twenty inches. And please believe me. There's nothing exaggerated about these numbers I'm laying down here. The needle was that long, if not longer; enough to tranquilize a stampede of cows in one clean stick.

Tigga was sitting on the other side, so she couldn't see any of this. Or, at least she never saw that syringe and needle, not even with as long as it was. Tigga had retreated to one of the guest chairs and was quietly sobbing, having moved on to the next phase of her concern. Even if Folana made the child the most beautiful person in the world, how would she raise it? She had no intentions on becoming a mother just yet. None of this was in line with the plans she had in place for her life.

But I was intrigued. I wanted to see just how Folana was going to redesign this child. I wanted to see her arsenal—the scalpels and sewing needles. And the fake skin and body parts. And, of course her techniques. How would she handle removing or hiding an extra eye? My suspicion led me to believe that that third eye was responsible for those extraterrestrial swings and punches, and the exorcist basinet moving around the house, slamming into walls and the likes. Get rid of that third eye and the child just might turn into a normal human being.

Actually, and to really tell the truth, I wanted to see the kid redesign Folana... a little. She, Folana that being, kind of deserved it. She thought she was all that... with them bodacious charges and dozens of mansions. Nobody likes a showoff!

The needle pierced the blanket, and evidently the child's tush too, because soon as it did, I blacked out. That is, one minute the lights were on, dazzling the small surgical office for all of a fluorescent bulb's worth, and the next moment the room was solar system pitch black.

When I came to I was lying between heaven and hell, *I think*, soaking up my tenth or eleventh beer. And yeah, yeah, I know it sounds like I've skipped over a whole lot, as how in the hell does anyone have a recollection they are in heaven, or hell, without first having some understanding of getting there, especially if they know they are on their tenth or eleventh beer?

Well, that's the thing about heaven, or hell. It doesn't work like regular life. See, most of us have been brought up with the misconception that heaven is all cotton balls and peace for eternity, and hell is one big inferno of fire forever. But that's not how it works. Both heaven and hell is one figment of the imagination, or perception for those who believe in God. Basically, it's a *'learn as you go'* type thing.

Like take Jimmy. And I know most don't know of him, but he was the dude on death row for murdering his family and sometime later, just shortly before he was put to death, going on one of them nightly news interviews talking about how God forgave him, and how saved he was. His in-laws refused to believe him, and later sued the nightly news for the grief they experienced hearing Jimmy's shit. After the hell he caused the family, no one wanted to hear Jimmy talking all wise and forgiven and saintly like that.

But guess what? I saw Jimmy a few days back, and I for one refuse to believe I'm floating up here in hell getting my drink on and relaxing the way I've been. Ever since I've been up here it's been nothing but peace and quiet. Every so often I'll see someone I knew from before pass by what could be taken for a window, looking all nonchalant, like they don't have a care in the world, which probably they don't. It's not like you have to deal with the rigors of traffic getting to work, or how about finding and keeping a job... or let's say hunting down money to pay bills and eat.

So long as your mind is at peace, your existence is guaranteed the same peace. I haven't heard a soul crying or praying, or wishing to go back, the whole time I've been here. At least not in the part where I wended up, because there is this one catch I must add. If I look out this back view on the other side of me, there are some hellified sights to see—

—Souls floating by this here back window is sho' nuff in hell. Now, no one came by here and explained the rules to me about living up here. After I saw Jimmy I figured all of this out on my own. Like I said before. It's a pick up and learn as you see and go type operation.

Them souls I caught on occasions raising all this sand behind me is dealing with some demons they carried up here with them; stuff they haven't cleared with God like Jimmy did before he arrived.

I must've cleared my conscience with God earlier as well. Either that or I wasn't a bad enough person in my other life to start with. Now I'm at peace sipping my beers, though there is some more minutia about heaven and hell necessary to explain.

That lane behind me with all them raising kane souls on it; *and just to note*, these souls don't all model people like souls. Hell, I glanced back there this one time and saw bison, and leopards, and quite a few rattlesnakes, among a number of other strange insects on this lane that's supposed to lead everything on it back to the physical life. It's crazy as hell back there. Wicked weather is on that lane too. Looks just like how hell was described in the physical life, except without the fire. The fire is all in the mind, I'm guessing...cause it's just about what all the beasts back there act like. Like their minds are all on fire.

At any rate, things *(and that includes people too)* get on that lane because they're trying to go back. Why the hell anyone would want to do such a fool thing like that, I have no clue. They get on that lane like I've seen theme park rollercoaster enthusiasts; waiting in long lines to have their jawlines knocked off track and brains whacked in half, apparently in the name of fun, or, as in this case, to settle a score...like dealing with some unfinished business. In other words, these fools weren't ready to come here. At least it's what I'm led to believe by stray vibes that's been blowing by my comfy nook. They wait on that stretch of road, or should I say, they go through hell on that road, all to return to the physical realm of life. The thing about it all is, they have to wait on this lift. This means they are waiting for someone, or something that can transport their soul back. This is where mish-mash gets real cooky; stuff I'm not so curious to prove or report my findings. I'd much rather guess at this thing, from what I've picked up from watching.

The only way a soul in a deadened vessel can get carried back is by 1) first wanting to go back. And 2) gettin' on that miserable super hell highway advertising you want to go back. And then 3) waiting on whichever physical vessel was about to conceive life to actually transport you back. This means after all your hell fighting other beasts on the super hell highway, your ass could end up going back as a fucking goat! Imagine that mish-mash. Getting a lift back don't necessarily mean you're going back nowhere near to the thing you were when you first transitioned.

Again, I don't recall when, or how, I picked up on all this, but I also know people have been on that lane many times trying to go back to the physical life they liked best, or in a form that allowed them to clear up this unfinished business. It really was pitiful. It's a sure way to stay in a permanent state of pure D hell.

I didn't want no parts of that hellish road...that being not until the day I rolled over and woke up to find myself wedged between heaven and hell...kinda' how I came by all this, as in how I learnt stuff.

4

I heard this commotion down beneath me, looked down, and all be-gosh-doggonit I saw a shitload of schoolyard children, at recess I presume, running around against the grain of bells and whistles going off. I couldn't rightly process whereabouts in heaven, or hell this visual was, what made me know for sure I must've gotten caught between on that lane I was explaining.

Down below where I was looking, about a dozen or so women, and one bald-headed man, hustled about to maintain some order with these kids that looked like busy bees from my vantage point.

Another thing I thought; *'cripes, I must be drunk!'* Normally it takes much more than ten or eleven beers to get me that drunk. I know how to hold mines...especially when it comes to the ales, something that affects me like a liter of soda, and that's both to my waistline and my head. But hey, I was up above, way up above...like I said, somewhere between heaven and hell, so the altitude could have had something to do with my hazy state of mind too. It didn't necessarily have to have anything to do with what I know for damn sure I was seeing.

I rolled off my milky silky white cottony roll-away bed and squinted, peering through layers of vapor to CLEAR AS DAY see my kid's face. I know it was her!!! It had to be; for who else would be standing all alone in the center of a schoolyard, sad and dirty, with a finger stuck in her mouth and hair sprayed over her head resembling a cave child that had escaped the forest?

I definitely knew it was her when I saw the croissant-tied lump in the center of her forehead. Plus, when she turned around I realized her dirty white dress was really a smock tied in the back like a hospital gown.

Yeah, that was our kid alright. Tigga would've had a holy fit if she saw what I saw, which speaking of Tigga...I got to wondering where in the hell Tigga was anyway!?! Actually, come to think on it, I did see Tigga once. At least I think I did. It looked something like her. From behind it did. You know...the long legs and nice ass thing. Sadly though, I had to see her on the super hell highway. And like I said, it was only the back of her I saw. Still...poor Tigga. I bet she wanted to go back. She was like that. The exact type who'd want to go back. For some reason I see a yellow jack snatching her up; probably had her on land pollinating a rose bush, or making ear wax or something.

At any rate, I'm up here looking down at a schoolyard of kids teasing our kid. They were pointing at her forehead, and opening her hospital gown from the back, and laughing. That was the part that riled me most. Those mean assholes messing with our kid. I knew this shit would happen. That's what concerned me the moment I first saw that third eye in the center of her forehead.

I got so mad I yelled down through the clouds, *'damn it, somebody get that fugly kid!'* And no, I *(of course)* wasn't talking about our kid. I was talking about the fugly girl who looked like zoo material picking with our kid. I wished I could have knocked the fuglyiness off that zoo kremlin.

Now I'm not majorily a violent person, but sometimes I do get emotional in stressful situations like this. Picking with others is my number one pet peeve. Like why the fuck do fugly people fuck with others anyway!?! And for no good reason! Like Why!?! Just tell me WHY!?! Especially when they look like zoo crud!!!

Unfortunately for me, but perhaps fortunately for our kid, which only time would tell, this was how I slipped up on that precarious spot, between heaven and hell. Not many get to exist in this spot, and certainly not for very long, because you have to both understand the existence you left and the state where you are. This means I had to make a choice... and make it snappy. Did I want everlasting peace, leaving what I knew from before behind? Or did I want to go back to finish up some business?

See now why so many want to go back?

In my case these assholes were messing with our defenseless child. And I know we didn't do much about defending her when she was born. First we tried disowning her, swearing we had nothing to do with her creation; throwing spreads and crazy looking scarves over her and whatnot. And then we had the unmitigated gall to try and fix her by taking her to 'ole good times felonious Folana, the facelift shrink. That couldn't have been right, not even in that day and time, even if we had convinced ourselves we were trying to do the responsible thing any caring parent would do under the same or similar circumstances.

I was thinking back on all of this when suddenly a little rugged girl appeared out of the crowd. She sort of blossomed like a petal opens into a flower. One minute I was thinking about taking the plunge, and the next I heard this angelic voice coming from what to me, at the time, was a beautiful blossoming rose.

"Don't listen to them dumbies," said the little rugged angelic-like girl. "They're just being mean. You wait and see. They're gonna get theirs," she said throwing a comforting arm around our tiny child's shoulder.

'You got that right kid!' I cheered from above. *'Yeah! That's what I'm talking about!'* Felt like I was at a Padres game. I even picked up another beer and popped the tab.

Our kid nodded but kept silent, dirty finger still stuck in her mouth, which speaking of her mouth, and the croissant scarring on her forehead, I had to scratch my own forehead of sorts trying to think back on our visit with Folana.

Had the surgery really happened? By the looks of things, it must have. Also by the looks of things, at least six or seven years had elapsed. Where had our kid been all that time? Could the operation have taken that long? And more questions...

Had Tigga and I transitioned together? For some reason I always thought we had. I also thought Folana came with us too. And I for darn sure had no reason to hold any hope in that surgery being remotely successful. During all of this the kid never entered my mind. That's because I never saw it as a real kid. I didn't know what it was, and consequently let its existence absolve with our transition.

Well Holy Toledo, somehow the kid survived! That's one thing about being stationed between heaven and hell. You automatically know things like this. In real life people refer to my knowledge as ESP, or reincarnation. But up here, you're officially known as being caught between heaven and hell.

I looked back down and panicked when I saw the school-yard had cleared. *'Oh dear FUCK! Where had our kid gone?'* My eyes flitted around, unfittingly searching for her.

"Ugh, Cummins," a force to be reckoned with bellowed, cuttin' the line and stepping in my lane. "I can get you on the Causeway," said the giant strapping voice made up of millions of muscular tentacles.

You had to hear it. That voice I mean. I never heard nothing like it. I always knew God had one of those booming powerful earnest tones, but this voice kind of sounded like all the things you'd hear at a stadium; like if the Padres was playing while a bull fight, an Olympic track meet, an Opera, and the National Anthem were all playing at once.

Like I said, you had to hear it, which I really didn't want to, not going by what I last heard. My ass didn't want to be nowhere near a Cause or a Way. Shucks, going on repeat. I'm a peaceable soul. I don't like to fuck with no-one, and I don't like to get fucked with!

5

"Chile, when we get you?" asked a stout grandmotherly type woman looking down on our child.

Now, although I can't rightly explain how I picked up the image, but there she was again. The child. Our kid. This time standing by a refrigerator, perched quietly before the squally rugged, but angelic kid, and the stout matronly lady...with that dirty finger still stuck in her mouth.

"She in my class, Granny," the little rugged girl smacked at the matronly lady pulling food out of the frig.

Our child said nothing, though I watched her pull that dirty finger out of her mouth.

"You don't have a home," Granny asked our child.

Granny reminded me of a grandmother I visited when I was a boy. These were the grandmothers I went to see where we had to load up the car and drive a whole day and all night to see. This matronly lady *(I peered down on)* looked like an elderly woman on my mother's side. The one who had the eye and a half; one brownish, the other grayish. The old woman I saw however, was big around the top to mid portion, and slight in the face. Reminded me of a bubbly lemon meringue pie.

"Her mama and daddy died," the little rugged girl spoke up again. "She my best friend. I want her to stay with me! Please Granny, please. Can Cuttie stay with us?"

Cuttie?

OH Man, lots ran through my mind hearing that name. Right away I got to thinking about why we never got around to naming our child. Or maybe I was wrong?

It wasn't too far fetched that I was up here dreaming. And let me tell you one thing about dreaming up here where I'm at. You Don't! That is the quickest way to land at the very back of the line on the Causeway; the last spot in all creation where no one wanted to be.

You know, I caught scalped souls back there. It's brutal at the back of that line. A person blessed enough to have his or her ass in heaven should not be dreaming at all. That's like telling Your Master, who's blessed you with peace forever, *'no thank you!'* Like what the what!?! Only a totally zonked out coot would throw their peace away! You're supposed to take that shit and go sit your dead ass down somewhere!

What I'm saying here is, what if this child was none of ours? I could wind up on that Causeway in a real dilemma. Like up shit's creek!

But I wasn't at liberty to think on things too long, nor too hard, least I be suspected of wanting to go back. So I did some quick tabulations. What if? I wanted to make sense of what happened. How had Tigga and I created whatever it was that doctors and that one nurse swore came out of Tigga, and was OURS? Was it the same child? Was this my chance to upright my wrongs? It didn't mean I wanted to go back. It was just me wondering—out loud. You know, I wanted some clarity. Some peaceable type understanding.

"Good Lawd chile, what happened to your head?" I heard the 'ole one-and-a-half lazy-eyed Granny ask.

Soon as I heard this, my next thought, which I'd be lying if I tried to rehash what it was, slipped up on a film of thick black vine that felt like electricity, and zapped my ass straight back to the real world. I didn't spend a second on the Causeway. I blinked and ended up fizzing through midair.

I landed on something, I don't know what, and got to looking around, looking for my arms and hands, and my legs and feet, trying to upright myself to stand.

But I saw nothing. I had no limbs, and from what I could discern, I had no body either. I don't know what in the hell I was, nor where I landed.

My next thought was *'Invasion of the Body Snatchers'*. I knew I was in the physical world, and I knew I was a being of some sort, because I heard and saw everything as if I was in my old self. I just couldn't see myself. Crazy, I know, though here's the real deal. I could move around, freely and quickly. Yeah, I had a whole lot of speed; something that would have come in real handy back in the days when I was a booty-catcher.

Suddenly I realized I was staring directly in our child's face, and I mean face to face with no more than a nose hair between us. She really didn't look all that bad. Folana, I must insert here, had done a fine job removing her third eye. I knew this because the EYE WAS GONE! Yet, to the raw ignorant eye the scar definitely was an eye sore. It resembled a slug, but lance that baby down and give it time, and it would flatten and smooth right out.

"Well, I guess it'll be alright...so long as no one ain't out looking for her," Granny sighed, causing me to spin around just in time to see her rubbing her hardened dark crusty hands on a soiled flowery apron.

"Come on!" And I spun around again, just in time to see the rugged girl snatching our child by the hand and running off with her.

I followed behind them, clumsily flying up dusty dark stairs they clobbered and clunked up to the top.

"This is my room," the little rugged girl proudly announced. "We don't have to share beds 'cause we don't have no whole lotta kids like my sister, and we ain't boys," bragged the rag doll.

Our child nodded but said nothing, so I shoved her. *'Speak up child! Let Daddy hear what you sound like.'*

"Are all these your clothes," I heard. And just like that I dropped to where the ground and my knees would go and got to boo-hoo crying.

'God,' I cried, *'this is our child. I know it! And I thank you heavenly Father for being with her and bringing me to her after I neglected the job. But as you are my witness dear Father, please let me step back in my rightful place and do right by her this time.'*

Next thing I know, I hear, "Hey Reba, what you do wif' my burner. I kno' yo' black ass been in my stuff and took it!"

I looked up from my tearful position to lay both my good vision on this ugly bulky misfit looking dude standing in the doorway. He had both arms, and that being elbow for elbow, propped up against either side of the doorframe. Long hairs dangled from his armpits like an orangutan. Other curlier hairs bubbled over the battered wife-beater stretched across his meaty torso. He did have pants on, but the waist of these pants hung on that ding-a-ling of his. He had his fly open too, and had natty matted hair, and quite crusty lips.

The rest of what I saw and did was a complete mystery at the time I saw and did it. Before Reba answered I had gotten off my tears and pulled a plug out of that chump's gut. Again, don't ask me how, cause again, I don't know how. From how I recall it, I was thinking bad stuff, and the next thing I know, I had a chunk of that fool's guts trapped in my tentacles.

"Ouua!" that fool moaned doubling over. "Aah shit," and he bee-lined his ass straight to the bathroom next to Reba's bedroom, slamming the door behind him.

A fantastic vociferous rush of gurgley noises were heard splashing in the toilet after that. Reba snickered and Cuttie smiled. I did neither. I was mad as a green hornet. I had seen those type men, *if you could call them that,* before. They were the type who wouldn't let our child get in one good menstrual cycle before she would be knocked up like other young girls living with them types.

Not including Cuttie I counted about fifteen to twenty parasites living in that little house; most staying in the cellar—like underground—3 cousins, 2½ uncles, and a gang-banging swathe of friends. This total didn't include Granny, Reba, and Reba's sister who had 9 children. Irene, Reba's sister was only twenty-one...so there...how about that for a father's intuition. You do the math and figure out what I was seeing.

Unt un... I didn't like this living arrangement not one bit, but not so fast Protective Daddy T. Cummins. While it occurred to me during this unceremonious introduction to my knew life...*or existence*...I had powers, these special powers couldn't pick up my child and plant her where I wanted. Her daddy...*as it turned out*...was still in the ethereal world, and she was not. All I so far understood was how I could get inside people, and most things, and make things happen. Like when I got inside that chump. I just flew inside him like I was my old-time self, running into him like a fullback. But instead of me bumping into him and cold busted knocking him flat on his back as I meant to do, I ended up crashing inside of him, and in a fit of rage pulling on veins and things as if I was pulling things out of a drawer, or snatching clothes off a line or something. At the time none of this computed, but now it did, except I'm still not sure how all my special powers work. Right now I only have two concerns. My first, and very first mission was to get Cuttie out of that house. And the second was to rename her.

6

I tried finding Cuttie a better living arrangement, but it wasn't easy trying to look around and keep an eye on her at the same time. There were a lot of mites running around that house and everybody I checked out, didn't check out. Reba was all she had, and so far seemed to be really good for my kid.

"You like my room? You like it here," Reba giddily asked, so proud of that raggedy room I was looking at.

"Yes," Cuttie answered in the sweetest curly voice I'd ever heard. Sounded like she was from the South, the deep South. Her voice could melt in your mind and curl up a tongue it was so soft and mellow.

But OH DEAR JESUS! I had to get my baby out of that scurrilous house and find her a proper home. That's the first thing I picked up on. My sweet innocent child would never survive that butcheress environment.

"Get away from the door Nookie! You know you ain't allowed in here!" Reba shouted.

Nookie was Irene's oldest boy. He was twelve, a few years older than Reba and Cuttie who were the same age. He also was hot in the pants, a little buster grooming to become a peeping Tom, typical for a boy his age.

"I'm still gonna bust your friend's cherry. She know she want this," Nookie laughed, darting away.

But I caught his little rusty dusty raggedy tail headed back down the stairs. He went down all right, head first, all thirteen steps. Came to a blunt stop without a sound out of him until medics arrived.

And don't be concerned about the boy. Medics that scooped him up were good. They revived him and fitted him in nice thick casts; one on one leg, another on his right arm... straight down to his fingers, after wiring his frisky jaws shut too.

Still, it was damn near nineteen more of them; a number steadily rising each time one of the nineteen brought another nomad in the house. I wasn't going to win this thing going at this escalating rate; not if I didn't find Cuttie somewhere safe to go, and soon.

"Chile, you gonna hafta' hep me out and tell me where you come from. Da school is asking all sorts of questions. Dey talking about calling da law on us here," Granny said all worried-like.

Lodus was Granny's name. Miz Briggs to most. And Miz Briggs, sweet as she was, surely did have a lot to worry about if the law came nosing around her nomadic palette. Between Irene and the welfare inspections, alongside the other drama she had going in her life, Miz Briggs kept a ton of rogue-some company, most who belonged beneath cells.

Them sons and grandsons, and friends of them sons and grandsons, along with Irene and hers had rap sheets thicker than fat ass dictionaries. Cop-brigades ran, and shot through that place by the day. And if it wasn't a cop-brigade, then it would be the medics, like the one that ended up carting Nookie off. Yellow streamers and flashing lights quarantining the house was no unusual sight. Them motifs looked like part of the house décor, and emergency vehicles their mode of transportation. No, Miz Briggs certainly didn't need any more law in her house.

"What the school wanna know Granny," Reba asked, in a voice that said she wasn't as concerned as mousing around in her closet more interested about what she and Cuttie would wear to school the next day.

"They wanna see papers on who she is, and if she done had all her shots, or else they hafta' take her away."

Reba dropped the blouse she was holding up to her flat chest and almost bust her head on the ceiling as she left the stool she'd been standing on.

"No! They can't take her! Granny, we can't let them take her!" Her small round eyes darted around the bedroom. "We have to do something. Let's hide her! And when they come let's tell 'em she's not here like we do with Butch and 'nem when the law come for 'dem!"

"Honey," Miz Briggs said sadly, "I wished we could but then Cuttie couldn't go to school."

Reba's eyes turned cobalt blue from black. "I bet that witch sic'd them on us. She mad cause what I said."

The witch Reba was referring to was a woman I initially thought Cuttie might do well, or at least better, staying with. Omega Cranberry was the woman's name. She had four kids in all, and a husband. Her oldest boy was off in the Navy. I checked while Reba and Cuttie were sleep. Her other three kids were at home. The oldest girl was about to go to college the following year. The younger girl was just a year or so younger than Cuttie. And the baby, a little boy, wasn't but a few months old. This family looked like they would've been perfect for Cuttie had not Omega shown herself to be less than a stellar woman.

Omega was walking by the Briggs house with another *stay-at-home* neighborhood mother, both of them pushing baby strollers, and stopped in front of the steps where Reba and Cuttie were sitting and braiding two of Irene's children's hair.

Omega leaned over to tend to her hollering child in the stroller, trying to plug a dinky in the kid's shute, when Reba and Cuttie drew her attention.

The girls weren't doing anything bad, other than giggling. But Omega must've assumed *correctly* the giggles were about at her. Huffing rather loudly she goes, "ump, ump, ump...I can't see how all of you live in that one little house," she said, finishing her snide snicker with the other *stay-at-home* neighborhood mother.

On cue Reba shot back, "Ump! Ump! Ump! I can't see how someone old as you still fucking and having babies. I thought Stanley *(Mr. Cranberry)* was done with your old worn out tired yella' BA-hind!"

"Ah!" Omega gasped, snatching around to exchange an incredulous look with the other *stay-at-home* neighborhood mother.

"Did you hear that...what she just said!?!" Omega gulped clutching her chest. Abruptly she turned to Reba. "You have a filthy mouth young lady. I wonder if..." and she looked up at the house, a monstrous brown brick creature with broken streamers from past incidents strung Helter-Skelterly around the porch and front yard, and realized she was arguing a hopeless point. No one in that house cared about Reba's filthy foul mouth.

Point proven the very next day when the school called Granny. The principal, a Mr. Sturgis Grover, wanted to meet with her, or the parent of *'all these children'* using her address as their residence.

This was the way a lot of kids got to go to the school of their choice; by using relatives *(or other peoples)* address without actually living there.

"Mr. Grover, you know darn well dese are my children's children, and dey all stay with me."

"Now hold on Miz Briggs," Mr. Grover said, "cause you do have one using your address that we have no papers on. Cuttie Brown."

'Oh, not for long,' her now loving daddy vowed.

7

Man, I was so pissed at that Omega woman! See how people wend up on the Causeway... the super Hell highway. It's vehicles just like me that drive them there. And trust me, had it not been for her children, and my sheer desperation to help Cuttie, I would've drove her ass there the same way I liquidated Reba's cousin, or uncle, or whoever he was, manners straight down the commode.

I had to do something. I didn't want to see Cuttie's living environment disrupted until I could be sure she was in a better place. Seeing her shuttled off to an orphanage, or stuck in an oppressive situation like that damn Omega's opinionated penitentiary was no option. She would've been miserable all over again, a vision I couldn't stomach. For the time being she was comfortable, even if I knew I had to act fast.

I landed on Omega's phone wire as she was whispering, trying to not let Stanley hear her gossiping.

"Girl, I wish they would just move the whole house off the block," she was saying, likely to the same *stay-at-home* neighborhood woman she was with on the offending day. "...Just get a forklift and forklift that whole wrecking wreck out of my sight!"

The female voice on the other end laughed. "I know what you mean. The other day Hank caught one of 'em crawling in his window?"

"Wha—you mean bald-head Hank who lives at the end of the street?"

"Yeah, Fay's Hank," replied the female voice.

"Oh yeah, that 'ole bow-legged man don't play! Stanley said he said he wasn't even going to bother with calling the cops if one of them came around his house looking for trouble."

"Well, he must've meant it," said the female voice, "cause last week he sure 'nough shot one of 'em right in the BA-hind."

Omega threw her head back and cracked up laughing. "Ha! Ha! Ha! Really? Which one?"

"That little egghead one. The really bad one that tried to burn down the school. I think he's one of Irene's..."

"Ump," Omega umped, "I don't know how you can tell one from the other. It's so many of them in there. Every day I see another one."

"Well, I know the small ones belong to Irene because—"

"—Unt un...not that latest one," Omega interrupted. I called the school on her fresh mouth BA-hind. I know Irene didn't have that one! And neither did Lodus. You ask me, I think they got that one off ebay."

"Off ebay?" asked the female voice.

"Welfare! You know! The government is paying up to $1000 for each one of them crumb-snatchers," Omega spat right back as if this info was obvious.

"Ump...ump...ump! What a shame," sighed the female voice.

"Can you imagine?" Omega continued like usual business. "That's why they keep having them, or stealing them. For the money. What I'm surprised about is why they don't kill and claim 'em. Ain't like no one's gonna try looking through that rat trap to verify any of 'em."

Honestly, that call really rattled me. I was unnerved and I was angry all rolled into one. But what undid me was when I heard Omega say, "hell, I wouldn't even want that ugly thing in my house!"

It was an accident, because I already know it was wrong, especially given how Tigga and I felt when Cuttie was born. So it was a mistake, okay? I just so happened to be mistakenly in the Cranberry's gas line when I involuntarily farted. That's really what happened; how their lovely home blew up in pieces. Omega no longer had to riddle herself with Irene's welfare kids, no one's raunchy kid, or our ugly kid ransacking it, because there now was nothing left to ransack. It was done. Finished. Laying smack flat out like a cut open cardboard box in the middle of Princeton Road. The block of houses now looked like a tooth was missing.

Mercifully, and credit goes to whoever else was watching out for the Cranberry's too, because they all had just climbed into the car, headed to the airport to meet the son returning home for the holidays, when my gasket mistakenly blew.

They were all happily smiling and looking forward to this family excursion to the airport when BOOM! —the roof to the house shot straight up in the sky, returning to earth in a showering flurry of snowy cardboard shavings.

"Ya'll missed it," Tebok grinned, sitting on a bike he built from parts picked off anything from cars to airplanes, hocked right out of auto shops and a hanger where a cousin worked.

"The Cranberry's house just got blowed up," he laughed.

"Unt un...no way! Boy stop dat lyin'," Reba said, excitedly jumping up off the stoop.

And "really," cooed Cuttie in her sweet super supple voice, looking around like the innocent wide-eyed child who desperately needed my protection.

"Yup...yup...ya'll should've seent it," Tebok confirmed, about to push off in the direction of where he'd come—the Cranberry's house of course. "I'm gone back over there to see if I can find me something!"

"Ooo! Let's go!" Reba said excitedly turning to Cuttie. "Let's go see if we can find something too!"

'No Cuttie! You stay right there,' I said frantically

scanning around, gaging a way to stop Reba from dragging her along. Honestly, at this point I still didn't know who or what I really was, or all of my special powers. This fatherhood bit went way over my head. In this early stage I was learning...and doing... on the fly.

"Reba! Cuttie! Ya'll come on in here and get cleaned up," Granny called from the doorway.

'*Good,*' I sighed. Saved by the bell...

"Awl Granny, where we going," Reba huffed, slinking back to the house and up the steps.

"Them state people comin' over here to check up on Cuttie and I don't want ya'll lookin' like ya'll ain't been cared for," Granny said.

Maybe this wasn't so good afterall. So much had been going on I hadn't had a chance to check up on that. I actually forgot all about it until Granny called them in the house. I had been over there trying to deal with that Omega woman conjuring up this bad energy. I was trying to free up her busyness, to give her real business to mind.

But Reba hadn't forgotten about Social Services. That's one thing I loved about that wild child. She had my little girl's back on more than dozens of occasions. From the schoolyard to the neighborhood, Reba didn't let nobody bother with her best friend who she was now calling a sister. I really liked her for that. When she heard Cuttie needed papers, she got right on it, and the child wasn't but 8 or 9 years old.

"Irene, how you get papers on all yo' kids for them welfare people," Reba asked Irene early the next morning after Mr. Grover apologized for still having to turn Granny into Social Services.

"Dey in the drawer over deer," Irene said stretching and yawning, lazily tossing her hand towards a nightstand where a drawer crammed with papers was missing its face.

Hurriedly Reba stepped over sleeping kids lying in a pile of clothes to dig around in the drawer. Papers fell to the floor and on top of the sleeping kids as she dug.

"And don't be wakin' up dese kids and fuckin' up dis here room," Irene growled. "I spent all day yesterday puttin' things in order." The man whose arms she had come out of grunted and turned the other way, just as the baby at the foot of the bed almost fell. Cuttie caught him, though he let out a loud wail anyway, screaming for all the world to know he existed.

"What da," and Irene threw the remote at Reba, missing her head by centimeters as she ducked.

"I told ya'll not to wake 'dese damn kids!" she shrieked, stomping out of bed as one child after the next, like a row of dominos, started crying.

But Reba had what she wanted. "Come on, let's go," she said, grabbing Cuttie by the arm.

"Where da hell you gone with my papers," Irene yelled after them, hissing and slamming things around when she realized she wasn't going to catch them.

"See, this is all we have to do," Reba said, standing in Ludlow's Public Library, at the copy machine, carefully putting the finishing touches on a birth certificate she doctored up.

"But what about the seal? Mines don't have a seal," Cuttie inquired, gazing down at the crude job Reba had done. They were only in the fourth grade. Reba's creative skills weren't all that great, or savvy.

Reba looked from Tebok's authentic birth certificate to the one she doctored up. "Yeah, this one does look a little too plain," she said as if that was the only difference between the two, perking up when another idea hit her. "Oh, I know where we can get some seals. And I know how to make them look real."

A kindergarten teacher taught her how hot rolling pins over foil embossed things, which Reba imitated, albeit using stickies her and Cuttie stole out of a discount store. Of course, Cuttie's birth certificate looked funnier compared to Tebok's, but it passed the sniff test.

"Uh un... uh un..." the nervous Social Services woman hummed when she finally got to the house and took a look at the obviously doctor birth certificate. That piece of paper looked like something a kidnapper left as a ransom note, trying not to be identified. But the only reason she didn't contest it was due to one of Granny's visitors, Mr. Luke, trying to sniff around her neck.

"This'll do," said the Social Services agent, fanning a hand at Mr. Luke and leaning over as far as she could, trying to shake one of Irene's kids off her leg, and peel another kid's sticky fingers off papers in her opened briefcase.

"I'm like a bumble bee," Mr. Luke drooled. "I lock on all sweet scents, sticking to them like—"

—CRACK! Granny whacked Mr. Luke upside the head with her slipper, dust particles poofing in the air. "Man, leave that woman alone and let her do her job!"

Mr. Luke rubbed his cabbage (head), and the nervous social worker finished the last of her *'uh un's'*, snapping her briefcase close and hurrying for the door. "I'll contact the school tomorrow," she said without looking back.

So that took care of that. So far, so good. Cuttie looked to be all set. All I needed to do was be half as good as Reba in fast thinking, and Cuttie might have a chance at having a little better future than this Briggs' clan.

8

But there was one major problem. For as much as I hated it, there just wasn't going to be another way around it. I was going to have to deal with Reba.

Reba didn't want to lose her playmate. All those people coming and going in and out of the house, none measured up to what Cuttie had been for her; a girl about her age who she could play dress up and make-believe, and make-up with. Someone she could get into trouble with and giggle late into the night and slumber with. They traded blood, making them more than pretend sisters. Cuttie was now a soul mate. They went skating together, and to neighborhood parties dressing like bobbsie-twins, and sharing music, or playing Chinese jacks on rainy days, and of course they also shared *'hope to die'* secrets. Cuttie and Reba were tied at the hip...and head, who according to Reba, were destined to be together for life.

I realized moving Cuttie out of the home at this point was going to be a problem, but hadn't considered just how major of a problem it would be until I overheard Reba talking with a classmate.

"Why you hang around that weird girl," asked the classmate. The girl's name was Syria. She was the most popular girl in the school, even more popular than Reba who only acquired her reputation by the unsettled home she hailed from.

Syria's infamy was different. Teachers and school administrators liked this girl because she came to class with her light bulb turned all the way on.

But Reba wasn't hearing none of what Syria was talking about. She flipped around and flat out told the girl, "she my blood!" And she made it clear nobody was supposed to talk about blood that she loved *'more than anyone in the whole wide world!'* "Plus, she tells me secrets don't none of ya'll know."

Now the child is my child and all, but the bit about her loving my child *'more than anyone in the whole wide world*' proved Reba had a slight problem with reality. No one or nothing in the whole damn universe loved that child more than I DID! No ONE! Not even that Damascus bending over scolding a child. And man, was her posterior not a delicious temptation for manly roving eyes. I couldn't take my sights off that teacher, though I'll get back to that honey in a minute. For a placeholder though, the teacher's name was June. Mrs. June Clapton.

For the interim of time, Reba admitting what Cuttie meant to her, meant a lot to me as well, though this in no way meant that I, as her soul mate's loving father, wasn't jockeying amidst a microscopic of cells to find my sweet and beautiful and innocent child a better station in life.

"Oh, and what secrets are they," I heard a child flanking Syria ask. This child was one of Syria's followers, so her name isn't important.

"I'm not telling," Reba spat back all sassy like, throwing a hand on a place where hips might one day go.

"Is it you're not telling, or you just don't know," Syria snapped back.

"Both!" Reba shouted back.

"Well how do you know she is telling you secrets if you don't know what it is," Syria asked like the smart clever child she was.

"Yeah!" huffed the follower, braced for a verbal sort of war. "Which one is it? You don't know or you ain't tellin'!?!"

"Leave her alone," Syria told the follower, pushing the girl away from Reba with the back of her arm. "I'll find out for myself," she said, rolling her eyes at Reba.

"Yeah! We'll find out for ourselves," the follower puffed, backing away to follow Syria.

This was where I took leave of my senses, overwhelmingly concerned about the prospect that Cuttie may have really told Reba some secret that could jeopardize her future.

For the most part I stayed on our child, like white on rice, *as it's said.* Bedtime was the only time I left her alone. I used this time for scouting out possible living arrangements. This being after assuring I had them nuts squatting in the cellar squared away. Make no mistake about it, I was a wheezing and a panting asthmatic busy father during this transition investigation.

This is one thing about living virally. There's no way to flip back to scenes you missed. You can't see into the future either, well at least not any clearer than the most skilled ESP practitioner. So, if I missed it, then I really missed it. Far as I knew at present, I only could avert or circumvent things happening in the now.

"Cuttie, I've got to get you home," Reba said when she saw her coming out of the girls' room. "Some girls are after you...they're planning to beat you up."

Now I know damn well I hadn't missed that one. I heard the entire exchange. Wasn't nothing mentioned about beating up my child. Reba was up to something, and as usual, she was about to drag Cuttie into it.

I listened intently, Reba lecturing Cuttie on their walk home about how to fight. "I want you to take this," she said handing Cuttie her personal secret weapon. "If anyone comes near you, I want you to flip this out like this," and she took the little gold keychain out of Cuttie's hand to demonstrate by mashing a lever that opened into a switchblade.

Oh Lawdt Jesus! This damn girl is about to turn my kid into a mother-fucking murderer. *Sweet Jesus have mercy please help me!* I've got to stop this maddness! Cuttie's life will be over if she ends up hurting one of these kids.

I was crying out so inconsolably loud that I liked to have missed the rest of the exchange.

"You tell whoever steps to you first, you'll trim 'em down so fast they'll be smaller than a bug! And say it just like how I just said it, too!"

Oh God Noooooo! Nooooo! Don't let my baby go out like this. Forget the fact how corny and ridiculous Reba sounded, I got to wailing so audibly I again nearly missed what I heard after that...

"But what if I hurt someone with that thing," Cuttie said, staring at the crooked hooked blade that came out of a small gold handle inscribed RKBB.

'That's right baby...that's right...you tell her,' I sniffled. See. Did I need more proof that this definitely was my child; a little girl with a golden heart, sweeter and more beautiful than anything in the whole wide universe?

"Awl, don't worry about it. Once they see this," and Reba ran her small finger over the inscription of her blade, "they'll likely back off," and she laughed noisily before adding "...if they know what's good for them!"

I watched Cuttie fanning away a black butterfly fluttering between them thinking, this could've been Tigga. But then Cuttie said, "that's okay. I don't need that to protect me. I'll just tell 'em to leave me alone," she shrugged, "or tell a teacher or something," she whispered.

That's when I knew emphatically that butterfly was none of Tigga. The Tigga I knew would've been handling that switchblade like a grand master chef. All them shallow wanna be pageant queens she dealt with, she expertly sized down. She was something like Reba. She didn't play.

"No Cuttie, you don't get it," Reba pled. "These girls are wicked. They'll hurt you if you don't do exactly as I'm telling you. I've seen them do it to other nice girls before."

After that pep talk I had no time to be out scouting down suitable residences. I had seen a few fights Reba was talking about. They were none too pleasant. Nothing like how boys fought, usually in one shot and that'd be the end of it. Them girls in that school had an art for how they pulled girls down to the ground and lifted their dresses all the way over their heads, exposing panties and whatnot, so the little boys could stand around laughing to later pull some similar moves. Repugnant. It was encumbent upon me to intervene.

I wrapped my tentacles around Cuttie that night, holding her tight, praying I could release some of my powerful kismet energy into her tiny body. Something so powerful that it might carry her on to where she would be safe, and happy, so that I didn't have to...

...Oh Lawd have mercy! One of them fools had gotten loose and done come up out the cellar. I felt the knucklehead trying to turn my ass over. Of course he didn't know it was me, thinking he was touching Cuttie, but it was me all right.

I gorged two prongs in his eyes so damn deep every light in the house, for the next fifty-sixty cities, came on. That fool, whichever one it was, hollered so loud, and for so long, an ambulance had to swing by and carry him out of there...and for good. It was all over the news. Paramedics claimed a rabid stray bat must've come through the window and attacked him. Nobody even tried to figure out what his ass was doing in the girl's room at three in the morning. It wasn't too much of a stretch as for why his draws' were found wrapped around his ankles. That's how him and his kind regularly dressed.

But see, I didn't want to have to go on like this for the rest of Cuttie's life. It wasn't fair to either of us. I wanted to see this child grow normally, and be a part of a normal, loving, nurturing home and community. Hell, if I couldn't get things straight for her, I might have to consider jumping on Hell's highway, just to have a chance at possibly being a part of her life in a corporeal way.

9

I was happy Syria was bright enough to know Cuttie wasn't worth fighting. The girl seemd hip to Reba's M.O. It was some of that blood sisterly stuff, like how gangs initiated new recruits. No witnesses. Only accomplices allowed.

This was the hard part. I understood Reba had no decent faculties to come up with a better way to form a decent sisterly bond. It's exactly why I had to get my baby the hell out of that toxic environment.

Mrs. Clapton was up at the blackboard writing math equations across the slate when I got inside of her. My, that woman had some lovely insides. And not to get freaky here, since I respect the fact she IS married, I entered her through a tender spot just below her left bosom, right near her heart.

The chalk fell out of her hand and broke in three pieces as I slipped inside of her. Her knees buckled and the students laughed, not understanding why their teacher staggered like a drunk trying to get to her desk.

Syria was in this class at the time, and thank goodness she was, because she got out of her seat and rushed up to her teacher. "Mrs. Clapton, are you okay?" she asked.

"Go...go...go get me help," Mrs. Clapton got out.

At this point the class knew Mrs. Clapton's condition was no laughing matter. Syria ran out the room and summoned help from the front office, and away their dear teacher was whisked to the hospital.

"Man, I wonder if there's something in the water," one of the paramedics remarked as the ambulance pulled up to the hospital.

"...Or in the air," mocked a paramedic hustling the stretcher Mrs. Clapton lay stretched out on in the hospital.

Okay, so maybe the ambulance trips back and forth to the hospital had increased upon my arrival.

"Ugh...please call my husband," Mrs. Clapton moaned, bringing one hand up to her forehead as she was wheeled to a room where staff immediately went to work prepping her for a battery of tests, while a Dr. George leaned over her asking a battery of questions.

"Where does it hurt?" asked Dr. George.

"Ugh..." Mrs. Clapton groaned. "Nowhere really."

"Can you see how many fingers I'm holding up?"

Mrs. Clapton peered through two fingers covering her eyes, more out of embarrassment than feeling pain. "Three," she whispered.

"Well, what did you have to eat today," Dr. George asked.

"Soup and saltine crackers," replied Mrs. Clapton.

Dr. George frowned. "When was your last menstrual cycle," he asked.

Mrs. Clapton froze. Come to think on it, she hadn't had a period in years. She gave up on having children of her own. Her biological clock had tick-tocked after the years she spent getting an education first, career second, and finding a loving man third. She was thirty-four by the time all the tocks fell into place, and thirty-five when she started trying to have children. But six years later and nothing. Seven years later, hot flashes, and now 53-years old, she couldn't recall when she had her last period.

Her reply came in a siren of sobs, as she turned her head from side to side, as if her soul was coming apart.

"Mrs. Clapton! Mrs. Clapton! What hurts? Where does it hurt," a freaked out Dr. George asked.

"Aaah...aaah..." Mrs. Clapton went on wailing.

"What's her EKG read," Dr. George turned to ask the medic who'd taken her diagnostics.

"Positive—690 over 117," someone behind Dr. George rattled, reading off a chart.

"Six-Ninet—" Dr. George started to echo before turning to see what was tugging on his sleeve.

"—Doctor please, did anyone call my husband," Mrs. Clapton pleadingly asked, the one tugging his sleeve.

This woman shouldn't be talking, was the look on Dr. George's face. He didn't want to answer, and not because he was busy trying to comprehend what he just heard. He absolutely refused to believe his ears. No one with a systolic pressure that high should be among the vocal conscious. No Exceptions! He could permanently lose his medical license if he reported what he was witnessing for the very first time in his free of court appearances 55-year old medical career. He'd be lucky if he wasn't institutionalized behind this as well.

"Can you read that EKG back to me again," he asked, ignoring Mrs. Clapton's clearly coherent state.

"Positive—690 over 117," the background voice repeated, that time with even more indignation in its tone.

"Doctor please," Mrs. Clapton cried, as Dr. George looked over her, completely ignoring her that time, to reach over a few heads to snatch the chart out of the medic's hands. He glared at the medic as he snatched the chart away too. How dare anyone working under him reply so cavalierly to such a reading!

10

It must be understood I had to do this to Mrs. Clapton. Time was of the essence. Less than 10 hours after I sent the fool on a one-way trip to the hospital, three more something like him had moved in. Cuttie was on her way to school when three of them jokers came trolloping up the street totting a garbage bag between them; not a one of 'em yard workers.

'*I was like, why Granny? Why?*' Gosh, just give me another week and I'll have my child out of there. But I couldn't even get in a lousy 10 full hours before the weed-whackers found a sure 'nuff hole in the wall to lay low in.

After making sure Cuttie got to school without any frays, I doubled back to the house to see what I could do to more permanently child proof that home.

Well, right there on the sofa I found a weed-whacker holding Irene's youngest and whining about how she always wanted one. Can you believe it? A dope head wanted a kid? Actually the part I couldn't believe was the fact that the dope head was a she!

I swore all three of those saggers I saw were the usual bums. But nope, one of them was a girl, just sagging like the other two trying to work on her transition, and not the regular transition to the other side of existing, but to a gender in an opposite direction.

She, soon-to-be he, wearing three thick cornrows braided diagonally across her head, and a gym bra to flatten her chest, started talking about how her mother always wanted a grand but didn't think she'd ever get one. Out of curiosity I zipped by this house the weed-whacker referred to, something I had exhausted myself doing, trying to keep up with all that was going on in this house while I scouted a decent home for my baby. Well, gosh be doggonit if this girl, and a young girl at that, didn't live an upscale civilized life at home.

LaDonna, her mother, worked for a private fortune 900 company, obviously a whole lot of hours, why she wasn't home to see what that youngest one of hers—the weed-whacking she/he—was up to. The weed-whacker's mother actually was a law-abiding regular tax-paying mother. She was home when I zipped by, so the Benz was out there in the carport. A birdbath was out there too, and as well a manicured lawn, white picket fence, and the loveliest mailbox to go along with all of this.

Inside LaDonna was sitting at a large glass dining room table with black rims hanging off the tip of her nose and papers scattered from one end of the table to the other. And just for reference, the table looked to be about ten-feet oblong, and maybe six-feet wide. You couldn't pass anyone sitting across the table a dish. You'd either have to kick it with your foot across the table, or perhaps tilt the table so the dish would slide across the table.

But there LaDonna was with the papers and rims resting on the bridge of her nose, I'm guessing, working from home. She was looking from one paper to the next while I hung around for a sec, amazed about this weed-whacker coming from this civil setting.

Did LaDonna realize where her child was, who incidentally, by an uneducated guess, should've been in school? Maybe she had already given up on the child, like her other kids the weed-whacker mentioned.

The phone rang, just as I was about to swing back to Granny's house, but I waited, curious to hear what Ms. LaDonna sounded like.

For the first few minutes I got to hear, "...umm hmm, um hmm...umm...un uh..." and then there was this unmistakable pause in the umm hmms. I saw LaDonna's expression change too. She went from a casual conversationalist, to a *what the fuck* expression, just before she exploded.

"It's no fucking way Ashley has missed that many days of school! Not when I fucking send her out of here every day! And—" and she broke her verbal stride caught by another bit of disbelief this caller was relentlessly and religiously trying to rinse her ears out with.

"What!" LaDonna shouted, surely without letting her caller finish this entire year-long lawless weed empire enterprise. "Why in the hell are you just calling me now to tell me all of this!?!"

With all of this filthy language canvassing the line, of course all on LaDonna's end, I started trying to figure out who LaDonna might be talking to. I knew most of them turds who worked up there at the school, you know...trying to find a suitable parental match for my little girl. This voice sounded uncomfortably familiar, when the fact was, given the weed-whacker's career, this person could have also been someone like a truant officer. Or maybe a probation officer? Or how about a narcotics agent, representing some kind of kid's weed-whacking round-up squad perhaps? I mean come on lady? LaDonna had to know that child was up to no good.

That's about when I caught the weed-whacker's school photo up on the mantle. Wouldn't you know it? The child looked innocent... just like a child you'd expect to see coming out of this type home. Nice big pretty smile. Bangs galore, and two fluffy pom-poms for a hairdo. Bright eyes. Bushy brows. Just the cutest little girl a loving, caring mother would send off to school while she worked an important job to ensure her youngest child had the best.

I wondered when the photo was taken because it sure as hell looked nothing like the weed-whacker I saw just an hour ago totting roughly 50 pounds of grass, not a blade of it from any regular lawn that gets watered twice a week and decorated by things like white picket fences. This grass was the type grass that grew in abundance in places like Colombia.

And still, if this woman wanted a grandchild, a grandchild she should have. I mean, come on now! I was desperate. I needed to do something to clear out Granny's house, and didn't have no whole lot of time to be engineering a woeful wonderful plot where all parties would agree upon my idea.

Without a second's more thought I jumped right into LaDonna's head and literally drove her straight to Granny's front door where right there on the couch sat weed-whacker Ashley, still bouncing Irene's littlest one in her lap.

LaDonna burst in the house, after asking up and down the block where Reba Briggs lived, shouting to the top of her Crowd Fund lungs, "what the fuck are you doing in this woman's house when you should be in school!?!"

Whack! LaDonna caught Ashley upside the head slapping the crap out of that child. She whacked Ashley so hard that I involuntarily flipped out of LaDonna's head and landed in Ashley's head.

"Momma, Irene asked me to watch the baby," cried the weed-whacker kid, leaning to one side trying to shield the baby from her mother's wrathy blows.

I wasn't quick enough to get back into LaDonna's head. Too much was happening. This turned into a highly volatile situation. For one, the other two weed-whackers who'd been sitting in the front room with Ashley had run down to the cellar upon LaDonna's entrance. While in the cellar, as I had zipped down there right quick too, just to make sure wasn't no real craziness on its way up the steps, I found a few uncles knocked out—a bad combo of drugs, alcohol, laziness, and probably mental illness. A cousin had made his way out of a 2x4 window, along with weed-whackers 2 & 3, fearing the police would soon be making their presence. The rest, I was left to mercifully assume, weren't home. I have no idea where that many people got off to, and at that hour in the morning, 9:22 am to be exact, but they were gone when I got there.

"Get the hell in the car!" LaDonna seethed.

"But...but..."

"But nothing! Get your ass in the car!"

LaDonna looked over at Irene's little boy just a gurgling and kicking his little chunky legs laying on the sofa where Ashley, obeying orders abandoned him, and looked around for a normal grown up. The uncles knocked out in the cellar didn't count. She didn't even try to rouse them. She merely stuck her head in the stairway leading down to the cellar and quickly backed away from the stench coming up from that level of the house. When I say no one was home, I mean, not a single solitary conscious soul. Not even Granny.

LaDonna went next to the bottom of the steps leading upstairs and called out, "Hello, is anyone up there?" holding little chunky butt Boom-Boom on her hip.

No one answered.

"Well, I guess I'm just going to have to take you with me then, huh?" LaDonna said to the child. She fished around and found some rags to cover the child with and followed Ashley to the car, with Boom-Boom on her hip.

Now me, I didn't know then how all this would play out, so I zipped back over to the school, crazily for sure, trying to figure out in this dour hour which one of those teachers I could help want to raise Cuttie. It was then when I zipped into Mrs. Clapton's class; her up there with her cute self, writing math on the blackboard.

Now, don't worry so much about Mrs. Clapton's trip to the hospital. That systolic scare she gave Dr. George was pretty much false. All that reading was, was my pressure mixed up with hers. Mines must have been over 500 with all that stress I'd been under ripping and running, zipping in and out of people. But hers was just fine. That was just a little mishap that took place there too... trying to verify Mrs. Clapton's fitness for long-term parental suitability when I suffered a major panic blow as I was fishing around inside of her. Before I realized it, I was smack dab in the center of her heart—full fledge panicking. She got better once I got out of her, which to her relief...and mines too, was before those practicing quacks wheeled her down to the morgue.

11

The kicker was this. As I scrambled getting out of Mrs. Clapton and back to the school in time to meet Cuttie for her walk home, I ran head-on into another commotion.

Zapping up the street, a little disoriented and dazed after my ordeal in the hospital, *that damn Dr. George nearly killed my ass trying to save Mrs. Clapton who already told his ass she was okay,* but later for that story as I zapped up the street to lo and behold zip through one of the two weed-whackers headed to the school as well. Surely they weren't headed that way to go to school. Oh no, that would be too ridiculous since these knuckleheads had no use for school, which was besides the fact that school was letting out, not just starting.

The knucklehead I was trapped inside, *(for the moment),* had a pulse that needed Dr. George's dutiful attention. His ass was scared, but about what, I was just about to find out.

"Hey Reba, you and Cuttie better lay low before going back to the crib," I heard. "The Feds just busted y'all house and might arrest y'all if you go in there now."

Whadt!?! What the hell was this little fool talking about?

"We ain't dealing, so why we need to worry for?"

That was Reba. I knew her voice, *and dialect* anywhere. And just in case you're wondering, well I had doubled back through weed-whacker number two and hauled BE-hind back to the house to check on things...just in case.

Wasn't a damn thing going on at the house. Granny was still gone, where, I still didn't know, but Irene and her bucket load of kids were in there, and as well the few uncles still conked out, plus a cousin or two more. All of them were in there doing what they normally do; sleep, crap, and yak on stolen burners while the littlest ones ate all over the house, dropping crumbs any and everywhere.

Back up the block I zipped, by chance passing the cousin who escaped through the 2x4 cellar window, hanging over a passenger window talking to some people in a silver Mercury.

"Yup, Sho'dy done put Boom-Boom up for fiddy dollas on ebay," the 2x4 cousin said.

The hellaciousness of the accusation slowed my zip to an automatic near screeching halt.

"You sho' 'bout that," asked a gold-tooth man I hadn't seen around before.

"Sho' as butta," replied 2x4.

"Lemme call Irene and see what she want done 'bout Sho'dy," said gold-tooth.

"No!" screeched 2x4. "Hole' up cuz. How 'bout we get somefin' like a ransom goin'? Dat way we can get mo' dollas outta it. We could be big in no time!"

Gold-tooth grinned, exposing more gold teeth. "Yeah, I like dat. Good lookin' out money. Irene owe me from las' week anyway...fo' that purse I let her hol'. But I think I like this gig betta'."

I couldn't believe what I was hearing. These fools were going to set their fool selves up in a twisted scheme marked for absolute failure.

I didn't hang around a second longer. LaDonna wasn't hardly going to keep Boom-Boom. After she cleaned that child up, and maybe fed him, after tearing a few new assholes in her daughter, she would return Boom-Boom to its rightful owner...the welfare agency. And good luck with accusing the government of kidnapping. That would be the biggest riot since Rainman opened at the Apollo.

Suing the government for stealing its own money? Ha! Ha! Ha! Where's the cane?

I almost made it back to the school, but met Cuttie and Reba coming down the block still fussing with one of the two weed-whackers.

"I'm telling you Reba, dey gone git y'all," weed-whacker two said walking backwards, as the girls continued moving forward.

"Yeah, why don't y'all come hang out in our crib," laughed the other weed-whacker, number three.

Whomp bomp! "Aah!"

That would be weed-whacker number three hitting the pavement. And just in case you're wondering, yep, it was me. Blame 'ole dad for making that fool trip... trying to get my baby girl in his nasty crusty cradle!

Reba burst out laughing. LOUD. And Cuttie smiled as weed-whacker number three pulled himself up on his feet, rubbing his arm and embarrassed for sure.

"Dang man, how'd you do dat?" the other weed-whacker asked, trying to ignore the girl's laughing.

"Dat's al-ight," the second weed-whacker turned around and huffed at the girls. "Let's see who gone be laughing when dey put y'all in dem cuffs!"

The girls arrived home where the house was in chaos like always. Granny wasn't there, and I still don't know why, or where, but I also didn't have time to go looking for her either. It was better I stay with Cuttie, since this was the craziest time of her day.

The girls reheated some of Granny's plentiful soul food—baked sweet potatoes, mac and cheese...my baby girl loved her some Granny's mac and cheese, and fried fish too, just not cold.

"Wanna split dis'," Reba asked Cuttie, speaking of the fish, the last piece left after Irene's bucket load had beat them to the refrigerator.

"Na'," said Cuttie. "I'm gonna git me a piece of ham wif' mines."

"Ya'll close that damn frigerator," Irene yelled from the front room, lounging on the sofa with her extra skeezy-sleazy self, drawing a long drag from a cigarette.

I mean, here her bucket loads of government swiss cheese were in and out of the *frigerator* all day, swinging on the door in fact, while her ass laid up, and here she's gonna yell at my kid who is doing nothing but getting an after school meal. I know I'm getting really worked up about my fatherly role, but that was one woman who I could really give something to yell about, which was just about when a psychosis jumped in the dead center of the TV, and this time I had absolutely nothing to do with it. Well, at least not directly.

Breaking News flashed on the screen, followed seconds later by an unattractive photo of Irene. One eye open, the other closed; one swollen, the other not; one purple, to match the top lip, also swollen, and the other *(eye)*, not *(swollen that is)*, this definitely wasn't one of Irene's happier pictures. Aside from the eye and lip thing, her hair stood in disarray all over her head. She appeared to be wearing a shoulder-less top, at least one shoulder was bare, the other looked like a hand-me down from Jane's collection...you know, Tarzan's soul-mate, and of course she wasn't smiling. In fact, she looked ready to spit...at the camera, or whoever was taking the picture. Yes, it was a mugshot all right, though I hardly would've recognized her had it not been for that name beneath the photo: Irene Louise Briggs.

I was surprised as anything seeing what I was seeing, but there was so much commotion and yik-yakking going on in the front room, to include my darling daughter laughing with Reba, that I couldn't hear the broadcast.

"Oool Mama," one of the kids sitting up close to the TV oooled, pointing and grinning glazy wild wide-eye at the mugshot on screen. "Mama look...dey put you on da TV," the child said just as amused as she wanted to be.

Irene's beady eyes widened as she slowly sat up

on the couch, dropping the cigarette in a can of diet Pepsi. "What da fuck—" Irene mouthed, apparently this breaking news, was news to her too.

"Where'da remote," she asked fishing on either side of her. "Turn dat shit up!"

Actually the TV was just about at its top-notch volume, but oh well...the chatter in the front room piped down and someone found the remote and turned that shit way up.

I couldn't believe it. Those fools actually convinced the law Boom-Boom had been kidnapped and was being held for ransom, though in that sure fire-plan I knew without a shred of doubt would backfire, had indeed backfired, though not like how I thought. *Father Mercy*, prosecutors had a warrant out for Irene's arrest. She was their *person of special interest.*

"How they gone say I'ma unfit mother!" Irene shouted at the TV, hurling the remote as she shouted. "Peekabug," she yelled in that very next breath, "go up deer and bring Boom-Boom down here!"

Peekabug scrambled off the floor and with his bowleg self loped up the stairs to do as told. No one else seemed too much concerned about why Irene was on the news, or what she had done, or the fact that Boom-Boom might be missing.

Lots of people were in and out of the house all hours of the day and night. Wasn't nothing too spectacular about one missing kid, or Irene being wanted. She was in and out of jail all the time anyway, something like a revolving door.

The thought seemed to be Boom-Boom probably was with Granny, wherever that was. It wasn't like these news people were the best at getting news right anyway. They got stuff wrong all the time. The poor weren't the only ones face-planting in the gossip columns. The so called yuppy-guppies fell into the hype they created and dispersed too.

I wasn't worried either. I expected any moment La-Donna would appear with the child and these bold-faced informants be found out. And if it didn't happen the way I expected, then I'd make it happen.

"Ma!" Peekabug called from the top of the stairs. "He ain't up here!"

"Why he ain't up deer? You check his baby bed?"

"Un uh..."

"Well check Granny's room."

"Granny not here," Reba quietly replied. "She tol' me last night she was stayin' wif—"

"—Granny gone too," Peekabug reported, confirming what Reba was about to say.

"Well call Brenda and see if dat winch dun stole my son!"

"Brenda!" Peekabug shouted.

"Boy, don't call her like dat," Irene shouted back. She looked over at Reba and Cuttie sitting crossed-legged in the floor eating. "One of ya'll go git Brenda for me," she said, kicking at Reba. "See if she dun sole Boom-Boom."

Neither one of them got up, both ignoring her, caught up in smacking on that delicious soul food.

"Ya'll here me talkin'! Somebody fuckin' go git Brenda!" And Irene picked up a magazine laying within reach and threw it at them.

"Why don't you go git her yourself," Reba snapped back. "It's your son!"

"Gurlll...don't be gittin' smart wif me! Now move! And go find out if Brenda dun *stole* and sole Boom-Boom!"

Reba huffed, and started to get up when there was a loud knock at the door. All of them froze, except for one of the kids who scrambled off the floor to answer the door.

"It's Peaches and Brenda," lil Audi said, another one of Irene's rug-rats.

"Irene girl, they fixin' to arrest you. You all up on da news! Girl you in trouble," Brenda wheezed as if she'd run over from the next country, instead of two doors over.

Irene leaned forward, arching her back so she could see out of the bay window. "All, dis shit is bullshit. Dey always tryna' throw a bitch in jail," she said, getting up off the sofa. "Bren—why don't you do me a favor and tell po-po you got Boom-Boom at your place... jus' til I figure dis shit out."

"How I'ma say dat? What if dey wanna check?"

"Awl girl, stop being a fuckin' scaredy-cat. They can't check yo' house if you don't let 'em in. They hafta git a search warrant first."

"Unt un Irene. I ain't gone down for some mo' stupid shit you done did."

"Girl, I ain't done nuffin' yet!" Irene spat.

"Well, where he at den?" Peaches asked, standing in place and looking around like she suspected somebody was about to pick-pocket her.

"Well he ain't da fuck here. We dun already checked. Maybe he—"

—And before Irene could finish her next guess the police pulled up in one, two, three, and four squad cars.

"Oh shit—" Irene took off for the cellar where the real rogues lived. Running didn't do her no good though. Her big ass couldn't fit through that 2x4 window. The police ran right after her, could've even passed her, pathetic as she ran, and dragged her right back upstairs and out the front door.

Now I'm going to tell you, even though it seemed like I was calm and loddy-doddy during all of this, I wasn't. I was pissed like nothing before when I saw one officer's foot stomp in my baby's plate. Broke the plate in half and spoiled my baby girl's meal. And the thing about it was, I know that bitch did it on purpose. There really are some f'ing mean ass people in this world. They fucking hate just to hate. But I got that one bitch. I had to. Stepping in my baby's plate like that, when the child hadn't done a thing to no one. Tell you about what I did though, after I sweep up the rest of this mayhem.

Lawd, I never bawled so hard thinking about how I had to get my princess out of this mess. I heard the phone ring during this plough, but thought nothing of it until I heard one of the kids trying to tell the caller somebody in the house was busy. Instantly I zapped on the phone wire, recognizing Mrs. Clapton's gentle voice right away.

"Does Cuttie Brown live here?" she asked.

I wished I had vocals so Mrs. Clapton could hear me shout back, 'yes!'

"Who dis? She in da flo' too," the child answered.

'*Lawd, praise this child,*' I whispered, realizing Mrs. Clapton assumed this meant Cuttie was hurt, or otherwise in need of her help. She hung up the phone and not more than ten minutes later was at the house.

Part Two

12

You had to see her, my pretty little princess with the two big pretty yellow bows tied on either side of her head, and the long bangs almost covering the sweetest eyes ever seen on a face as tiny.

Cuttie's eyes looked just like pearls, turned sideways. Plus she had the cutest little button nose. Reminded me of a Pirate's hat by the way it was shaped, only much, much tinier; about as big as the tip of my pinky finger, when I had fingers of course. I'm surprised the child was able to breathe. And you couldn't convince me she didn't look like the perfect angel sitting there between Mr. and Mrs. Clapton. That family belonged together, and as every god was my witness, they were going to be together. That was my mission.

"Mrs. Clapton, may I speak with you," a tall slender perfumed woman came out of an office and said. She didn't bother to address Mr. Clapton. She looked all over and around him, and Cuttie too, sitting there smiling and swinging her legs, just as cute as she wanted to be.

June got up from where she was sitting beside Cuttie and briskly followed the tall slender rose scented woman.

"Mrs. Clapton," the tall slender woman began no sooner than all of June was in her office. "I understand how you feel about this child, but I just got off the phone with the Social Services department and I'm afraid we're going to have to keep that child with us until you go to court and *we* get a ruling from the court.

'Whhhhhaaaaaaaaaaaaaaaaaaaaaaaaadtttttt!!!'
Every man, mammal, and extraterrestrial living in the furthest galaxy had to have heard that cry. After all I had been through...all Cuttie had been through, wasn't no MOTHER FUCKING WAY!!!

"Miss Whatuchi," June crisply started, jaws tight and teeth clinched, "I know you don't have any children, or understand what it's like for children to be shuffled around from home to home, uncertain, unloved, scared, and in desperate need of something stable, but every minute...every second that child is tossed around, is another ten years off her life!"

That's right June. I knew I liked this woman the first time I laid eyes on her. There was just something special about her. And damn it, I would have said just about the same thing.

"Look," said Whatuchi, "I know she'll be sad and all that, but there are rules to be—"

"—All that!" June hissed, glaring daggers so razor sharp at Whatuchi that even I ducked.

"Let me tell you something Mizz Whatuchi," and June really sneered that woman's trunked up surname. She made that mizz sound extra ugly, and Waah-too-shee too. That broad wasn't from no other place than tiz of thee and land of the free. Straight up. Her people were from Washington's stock, now trying to pass off as a Hawaiian, as if that would absolve her of the unmistakable ignorance and disdain she had for my baby, and all children sharing her culture.

None of this dissuaded June from going where she had every right to go. She jumped all in Whatuchi's put-on, recounting the *'one hundred-sixty-three days Ashley Priest had skipped school'* while she, specifically, gave not a red damn about Ashley, or any of the other kids who drank, smoked, had sex and hookied school together.

"...And don't you dare get to holding your breath," June went on, sneering through a veneer that could shear steel. "You're not winnng this one!"

June, of course, had proof. She had personally reported Ashley's situation directly to Whatuchi, right in the very office where she stood giving the lip-sealed woman the Siberian cussing.

But MAN! If mortals could see living cells, they'd seen me going *'Yeah! Yeah!' Punching the air and whatnot. 'Tell her, June! Tell her!'* And I swear June looked around as if she heard me. I piped down some after that, but boy was I sure glad June kept some sort of record of all that madness I'd gone through.

To be fair though, poor Whatushi couldn't have been more than a year or so out of school. And I'm thinking undergrad out of school. She might've even got her deflecting skills from one of them community colleges. That name, Whatuchi, sounded like the type. Rich people were proud of their ancestry and thus kept their names. Like the Queen of England and her clan. You ever heard of a sudden break in their names? Hell no you haven't. That stuff can be traced. I know, because it's how I learned all this...straight from historians. They don't play. They were the ones who tracked down and traced all men, and women, right back to the heart of the motherland. Now, of course, this Whatushi, for as young and ignorant as she was, was clueless about all this. She only took the ESL history class. The class where the teacher made stuff up and read them fairytales so no ones feelings got hurt. Poor Whatshername would probably even try to sue someone, claiming defamation, not knowing her dumb ass was all along a Washington.

Consequently, Whatushi didn't know what the hell to say after that verbal ass whipping. But she did know what to do.

Hastily she scribbled on some papers and without looking at June said, "here," snatching papers off her desk to hand them over. "Take these over to Social Services. They'll draft up the formal adoption paperwork."

13

It would've been so nice if things could've ended right here, except nooooooo...by my take, and I've been around plenty, there are troves of bored folk who live to fuck shit up! These are people just plain tired of living and aching for me to sit their asses on the super hell highway.

"June, you really need to think about this move honey." This was Eric, June's husband, trying to caution his wife before drafting his final notice to a company he'd worked for, for over 35 years.

"I'm sure," June sighed, really not sure, yet keeping hope alive. "I want Cuttie to have a fresh start, why I'm so concerned about these busy bodies who keep stirring pots. I just don't want them to ruin things for us."

I knew just who she was talking about too. Ethel fucking Jenkins. I didn't care for the woman from the get go. Too phony. And much too righteous for my average tastes. I like plain people who mind their business. This was not Ethel.

"You really should consider coming back," Ethel told June one day, actually the same day June made up her mind she wanted to move.

"And just what were you thinking, adopting that child like that? Do you realize how much trouble you could get into if this gets out?"

'Get out? Like, get out of what, or why...OR HOW!?! Ethel and June had been friends for 20 of the 23 years they worked together. The gap accounted for years they spent getting to know each other's work ethics. That's a long time

to be learning the habits of a two-faced, backstabbing, double-dealing, snitching bitchy hypocrite!

I bit down on my anger to keep from knocking Ethel off that pedestal and flat on her flat ass. Cuttie didn't need no more problems, and neither did I, or June. I had to be a big boy and behave myself.

"Oh, Ethel," June sighed, "I'm passed all that. This child is special. I can feel it. She belongs with us, and I will fight for her with everything I have to keep one more from falling through the cracks."

"The cracks," that (---), *woo...almost called that lady out of her name*, had the gall to *tisk.*

That's a sound people make when they think they know something, or think they are above the righteous bar, a concurrent problem running in this Ethel woman.

"June, you know as well as I do that some of them have to fall through the cracks so that the *rest of us* can succeed. Not all of us were meant to make it." And the fucking snide BITCH said this as if June was her pupil...her 2nd grade pupil!

I liked to have puked and made my presence known. It probably would've killed them both to see puke coming out of thin air, which wouldn't have mattered if it was only a matter of Ethel that I was dealing with.

Fact to the matter, so far June, and Eric, had been good to my little peach. June alone was doing a mighty miraculous job holding her own to help my little sand castle thrive. Eric was a little wussy, but so long as that man kept his hands, and eyes, off my little princess, then he was a good man. I wanted to see this thing through. Yet to hear this shit coming from a teacher—*a mother fucking teacher, you hear*—ticked me the WHUCK OFF!

Thankfully June beat me to it. "Not this one," she angrily spat. "This one is going to be someone. I'll bet *your* life on it!"

Ha! Ha! *Good One.* That brought ms. self-righteous, yes, all lower case letters, up in the chair. She shot up like an arrow, which straightening up like she did had to be difficult with that hump in her back.

Still ms. selfish left June's house and got her back-stabbing flat ass on the phone to share June's affairs with another teacher.

I was on the line when they got to talking, *you know... minding MINE and my child's business!*

"Can you believe it? She quit her job for one child," said one nosey meddling bitty to another nosier meddling bitty. "And one of them Briggs kids' at that!"

That was not the reason June left her job. June retired early because of that heart scare, and that happened several months ago, not the other week, or that day. See how rumors got started? By JUDGEMENTAL backstabbers who don't know shit! *Woo...I wanted to wring her neck like a chicken.*

"Well, if you ask me, I always thought June was a red flag, making waves from the first time I met her. But mark my word, just you wait and see...when that child stabs her in the back, which you know is gonna happen sooner rather than later, she'll take off them rose-colored save the world glasses."

"Yeah, but that's just it," the ole bitty Ethel inserted. "She's having her husband...quit.his.job," and she enunciated quit.his.job, with just that emphasis. All three words came with a period on the end—strung together.

Aww, these bitties needed real troubles to concern themselves with. That, of course, was me. My thought. Which lifted my karmatic energy, expotentially. Immediately I got to work on helping them fill up their shallow down time.

Sturgis Grover, the principal of Princeton Middle School, needed to make some budget cuts. Now, because these two bitties were union, he couldn't fire them, but he could send these two packing off to another school. His only problem was he needed help selecting which of the union bitties he could axe...and guess who was more than willing to oblige him with such help?

I rifled through files kept on these two, sure I was going to find some dirt. Everyone has some dirt on them, even the cleanest person, which there was no doubt these two were far from clean.

Zappo! There it was...believe it or not, Ethel was the easiest. That's right! You make trouble for my sweet little poo castle, and you're making trouble with her daddy. I learned a long time ago in my past dealings that don't nobody in this whole wide fucking world too much care to be wearing shoes on the other foot. No one. Talking about my child slipping through some fucking crack. Well, watch while I open this fucking crack!

That's right, I sure did. I opened a crack wide enough for two bitties at once to fit through any way they went through. Slip, slide, somersault, cartwheel, jackknife...whichever way they rolled.

Umm um, turned out 'ole precious Ethel had gotten into an altercation not once or twice, but three times in the two sheets of notes I thus far came across. Umm um; students, parents, and fellow teachers were involved. This woman had a problem with her hands. She couldn't keep them to herself. Someone this bad and tough would work well in a more correctional type environment; not a regular school were poor kids attended.

And by the way, Cuttie no longer attended Princeton Elementary School. June pulled her out the day she brought her home to live with her. She home-schooled my child.

14

I put my plan in motion when I saw knucklehead Malik Smith holding a gym shirt up to his head, headed towards the nurse's office.

'*No Malik, No,*' I spoke softly, getting all up in this challenged kid's head. '*You're too dizzy and hurt to see that nurse who's not going to do anything but give you an aspirin and call your parents to come get you,*' I said. '*You want the principal to see JUST how hurt you are so he will get angry and really punish that boy who hurt you.*'

Malik stumbled right into Sturgis' office holding his head with whooping-cough tears blurrying his eyes. Now, earlier I had paid Sturgis a visit. I paid Sturgis a visit the second he sat down at his desk, a full 3 hours before the first kid arrived at school.

He sat down at his desk, and I sat right down in his head too, reminding him about the budget cuts, enumerating Ethel Jenkins's name far more than I cared to hear it.

The recital helped push him away from his desk, though he stood and schlepped over to a metal filing cabinet much too lethargic for what I'd call a man worthwhile. I mean, what is with all these pussified-out men!?! Just looking at this nimble thimble told me I was going to have to keep all my essence; hooks, daggers, venom, and whatever else I could conjure up, deep in his risible tail.

He opened the third from the bottom drawer, one that required bending a little. When he stooped over, he grabbed his back. *Aah, the old pony must've been a little sore. Gee Whiz!*

The painfully pitiable looking principal, trying to support his back with one hand resting on it, used his only available hand to rifle through files packed too tight to accomplish with one hand. *Gosh! Can I kick him in the ass and send him through the file cabinet, shut the damn drawer and then kick the whole thing through a wall?* You know I was mad enough to do it, except I had no feet. Plus, it wouldn't have helped my angel. I had to be patient with this pontz.

'Ethel...Ethel...Ethel Jenkins,' I recited over and over as he listlessly went through these files. He stopped once, but not on Ethel's name. Still, he pulled the file out and stood, and arched his back to get in a little stretch. What the hell, he had to be thinking, because he reached into the cabinet and grabbed a handful of files, using both hands, holding whosever file he first pulled out between his lips.

Sturgis was now annoyed. Having to bend over that file cabinet started it, but having to tend to this chore finished it.

A heap of files stood on his desk, not quite burying him from view had someone walked in and caught him reading, but enough files to keep him plenty occupied for the next few hours while the children assembled outside his office waiting for the bell to ring.

I stayed with Sturgis, though I slacked off with the repetitive name recital, since he appeared to be getting overly interested reading the personnel files.

A few times he shook his head. Once he slapped a file down, turning it over so that I had to get up underneath the stack to see who he turned down. Several he tossed aside, and maybe one or two, but no more than three, he gingerly laid on the tossed aside stack. Ethel's file, much to my delightful surprise, was in his hand.

When the bell rang he was angrily reading Ethel's file, rolling his eyes each time he flipped a page. He scribbled a few notes right there on the folder—*schedule a meeting was the note he underlined*—just as he came to a brighter idea...just as the school bell rang.

On cue I told Sturgis he needed to find a place to put that file so that he could access it without having to bend over and hurt his back more trying to pull it out of another file cabinet. So, about to find a convenient place to put the folder, Malik Smith, holding his head, stumbled in his office.

Re-staging the scene: There was Sturgis, already annoyed. Not feeling his chirpiest given his back pains, and angry about something he read in Ethel's file, when Malik stumbled in.

"Oh my goodness," Sturgis said, hastily rushing over to the youngster. "What happened son?"

Malik wasn't Sturgis's son. It's what he called all young boys.

"Tyrone Briggs hit me with a brick," Malik brooded, covering a baseball size knot on his head.

"Oh, Lord, Jesus," Sturgis huffed. Of course you know exactly where Tyrone Briggs came from. Sturgis knew too. It's why he didn't have to question Malik any further on what happened. Saying Tyrone Briggs, or how about Briggs all by itself, was enough information to fill in the rest of the story. Many courts bought this type testimony as well.

It'd be like Briggs vs. *fill in the blank*, and a gavel would slam down on the docket and a big voice boom, "GUILTY!" Of course in favor of fill in the blank. This was such a popular verdict that it became the Briggs's most used defense.

Sturgis rushed Malik out of his office, Ethel's file still in his hand, and ushered the child to the school nurse where he first started to go.

"Sandy," he said to the school nurse, "can you look at him and make sure he's okay. I'm going to speak to Laticia."

And here we go. Laticia Freedom. Two names that went together, stayed together, and everyone agreed together to steer clear of her path.

Laticia was the school dean. In grade school the dean was IN NO WAY associated with academic counseling or advising. In this grade school, Princeton Elementary School, the dean was the custodian of levying discipline. And Laticia Freedom who... did believe in eating flesh, but NOT abortion, and hated companies breaking child labor laws, rallied for MADD and started the first anti-bullying campaign, plus dimed on anyone habitually calling out, or reporting to work late, and rallied for women's libbers rigourously, along with wearing pink ribbons religiously and regardless of the color suit she'd worn, and had wrote Congress twice derailing two careers simultaneously...and permanently, and listed her favorite book as the Bible, DID in fact believe in setting people straight, especially knuckleheads like Tyrone Briggs. She may have very well been the only school administrator who was not afraid of them Briggs.

Sturgis rushed to Laticia's door, folder still in hand, and sort of braced himself against the doorframe.

"Laticia," he said highly agitated at this point, "will you please pull Tyrone Briggs out of class. He just hit a kid in the head with a brick, and I think the kid might really be hurt."

Laticia looked at Sturgis out of these bulging eight ball eyes bucked against thick black framed lens, and with her thick, *very thick,* red lips...*and nothing sensual here,* said, "sure."

I was in her head too. She was concerned about Sturgis. She never saw him this agitated. He was a pussy to her as well. One time a kid had been robbed by a Briggs kid, stripped all the way down to his birthday suit and 'ole Sturgis simply shrugged and mumbled, "oh well, what can we do?"

So Sturgis breaking into her office and demanding that she do something about this Briggs kid, something she'd been wanting to do since the first Briggs showed up

in the school, something like 23 years ago when she started and met Irene for the first time, made her warily concerned about Sturgis' mental well-being.

Sturgis saw that look Laticia was giving him, so I
helped him explain.

"Look," Sturgis said, releasing the doorframe to
step inside her office. "I'm a little fed up with these Briggs.
Every day it's the same thing. This nonsense has to stop,"
he added letting his shoulders droop a little.

"Well, it's about high noon time," Laticia spat.

And this woman had a way about spitting words
she spat. First of all, her voice sounded like a frog with
alligator lineage blowing through a fan. She had a non-
inviting husky drone, as if she smoked heavily, which she
didn't. *Oh heck no, she didn't...and never did.* And yet it was
her look that was even less inviting.

Ever seen a baboon? And I'm talking one light-
skinned baboon, with really thick red lips and puffy jaws.
Well, circle a lot of mascara around its eyes, and put a
little curly wig on its head, and make it wear a pair of
thick black-framed lens. That's what Laticia looked like.
So, between this and her voice, plus Ethel's file, which he
still held, even if in the heat of the moment he'd forgotten
about it *(wink, wink)*, all of this ruffled his feathers more.

"Listen here Laticia, I'm in charge here! Not you!
So I'd appreciate a little more respect when you speak to
me!" he spat back.

Whoa...whoa...this was not Sturgis at all. Admittedly,
I was inside him pulling every chord I could to rattle this
spineless wuss, but to Laticia, she must've thought 'ole
Sturgis was really going through some things. The scene
was off-script he-larry-ous! And yes, I was laughing like a
hyena, outside both of them however.

Freakishly Laticia rose from her chair and punched
both fists, knuckles first, down on her desk. "With all due
respect Mr. Sturgis F. Grover," she hissed, glaring at him
like a honey badger eyeballing an intruder while eating,

"...you did NOT let me finish," she snarled. "As I said, and would like to add, it. is. about. high noon time you decided to grow some balls and deal with these recalcitrant children!"

First of all, he wasn't going to be dealing with anything. It's why he enlisted her. And secondly, "ah, Laticia, I'm not here to fight," he explained trying to pipe down, raising his hands to signal a truce. Only problem was, while raising his hands, he absentmindedly laid Ethel's folder on her desk. He was going to pick it right back up, except Laticia had more to say.

"Well I think you did come in here to start a war because no one barges in an office I occupy to question my ethics!"

"I never questioned your ethics. All I—"

"—You absolutely did question my ethics! You accused me of disrespecting you!"

"But—"

"—Excuse me Mr. Sturgis," interrupted Sandy the school nurse. "I have Mrs. Smith on line one."

Sturgis released a loud, long beat the hell down exhausted sigh. He glanced at the telephone on Laticia's desk, line one just a blaring, but decided to take the call elsewhere after meeting the dare in her glare. Touch that phone and he was apt to lose his entire right side.

15

It should be no guess about who had Ethel's personnel file, and exactly what was being done with it. And just so that it's all laid out there clearly, Sturgis did put an APB out on finding the folder. To his defense, a day later when he discovered it missing, things got hairier than expected dealing with Mrs. Smith and them Briggs, and of course Laticia on top of them all.

Initially he thought he misfiled the folder somewhere in his office. But a hairy call from Ethel herself, and the school board, he knew exactly where he last left that file, and exactly who got their paws on, and into it.

Now, I'm not even going to indulge on all the liberties, and improprieties Laticia took in disseminating that one file. Just keep in mind, it was going to be some time before Ethel got back to minding anyone else's business.

My plan worked like a charm. Ethel was so busy she had to wave the other bitty away when she tried to get back in my child's business, asking more questions about June and the adoption. The bitty wanted to pass this info on to another party who was very interested in that strange child who used to attend the school.

But Ethel was so mired in fighting the school and collaborating with attorneys to take legal action against the Board of Education, and Sturgis *personally* for misusing her personal information that she had NO TIME to get the digs on June and Cuttie. Her ass had to abandoned that scandal, to spare the remaining parts of her hide from sheep partying on her grave like it was the year 10,000.

Someone just mention June, or Cuttie, which no one had, and it'd be like *June who? Cuttie what?*

So I credit myself for having done a fabulous job dodging what could've turned into an abusive nightmare. My problem now was my darling daughter, and helping her settle better in her new home.

"I thought I was gonna go back to Reba and dem for the summer," Cuttie innocently said to June.

My child didn't know any better. She never had a chance to see better, all except for what she experienced moving in with June and Mr. Clapton.

Cuttie had it all. Her own room; a beautiful princess bed, with the canopy, draperies, pretty shag carpet and the whole nine. No more matted carpet that looked and smelled to the soles of feet like walking on guts, puke and big brown dumps. June even went out and bought Cuttie a new wardrobe, plus all the electronics she could ever want. Her own plasma TV. A cell phone which (she really didn't need, but June smartly restricted), blocking Reba's number. She also had her own laptop, an ipod and ipad, and plenty books to read on her Nook. It's mostly what kept her occupied for those six months she'd been there; only every so often asking about Reba.

"Oh honey," June answered, sweeping Cuttie's bangs away from her pearl-dropped eyes with one finger, "the state had to relocate Reba and her family."

I saw inside June's heart. The hurt and worry. She hated lying to Cuttie, but in desperate times, fudging the truth sometimes remedied problems where philosophy didn't always work. Yeah, so save that bullshit talk, I had every confidence June would eventually get around to telling my darling the truth.

"What's relocate," Cuttie asked. See. *Right there, my sweetie was learning big new words.* She would've never known this word had not June done what she did.

The night June brought Cuttie home with her, was the night that large foot officer stepped in my baby's plate.

June arrived at the house, alone, to complete chaos. And trust me when I say, it was utter bedlam on Princeton Road; because I made plenty sure of it.

I couldn't risk June walking off thinking Cuttie would be alright hanging in that house for another day. So when she pulled up in her black SUV I made sure that house looked like what I remembered of the Gingerbread house, except instead of cookies, tinsel and most things yummy, I had weed-whackers spilling out of that ill house.

Weed-whackers one, two, three and four were crawling out of that 2x4; Peekabug and Audi, plus two more unidentifieds were in one upstairs bedroom window yelling down to the street, "Mama, kick 'em in da nuts! Kick 'em in da nuts!" Meanwhile Reba and her wild self ran up and down the street ranting about police brutality and, "here, sign dis'...sign dis...yup, yup, you seent dit... here sign dis!"

And this was all minus rubber-neckers responding to cries of *'kick 'em in da nuts,'* and *'here sign dis.'* Many of them were acting plumb fools too.

But my baby, she stayed inside, curled up on the sofa Irene vacated, *and I almost forgot,* while I made sure Irene had her tail all the way bent over the trunk of that squad car, since the police had dragged her out of the house dressed in only a robe; no undergarments. It was a living nightmare for sure, to include that officer who I also forgot to include in this mayhem.

Yes! I helped her walk right into the homemade rat-trap, *courtesy of Tebok* who liked tinkering with shiny metal gadgets.

Listen, that child might not have been the brightest coin in a bucket, but he was the certifiable next up and coming engineer. Trust me on this. Not only could he make a whole bike out of scrapped metals, but he could set some hellified rat-traps that worked on all rodents of any size, to include rats with size 10 boots who liked stepping in children's dinner plates.

Whenever the police showed up, or got word they were showing up, Tebok, or one of them would throw down a skid *(they called it)*, strategically placed in spots around the house; namely that 2x4 window. It alerted them of visitors. Sort of worked like a doorbell, except... well, you get my point. The thing was totally legal, and assuredly warranted, besides, the heifer shouldn't have stepped in my baby's plate, and that was the long and short of it. See, if it really had been an accident, then the way I saw it, her foot would've never found the trap. Of course her yelling out over trees, many over 75-feet tall, told me this was no accident. Her buddies had to summon a damn near zoo trainer to undo that trap.

At any rate, the point I was getting at, was how all this bedlam helped get my child out of there without either Reba, or Cuttie being aware of what was happening. Really, neither June, nor Granny who arrived just as June pulled up—on foot albeit—via the number 22 bus—knew what was happening. June hadn't gone to the house to take Cuttie that night. She'd only been thinking of Cuttie— a lot, *courtesy of you know who*—and wanted to make sure she was okay. She really wasn't sure what she was going to do. It, ironically, was her conversation with Granny, and *of course at my inspiration,* that got the ball rolling.

16

"You don't like it here," June asked Cuttie in answer to her question about visiting Reba. "You don't like your room?" wondering why in the world Cuttie would ever want to go live with those dysfunctional people. You had to have seen the night I pulled my child out of there.

Cuttie nodded her head up and down, idly sliding her slim finger back and forth across her iphone. My poor child was in deep thought. She was trying to assemble this wacky picture too. And poor June wasn't able to make any better sense of things either. Granny's lecture that spoke to why Cuttie didn't see the way June, and others did, had rested on juvenile ears. She hadn't understood a thing.

"Chile," Granny told June on that blistery squally night she left out with Cuttie, "don't feel sorry for us. What most of ya'll don't understand is we's fittin' ourselves for survival. Cain't all of us be on top."

Well darn it if that wasn't what Ethel had said. But those words made no sense the way Ethel put it. Sounded cruel in fact, but not by how Granny said it.

"Our pain ain't yo' pain. Same way yo' pain cain't be ours," Granny went on. "We sho' nuff done been through a lot worse, but countin' plenny mo' happy days ahead," she smiled with that one and a half eye. "Jus' hafta' trust in Him," Granny added. "We not sufferin' like most like to think. We'll be alright."

At that very moment Granny was speaking, Reba was still running in and out of the house lobbying for petitions, for Irene's supposed police brutality case.

Funny thing about all this was, both Granny and June sat in naked sight of Boom-Boom showing up with LaDonna. I have to admit, myself, to the lunacy in how things unspiraled. That fool child Nookie had put himself up on the back of one of the police cruisers, trying to join Reba's petition, jumping up and down on the trunk chanting to the top of his lungs, "turn her loose! Turn her loose!"

Well, police turned him loose all right; two of 'em churned on him like a bowl of mashed potatoes. Last I saw of him once they finished turning him loose, he was laying like Jello on a gurney, on his way to Grand Mercy hospital—again.

LaDonna had pulled up to the house in midst of this circus, walking right by Reba, and the child's mother... IRENE! I heard Cuttie's soft purr telling Granny, "'der go Boom-Boom right deer."

Investigation in full swing, the house in complete disarray, and LaDonna swayed right up to Granny as she was talking to June and she sat happy well-fed and cleaned-up Boom-Boom right in Granny's lap. Obviously LaDonna hadn't seen the news either.

"I would've brought him back earlier but I was thinking about keeping this one for myself," she teased.

"Hmm umm," Granny hummed, letting her sit the child in her lap as if he was the thousandth child she held that day.

I caught June wince, but missed what that was all about. Honest to goodness there was so much going on I couldn't keep up. I mean, between Reba's raucous yelling about signing a brown paper bag in red crayon *(because she couldn't find one sheet of loose-leaf notebook paper or pen to write with)*... and the kids hanging out the window yelling at the cops making arrests and banging heads on the curb, I lost my place scheduling whose head to bounce into to figure out what everybody was thinking...or about to do.

So, aside from the fact that the upheaval could've been dispelled right there had one person corroborated what my baby was trying to tell them. Granny had the kid everyone was hollering about sitting right there in her lap. Unfortunately however, June didn't know the missing child from Adam to Felipe.

June looked around, soothed by Granny's calm and rich affable pitch, but baffled never-the-less. She couldn't get out of her pretty little head how anyone would want to be mixed up in this upheaval.

So I helped clear up a few of the fuzzies by allowing her to take two deep breaths to prep for taking that final step that wasn't in her original plan.

"Well then," June sighed deeply, "I'm sure you'll consent to letting me take Cuttie to my home so she can participate in a science camp program?"

The science camp program didn't exist. I made it up. So this came to June off the cuff, on the fly, *via yours truly and you know why.* I had to. I got to throwing them words on June's mind faster than atom ape whips on his cape. Hurriedly I shoved them thoughts down her thorax like I used to punch my feet in socks. June had no idea what she was talking about. She thought she was acting on instinct.

Granny looked around laying that lazy eye on Reba going one way, then the other, and back out the door, and gave her consent, just as unexcitedly as she shopped for pampers. The state wasn't yet giving her funds to care for Cuttie, though Irene had been working on it.

"Now, is Irene Cuttie's mama," June slyly slid in. "I just need Cuttie's guardian to sign this permission slip."

Slowly Granny turned that lazy eye loose on June and replied just as noncommittal as falling rain, "baby, dat chile don't belong to none of Irene's. She been orphaned to us."

June frowned. Was she denying the child? Telling her Cuttie belonged to no one? *And trust me, if I wasn't in there to field those questions.*

"Well then, would you mind signing for her," June

cautiously asked. She wasn't sure how accurate Granny's intel was, given the old woman's listless demeanor, but she was sure that sweet child with the scar on her forehead belonged in a safe, nurturing environment. *Ahem... thanks to that child's daddy.*

"I guess it'll be all right," Granny lazily shrugged, patting Boom-Boom's back, every so often looking around at another foible passing by. "I'll hafta' sign an X tho'. I ain't never learned to write."

June wanted to ask more questions, except I urged her to cut her losses and take Cuttie and get going.

"Cuttie, sweetie," June said kneeling to speak to my snookums eye level. "Why don't you run upstairs and pack a few things. I'm going to take you to Disney World tomorrow," she smiled.

Cuttie's eyes brightened and widened. She never heard of the place but was enamored that her favorite teacher was taking her anywhere.

She sprouted off the couch and darted upstairs, meanwhile that lunar model Reba was still running around paying no mind to either of them. The house activity was at an all-time high when Cuttie left out holding Mrs. Clapton's hand.

17

I made sure my baby got the best of the best while June and her husband talked over legally adopting my child and moving away with her.

"But honey, are you sure what we're doing is the right thing to do...for us...and Cuttie," Eric Clapton asked, being the utter puss he was. He racked up over 35 years working for Pinecroft Publishing, editing scores of best sellers, being just that puss. But then how was I to complain about a good-hearted man being a major faculty in my sweetheart's life? Even if he was a little puss in boots, I had to take what came along with June's fine package. I had to take what I could get.

"Oh, I'm sure," June said, more convinced than she was the day Ethel left out of her house.

"But what if her mother, that Irene woman comes after us looking for her," Eric asked with both hands on his hips, looking all worried, wearing down the carpet pacing tracks back and forth past June.

"Sweetie, I've done my homework. That woman can't be Cuttie's mother. It would mean she gave birth to twins that year...three and a half months apart. That's impossible."

June was talking about Reba and Cuttie being twins. That was some of the gossip milling around the school, before Ethel ran up on her claw-digging chest of troubles, and long before June walked out of the house with Cuttie.

Rumor circling the teacher cooler, gossip scraped

off the counterfeit birth certificate Reba forged, and social services turned over to the school, had Cuttie born a few months after Reba. But had anyone even bothered to inspect that document they would have seen the name cut and pasted on the form was born 4 years and 3 months BEFORE that wild child. But of course, those people could care less about the truth. They didn't even bother to look up Reba's birth record. Had they, and they would have discovered Reba and Irene were not daugher and mother, but sisters!

See. Right there. All they cared about was feeding rumormills, even though I must admit, dealing with them Briggs to separate truth from fiction was a lane where perhaps assumptions were preferable.

The door chime sounded as June and wussified Eric were discussing the matter. An agent from Social Services had been assigned to assess the home, to put a preliminary seal of approval on the adoption.

This would be it. Unless June, Eric, or both of them bungled this interview, or unless someone with a lot more information than even myself barged in and challenged the adoption, Cuttie Brown would officially be on her way to becoming Caitlyn Marissa Clapton. June decided to give Cuttie the family name, trying to shave off as much of that Briggs connection as she could.

My sweetums said she liked that name—*and I liked it too*. Soon as the interview was over June vowed she would forever refer to my poo bear as Caitlyn...*and you know damn frankin' well I would too!*

18

I'll be damn! The same social service agent who accepted the Briggs' phony birth certificate, was the same woman who showed up for the interview! *WTF!*

The heffa walked in the house a whole new social worker. She wasn't that shaky small-time official that ran out of the Brigg's house fighting off rug rats and a snaggle-tooth old man trying to hit on her.

No! She strolled in like a boss, trying to start some shit, going by what I saw. I could tell by how far her nose was turned up in the air, sniffing around prepared to upset June...and her puny husband.

Look! I didn't need any hold-ups or marbles rolled into this situation! Rumors were already flying a mile high when this interview got underway; why Eric was so concerned. By this time Reba was off the chain about Cuttie... tweeting what she planned to do to whoever was holding her sister soul-mate hostage.

I tried to thwart as much of this ugly anger as possible, the same way I dealt with Ethel, but it wasn't easy being in 99 places while trying to get in a little quality time with my sweetums.

After introductions were made, and the well-bred social services woman insisting on being called Loretta, and don't ask why *(with a name as dowdy),* I almost missed the point of this exchange.

Did she just say Irene was contesting the adoption!?!

Now hold the Gillette ON! This is where shit got really contentious and wicked. First off, how can some drugged-out, thugged-out, busted every other week mama a few dozen times over, *(Irene had a few abortions, and many, many miscarriages)*, CONTEST ANYTHING...much less an adoption!?! And more than that, LO-retta saw what type home June was trying to save my sweetums from. Everyone saw that home, and not one MOTHER FUCKING day did any one of their contentious pretentious lousy asses try to save by bookums from its ugly horns.

Not one MOTHER FUCKING day!

No! They let my lovely russet stay there, reel in it, scorned her for the way she talked *like them,* snickered because she couldn't get *their smell* off her, ridiculing her for the way Reba had her dressing *like them...*damn near that one hundred and sixty three days Ashley missed school! And now THEY THINK they're gonna FUCK UP the rest of my sweet tater-tots life by throwing her back into the bowels of hell!?!

Oh, you betcha' bare ass I was showing mines if they thought for an asshole hair of a second I was letting this go. Whatin' NO way! WHATIN' NO MOTHER FUCKING WAY, to be clearer!

How the hell did Irene get an attorney anyway!?! Much less find one, and one that would represent her unlegislated ass? I zipped around and tried to find him, or her, right while this conversation was getting started. I just wanted to see what the fool looked like. Trust me, I was coming back for this imbecile when all of this jumbalaya got squared away. I was learning quick. I was dangerous when I was desperate.

That's how it kicked in, I didn't need to see a pile of bile when I had special powers. I got my ass back to the house, straightaway—to deal directly with LO-retta.

Loretta grabbed her head the moment I zipped back in the house. She grabbed her head as if she had a headache, cause sho' nuff I was already inside, punching and kicking her in the skull trying to bring some sense to this woman.

She could've found the right paperwork to shut Irene's case down. How many times had she done this before? She filled out that DSA 1127 form some 2019 times. I'll have you to know I zipped through her office on my return trip from hunting down Irene's attorney. No, it's not right, possibly unethical, and definitely illegal, but I rifled through her file cabinets anyway, like I went on to do with Sturgis.

The bottom file cabinet was crammed with these forms; all 2019 completed you hear!?! I don't know who all those kids were, or exactly what type environments they came from, but every last one of them had a big red bold block of letters stamped across the first page: UNFIT HOME!

"Would you like a glass of water," Eric asked, the puss he was, more concerned about Loretta's sudden headache, than my headache trying to sort through, and straighten out all this madness.

"Yes, please..." Loretta whimpered.

June, at my insistence of course, didn't budge. She glared at Loretta the same way I was inside Loretta, glaring at this one membrane I was about to rip apart. It was a good thing for her that it dawned on me to calm the hell down. If it wasn't Loretta, then it'd probably be someone else. While I had this woman, I could use her, I realized. Who else better could end up being a louder advocate for my precious tookums, than someone who'd interacted with her, and was familiar with where she came from?

See, LO-retta's problem was this, which I caught wind of as I zipped through her files. She, like many other workers *(in all fields)*, needed to keep systems good and clogged, or risk finding themselves on the unemployment line...where incidentally in her case would feel like lounging in heaven, compared to where I booked her next destination... if she f'd over on my sugar plums.

To keep that luscious precious job of hers, she went around unfitting homes to keep punching clocks. In fact that's what her title should have been called; Unfit Social Worker.

Obviously after taking one look around June and Eric's fit home—beautiful whole wooden doors that didn't look...or work like rat-traps. Cozy furniture and clean soil free carpets, an expansive library filled with pristine kept books—this home resembled nothing near to unsafe...or unsanitary.

"Mr. and Mrs. Clapton, I understand how you both must feel, but my hands are tied—"

—well untie those crusty hands LO-Retta, or should I say LOW-retta! You do have the power to use that stamp. I know, because I've seen those files in your bottom drawer. 2019 TIMES!

Loretta drank that cold glass of water and finalized them papers was what she did, though not before this big windfall of incredulity came tumbling out.

"Cuttie, how are you feeling today," Loretta asked once she and June finished their terse exchange of words, and after the cold glass of water settled her anxiety attack.

"Fine," my darling tweetums purred.

"How are you doing in school?" Loretta asked, abruptly interrupted by June.

"She's being home-schooled now. I'm a licensed certified teacher," June said before Cuttie alarmed the woman, about to tell her she hadn't been to school.

My cupcakes didn't know those lessons she and Mrs. Clapton worked on at intermittent parts of the day accounted for regular classroom instructions. Actually they were better than what she learned in regular school. It took Princeton teachers a whole school semester to teach what Cuttie learned in a day.

"Oh, that's great" Loretta smiled, encompassing the great nerve to want to call June snooty. I saw the epithet scrawled in her balled up clenched tight heart. I started to stretch it out, her heart that being, but decided to let it go seeing things going mines and my snookums way.

"Cuttie, why don't you run upstairs and get your workbook, so we can show Mrs. Palmer what we've been working on," June as well smiled.

I wasn't smiling however. I was busy trying to keep my distance from LOW-retta's main heart valve. Almost anything was liable to set me off. So to prevent me from busting this woman wide open on one of my tension jerks right there in the Clapton's home, possibly in front of my snookums, I made sure to maintain a distance.

What I did question though, was why June thought it was anywhere near necessary to appease the woman. I already saw her check off that little square box, which would hand my little Tony-the-tiger over to her and Eric, hand in hand, fair and square, permanently.

"No, that's fine," Loretta said, just about ready to make her departing remarks. "That won't be necessary," and then she turned to my darling doll, smiled again, and reached out moving aside her bangs.

"How did you get that scar," she asked, turning her head in such a way that she could follow the 3-inch scar that ran from Cuttie's hair line, down to the top bridge of her nose.

"Mommy did this to me," Cuttie sweetly replied.

See why it was a good thing I kept my distance? I was shocked! Had I been in that woman's heart when my darling sunshine said what she did, LOW-retta would've been fanned out in many directions, spread all over the Clapton's beautiful peach Indonesia rugs.

Loretta looked quizzical, and so did June, though June's look was more on the side of absolute horror. *Who was Cuttie referring to as her mother?*

19

"Cuttie, who is Tigga," June asked after she let Loretta out of the house.

"She my mommy," Cuttie said like nothing, doing one of her daddy's moves, wiggling her head and the top half of her body, dancing to a tune she had playing on her ipod.

"Honey," and June pulled the one plug Cuttie had in her ear out. "You never told Auntie June about Tigga..."

My snookums wasn't like most bratty kids who would've whined about a toy being taken away from them. My peaches just kept on wiggling her head, and the top half of her body, as if she could still hear the music. And she kept wiggling and jiggling until June gently shook her by both arms.

"Cuttie please, tell Auntie June who Tigga is?"

My snookums looked at June out of eyes so cold, lifeless, and deadened, it frightened me. "She's my for-real mommy," she flatly replied.

June was very concerned, *and so was I!* To hear Tigga's name come up so casually, and jarringly, and by the one and only sweetums who could really jar me, I buckled.

"Sweetie, do you know where your mommy is? Where she lives?" asked one very alarmed June.

For too long June wanted a child, but never conceived one of her own. It now was too late, and surely too late to have a child like the one she just plied from LOW-retta's files to have; a child who passed the stage of diaper changes and keeping late hours to tend to high temperatures and colic bouts.

The more she got to know Cuttie, and of course the more she heard from her daddy *(though she didn't suspect it, me riding her conscience like a colicky barrister)*, the more she fell in love with the idea of having a little girl just like Cuttie; soft, sweet, innocent, and not a soul who materialized to claim her.

And don't think June relied solely on the school, and the states' half-hearted investigation looking into Cuttie's birth. She, with sheepish Eric's help, contacted the Board of Vital Statistics on every single birth reported in the year physicians surmised Cuttie would've been born. They as well talked to people in the neighborhood where the Briggs lived, albeit careful not to raise their suspicions greater than thus far raised.

Surprising, and then not surprising at all, it was Omega's nosey busy-body, homebody self who gave June the biggest earful, claiming she was washing her child's hair over the kitchen sink when she looked up and first saw my child. "I recognized the gown," she told June. "It was right before Easter when the kids were on break," she added.

Now, this would have been well after I first saw my baby...*you know*...after the whole face-lift incident, which incidentally first clued my dumb ass in, this hospital gown situation would've had nothing to do with the last time I saw my child...*when she wasn't even a month old!*

But this didn't heal June's curiosity since I didn't bother to enlighten her that Omega with her 8-inch gums had no useful information. June hung on Omega's every word about how she *supposedly* called police who *supposedly* took a report on *'the strange child'* who showed up in the neighborhood wearing a Grand Mercy Hospital gown.

"I never heard back," so said Omega. "But then that shouldn't be a big surprise coming out of that house," she laughed. "A mountain lion could walk out that place and I doubt anyone around here would fall over."

June wasn't humored, and neither was I, though I used this *'going nowhere chat fest'* to get my nap on. Did I not mention all the zipping in and out of heads and bodies I had been doing!?! I only intervened when I heard June start her car, about to take her curiosity to the hospital.

'No, June. Leave it alone. You have the child you always wanted. This is your chance to take her away from here and live happily ever after'!

20

This part may raise the hairs on many backs, so proceed with caution.

Unlike June and other mortals with the insatiable curosity streak, when my streak kicks in, there's no bounds that will stop me from seeking what I want to know! This means, as much as I didn't want to, I had to take a deep dive inside my darling. Her mentioning her mother told me this trip was necessary.

But see, I don't like doing this for fear I could get spooked and end up really dismantling her. Actually, aside from those on my DGAF list, I really don't like going inside anyone for this reason. If I get upset I could accidentally explode and end up shutting down vital organs. I don't want this to happen, especially not to my snookums.

But this night I have to know. I must know if Tigga is in some way living inside our child. Obviously that woman, with her history—a scheming rogue felon, belongs nowhere near our child...least of all inside her. Lawd help ME and my child if that shallow rogue felon was inside my snookums!

Now, here's the thing. The way it works with this life and death thing, a soul can only be one thing. For instance, I am a living cell that lives in the air, with the privilege of entering bodies, or other living things, which includes organisms both on land and in water. Apparently I also left the ethereal world with some unfinished business, how I ended up slipping between heaven and hell, to end up here. But Tigga, as my instincts tell me, and yes,

I'm privileged with those things too, would've lined her gold-digging self up to return whole; as in a full human body, and better than she left. That's how Tigga moves and thinks. She was one of them types that liked the best in life and thus highly unlikely *(for the type person she was),* to take up residence in our child without some very ugly and unholy unfinished business to tend to. I know Tigga. I know how she moves and thinks. Some things never change, even amongst the immortals.

Now, exactly what unfinished business Tigga had left to squash, I didn't want anyone having to die to know. This is why I emphasize proceeding with caution.

Cuttie got dressed in her cute little pjs June had laid out for her, and hopped in bed after June and Mr. Clapton kissed her goodnight on the forehead. They turned out her bedroom light and left, closing the door behind them.

I quietly ease inside my snookums and move just beneath her heart, in a spot where I can lay low and not disturb any vital organs should I encounter a problem that causes an immediate reaction.

Instantly I see Boom-Boom reaching out for my tookus, and her reaching for him, though neither could reach the other. Their arms weren't long enough. The kid must've loved her, like this other child I didn't recognize, but also likely a part of that rogue Briggs crew, reaching out for her. The sighting, touching as it was, I disregarded. I definitely disregarded Reba, hollering and putting up a large fuss looking for her *sister soul mate* who, according to her, had her blood. The girl was crying like a damn fool looking for Cuttie. But swinging that switchblade the way she was, I had zero sympathy for her.

A few minutes went by and it started getting deafening quiet. My poo bear had to be drifting off, out of that lucid dreamy stage and off into a deeper REM sleep. So I drifted off too. It had been a long while since experiencing a peace like this... where the world was one with I, and I one with it. Wanted this peace to last forever, except you know how this part of life goes...the up and down, back and forth, opposite attraction of physics.

No more than 20 minutes later, after a wooing nap, I heard music playing. It wasn't rap or that hard R&B rock; excluding Reba from the possibilities of what may have been transpiring. The soft classical piece, a sound I don't care too much for, lifted me up...and not in a too pleasant way. Yeah, I was waiting on the screeching stabbing pitch to weave into this calypso and start tearing up my hearing. Worse than niggas drumming up a rap ho bitch beat down. Neither do a thing for me.

Thankfully that noise never came. Instead I heard what I guessed was a Sonneto number 5; a cheesy mousey sound reminding me of when I was on cloud nine, willy-nilly-chilling *(in heaven)* nursing them ales. Came across like one of them sleep app noises.

So I looked down, into a dark abyss. At a glimpse, in a grave distance it looked like a small mass sitting on my bookums liver. Normally, in any other body I wouldn't have paid a mass like this any attention. Like I said, when I go in bodies it's usually for an immediate purpose. I'm pretty focused on my intentions, which rarely includes seeking to spare a life. June would be one such exception, and my bookums was an absolute exception! Yes, noticing this mass inside my baby shook my orb up.

Look, let me break it down. A lot of shit is going on inside bodies. I've seen whole wars taking place. In the mortal world these wars are called diseases. But in the immortal realm of business, smart cells like myself see this tripping out like Star Wars. In other words, it's a game. I know how to dip, weave and bob, and thus don't get riled...unless of course, we're talking about my snookums. Now she, I care about.

Right away, feeling Tigga's presence, I called out her name. I knew that shallow gold digging essence and picked up her scent...plus some other odd odor... prompting me to investigate.

As I started moving towards this sound...and scent, the mass started lifting up. That's when I heard my sweet bookums cry out.

"No! No! Tigga, don't move," I urged.

Funny thing, and not laughable funny, but odd in how I instinctively got to calling out Tigga's name knowing it was her ass causing this chaos. Whatever it was, *and I do believe it was her,* responded by folding over somewhat.

From inside I heard June's voice asking my poo bear if everything was okay.

"My stomach hurts," I heard my poo bear sniffle.

It got quiet for a minute before I heard, "here open wide and swallow this," and "here, now drink this."

Seconds later it looked like snow falling. Though I couldn't feel anything, it smelled like how I recalled gas smelling. Basically like a chocolaty fart.

I looked down and saw the mass shrinking, like trying to shield itself from the snowy substance. Whatever June gave my bookums, I made a cerebral note to find out what type agent it was. While it had no effect on me, it definitely affected the mass.

Once my tookus got settled I zipped down to this mass and settled right next to it, curled up in a black hunched-over knot. Reminded me of homeless people hovered in doorways shielding themselves from the cold.

Right off I sensed a stale bad presence. This mass was on its last orb. And an orb would be leg for humans. Now, don't try to figure out how I'm coming upon this knowledge. The ethereal world IS and IS NOT like the mortal world. Metaphysical life doesn't require spending goo-gobs of years in school learning about antigens and pathogens, though it is necessary to leave the real world with basic common sense. Just for the record, I LEFT LIFE *(in my old form),* as it's said, *'smart as a whip!'*

Really smart cells like me catch on real quick. I don't question when knowledge hits me. I just run with it. Like take China, who many think has a humongous population. Well, listen at this here. What's going on inside the human body is like a million China's sitting inside a million Chinas. This is why it's unwise to waste time doing like scientists trying to figure out and solve every damn thing. Instead you do like I do, and learn on the fly.

So, sitting beside this mass, I'm sizing it up carefully for a weak or strong pulse, and that scent I once smelled but no longer detect.

Up close this mass looked like how I imagined a million year old dethroned royalty would look. You know... bent over, spineless and homeless, and wearing the same robe it was dethroned in, except with a million year old quality to it. The only uncertainty I got was inspecting its gooey coating; wet and signifying it possibly was once a healthy mass, maybe with a rapid pulse, that was trying to give up.

This had to be Tigga! This mass was old and on its last placebo, with a pulse beating slower than a calendar year, but it all fit with a spirit that once had it all.

I took my chances and inched closer, getting right up on it to see if I could look in its face. Bet you didn't know that even the tiniest organism has a face complete with eyes, ears, nose, mouth...the whole kit and caboodle.

It was cumbersome, looking through this corroded shell coagulated by atrocious blackened bile, but I made out the hollow eyes and a sunken space where a nose ordinarily went. No lips, or mouth however, but it could and did speak.

"Go away," it groaned at me.

I KNEW IT!!! It indeed was Tigga! Recognized the voice instantly, despite sounding every day past a trillion.

"What are you doing here," I asked.

"I said go away," the trillion year crotchety voice angrily repeated. She sounded like a scratchy throat trying to scream.

"No Tigga. I'm not going nowhere. Do you realize you're sitting on our child's liver!?!"

I know this is no way to greet your wife who you haven't seen in a while, forget having departed the way we had, but I have a better grasp of life and death, so I'm not so concerned about modern mannerisms.

"I can't kill her Curtis. She won't die," Tigga said, speaking in this very ugly moldy old voice.

'She won't die,' I muttered, haphazardly thinking why in the fuck would my snookums' mother want her child to die!?!

"You heard me," the old ugly bag said, her words that time sounding like lumpy vomit.

"Why do you want our child to die," I asked anyway, wanting to puke myself. "Have you seen her? Our daughter is beautiful."

Look. I was working on something. Trying to figure out on the fly how to handle this situation. Had this mass been anyone-or-thing other, it would've been gone. I didn't play.

Problem was, this was my snookum's mother, and there was no telling what kind of relationship they had.

"No Curtis...I fucked up," said that hideous voice.

"No you didn't. You have to see her," I replied in a hopeful daze. *'Maybe if what I now discern as stinky Tigga knew how pretty our kid looked, she'd know she hadn't f'd up.'*

"Kill me Curtis. Just fucking kill me so this horrible thing can die," Tigga growled.

UGH! I could feel something wretched starting to overcome me. I think a membrane in this mass broke, releasing a wicked odor, because I know damn well it wasn't me. This vile miasma permeating my soul made me sick with fear, so I slid a piece away...just in case.

I listened for a sec, to my own reasoning. It had been a while ago, but I had been this shallow mass. Well... maybe not as shallow, *apparently*, but I was cutting it pretty close to marry it, and then go in on a ball-brained scheme to take our snookums to that face fixer—'ole good times Folana!

Doing shit like that is pretty damn shallow, even if our child *(at least from my slow recall)*, wasn't wholly normal. But God! Still! We were low! What was I thinking!?!

No matter. I've since repented, evidenced by the fact that I...and no sooner than this thought came to me, was it when I heard that ugly yowl again.

"They sent me here Cummins," she growled in that drunken voice. "This is called judgment! I shouldn't have eaten that octopus," and she hesitated, "...or given that child that egg!"

Okay, so throw me off the fast train and roll me under the slow bus. *Eating an octopus?* 'Wow. I mean, what bum luck to get a sentence like this over a damn octopus and an egg!

"So, what the hell are you then," I asked. I still couldn't figure this part out, which I needed to know to make my next move.

"I'm the child's reasoning servant," Tigga grouched. "I live in her spirit, as her damn maid!"

Wow. And again. What rotten fucking luck. Like DAMN! Wonder how she got that judgment, *and I didn't?* Compared to her I got the deluxe deal, although like I said too, my intentions were never as shallow as Tigga's. Guess she had some real shoe trading left to do.

"Way down here?" I asked anyway. This servant business didn't make any sense, as if much else really did.

"It's my sentence," she groused, releasing more of that horrible fungi. "They're teaching me a lesson," she bitterly snarled.

Suddenly it became intolerably difficult to think... due to intoxicating fumes litigating the air between us. My poor snookums could be in danger, far beyond my powers to extinguish. Ordinarily I could flick off germs and worms (basically anything that got in my way...or on my nerves), and keep it moving. But see, squashing the mother of my sweetums, an entity delicately connected to her, was tricky. I could end up washing us all out!

As many in the real world practicing medicine and science don't know, living in an ethereal capsule is a whole 'nother ballgame. It's why mortals think they can spare...or kill anything; such as nuking germs, diseases, people, ideologies and such, with chemo, radiation, bombs and whatnot. They have no earthly idea how we, yes 'WE' work. In the ethereal sense a lot of these masses and cells are carrying...as in pregnant. In other words, if I blasted Tigga while inside my baby trying to kill her, she could burst wide open and leave so many version of herself in my child that I'd have more success counting the number of threads in a million beach towels.

Now, as mentioned a half dozen times already, had this been anyone else I wouldn't have given two damns. But this was my snookums I was concerned about.

So far Tigga seems fairly incapacitated, and harmless, but I prefer to have her removed—entirely. Just lance her BA-hind the hell off my poo bear's liver and be done with it is the way I'm seeing things.

"Look, why don't you catch a ride on out of here on the next thing humming," I demand. "Just get the hell up and go. I've got this!"

I'm trying to give Tigga the benefit of the doubt. Basically I'm hoping she'll believe there were a lot more hells than the one she thought she was trapped in. See, although I have to proceed cautiously, I've already come up with a strategy.

Oh yeah! One way or another she was coming the hell up out of my snookums. Her rotten luck hadn't begun to begin if she thought she was hanging out in my tookus with that foul aroma she had working around her!

"Did you not hear me," she growled, and the fungi that came out that time nearly turned my bits outside in. I actually saw maroon lights blink on and off twice.

"I said I'm sentenced here. I can't go nowhere. This is it. Unless I can convince the child to die."

"For your info, that child has a name!" I zap. "Her

name is Caitlyn. And my snookums—"

"—Snookums," Tigga grunted sarcastically.

"Yes, snookums," I said. "I have lots of nicknames for my bookums. And I can tell you this too, snookums don't want to die. She's living a very comfort—"

"—Yoooooooooooowwwlllll," and that yowl was me, just after Tigga opened her yap, aka...an area below where her face was supposed to be, where she used to entertained me.

I couldn't see shit! Went totally blank! Completely lost sight of my strategy. I zapped out of my snookums, just so I could breathe... and think. Wasn't no way I could think rationally in all that fungi.

Landing on the pillow beside my snookums I just stared at her perfect little face. She deserved none of this. A child with her arm wrapped around a Power Puff stuffed doll should be able to conquer the...

...when it hit me!

Forget whatever strategy I had in mind. Yeah, scrap that plan! Didn't need it. My snookums wanted to live! Now how about that!? Required no bribery or extensive use of energy. *Damn.* What a shame... for Tigga that being. She never had a lot of smarts, typical for overly attractive people. But what ugly fuggly luck she ended up not only in her state, but subjugated to be a reasoning servant to our child who wanted to live!

Oh man! I cozied up next to my snookums after this realization. For the time being I could put the past in the past, forgetting all about mines and Tigga's shallow past. All I had to do was keep my baby safe, loved and looking forward to a bright future. How blessed were we?!

21

I slept peacefully, something I hadn't done since seeing my child, but awoke to some noise I felt needed my undivided attention.

As it turned out, June had settled on believing my buttercup made Tigga up. Lots of abandoned children do this; make up playmates to keep them company. Besides, June wanted a child so badly that she could easily put that episode behind her.

It was that damn husband of hers, Eric, that had a problem!

He liked Cuttie and treated her fair enough, but didn't like the idea that they were unable to figure out any part of her background, other than what the Briggs told everyone.

Listen, it gives me no warm cozy feeling referring to the woman I gave my hand and uttered 'I do', the beast. But I didn't need that damn Eric poking around to find that beast. A little part of me however, did want to know where my sweetheart had been those long 8 years. All tallied, because of this damn Eric...and too...my own inquisitivity, I was going to be on the zap-zipping road again.

You know, as it's said, in order to move forward with any logical progress, you have to be willing to go back. Now, I probably should've left off that word logical, because I'm no logician in my best mood. Like, since when has a scientist ever recognized a *logical* cell!?! I'll answer that for you. NEVER!!! Living cells don't do logic, why mortal doctors always *'be in practice'*!

I overheard Eric calling a meeting with his boss to speak in private, *and off the record,* despite having turned in his resignation in preparation to pursue a new life that would allow him to help June raise Cuttie.

Turned out he was talking to Mel Gallagher. I didn't know the guy...Mel that being... but got the vibe the two of them seemed to be cool with each other.

Mel was a little sloppier, and a lot louder, but the man had a penchant for calling it like he saw it. Over the years, *(and I'm only taking this vibe at its word)* Mel had been nothing but loyal to Eric...that being so long as he didn't feel double-crossed. Double-cross Mel and he would deal with the double-crosser exactly how I planned to handle anything or anyone that upset my child in any shape or form. And this included 'ole Eric...and Tigga as well. Oh hell yeah. Don't think for one minute I wasn't still thinking of a way to get that beast off my sugar plum. If things got repugnant I had to be ready. Exactly why, OH HELL YEAH, Mel from jump street, was my type guy.

"Come on in here Lonnie," Mel said in his blustery loud voice, "and shut that door. I've been wanting to talk with you all week about your leaving the firm," he said.

Mel was that type too. I don't know where he got that name...*Lonnie,* and frankly didn't give a damn, but just to speed things up, Mel didn't care for guys named Eric. Nothing personal. He just thought it was a wimp's name, which of course Eric was.

"Aah yeah," Eric moused around, sheepishly grinning and nodding, "I been meaning to..." and right there his quibbling blather was churned and mauled by Mel's no nonsense habit of getting straight to the point.

"What happened Lonnie? The mob or someone out after you? Cause you know I'll help you settle any debts you've got right now," boomed Mel.

"Aah no, it's nothing like that," Eric continued in his little mousey soft voice. "Me and June just..." and again his words were churned and mauled by Mel.

"How long you've been with us," Mel asked. And by the way, Mel was the president of Pinecroft Publishing. He swore in five years after Eric was hired on as an acquisitions associate. Fast forward a few dozen years and Eric had risen all the way up to Chief Editor, about the tenth down the line beneath Mel who was at the top of the line.

"Thirty-five years," Eric replied.

"Yeah, I suppose that's long enough," Mel sighed settling back in his high-back office chair. "Guess you already have a place in the Keys all staked out, huh?"

"Well..." and Eric himmed and hawwed here too. But not because he didn't have a vacation home all set up for him and June to retire with Cuttie in. He was there to solicit Mel's advice on helping him find out where Cuttie came from. He just wasn't so sure how to start off asking for his help.

"Well umm...not exactly," the 'ole chump-chumpy Eric stammered.

"What!?!" And Mel leaned forward, eyes bugged wide open and looking Eric so forcefully in the eye it scared me. "Look Lonnie, if there is a problem just spell it out. Why are you cutting out on us like this if you have nowhere to go? You know we could still use you. You don't have to leave."

"No...no..." Eric blubbered before quickly clearing the air so he wasn't interrupted again. "I'm all set. We have a place. I just wanted to get your advice on something."

Advice hell. Eric wanted this man's help. Those agencies and hospitals that couldn't tell him anything had already given him enough advice. Basically, *'go look elsewhere,'* was most of the advice he'd been given.

"Sure, Lonnie...anything buddy. You name it. How can I help you?"

"June and I just adopted a little girl...Cuttie...I mean, Caitlyn," Eric started as Mel nodded and umm hummed him. "It's the reason I decided to retire. So umm...

we can raise her in a proper new environment," he said.

"Ha! Let me in on that secret," Mel chuckled. "Wonder where's this place. Utopia?" he laughed.

Eric didn't join the laughter. He was serious as a heart attack the adoption rubbed him so wrong. But he did manage a stiff chuckle before looking down in his lap and shrugging to get back to where he was.

"No, it's actually a small city out West by the ocean. Nice and quiet. June picked it out," he went on.

"Oh okay, sounds fabulous," Mel remarked, taking notice of Eric's discomfort, and his annoyance that the man was acting like such a putz. Damn, he was big, about 75-pounds overweight, and had been known to shake many up by his voice alone, but Eric had nothing to be frightened of. Hell, hadn't he signed his damn walking papers!?!

"Yeah, it really is," Eric said loosening up. That was the thing. He just needed a moment to ease his way into things. Mel had been an alright boss and all, but he wasn't the most polite human being he'd ever known. It was rude to get right to the point the way Mel always did.

"I got it for a good price too—"

"—So, you come in here to rub my face in it, or do you need my help with a down payment?" Mel broke in again.

Eric cut the sheepish grin and looked Mel straight in the eye. "No Mel, I need help finding Caitlyn's parents."

22

Initially Mel was confused, though he said nothing to Eric. Many thoughts came to him, one of those thoughts being Eric trying to pull a fast one over on June.

The trauma Eric endured was no secret during the years June was trying to conceive. His co-workers teased him mercilessly about June calling and screaming in the phone, "I'm ready, we've got to do it RIGHT NOW!"

Along with working late, to avoid the barrage of temperature and penis checks, had to be humiliating. Doctors tried to inseminate June with his sperm, not once, but twice, which even that technique didn't work. June drove that puss nuts trying to conceive. She had nineteen miscarriages in all. His colleagues counted every one of them, how I got to know this part of Eric's story... and why Mel was smelling a fish.

Talk about pressure. Eric was sweating like he had smoked up all his boss's profits. Naturally Mel assumed Eric wasn't thrilled on the idea of adopting a child, period. Maybe he wanted to rig something up to force June to return the child.

Mel called Paula Broaddus in his office after Eric left. Tall and attractive, and one of Eric's colleagues who'd been serving up the brunt of 'I'm ready' jokes she slid in Mel's office with her notepad out.

Unable to look Paula in the eye, seeming ashamed himself about *the penis jokes* circling the office, he sighed. "Hey, look Paula, can you do me a favor and see what you can find out on this kid Eric and June just adopted?"

And just to note, I was in Mel's office, and zipping around Pinecroft while this chit-chat was going on. None of Eric's colleagues disliked him. He was a likeable guy according to convos and vibes I caught. These people liked him a lot. They also hardly thought being unable to conceive was that funny. It was just the way Eric handled it that tickled them.

Paula stood frozen in Mel's office, reluctant to turn on her heels. She wanted to hear more, and knew Mel had more coming, so she waited.

"And keep this quiet," Mel said glazing over her surprised look. "You know how sensitive Eric is about this whole child thing, so I don't want this getting out."

Paula backed out of the doorway, without asking one question. She knew why Mel summoned her to the job. She and June knew each other well. They talked just about every day.

23

Getting Mel in on this wasn't an altogether bad thing. I just didn't get why he handed the job to Paula. He knew Paula and June were sisters, or rather stepsisters, related by a father who spread his genes something like him. You know... the rolling stones who had scores of kids spread over the globe like sea salt.

The relationship between Paula and June wasn't the best, but it was a familial bond built on the household they once upon a time shared. Overall both had done relatively well in life; June a retired teacher married a *(also retired)* journalist, and Paula who had worked with that journalist...as she continued raking in credits and dollars. Still, Paula was a little jealous of June. She never got over her father choosing June's mother over her mother to live with. *For a place holder, June's mother was cuter,* though none of these people were alive. You'd think the hatchet would be buried, but I'll get to all that moolash in a sec.

Thing was, I swung by June's crib *(where she was keeping my snookums...and of course living with wimpy Eric)* to wait on Paula's call. *Note: This is how I picked up on the veiled jealousy.* Except while waiting on this conversation to take place, I caught my tookums running her tiny little fingers over a piano June had her taking lessons on.

I heard her play before, but not like this. Them keystrokes sounded really good beneath my princess's fingers; so sweet and delicious in fact, I found myself wrapped in a dreamy state. I decided to catch up with Paula and June later. I wanted to feel proud for a while.

With my visors down, and dark wrapped around me, *(meaning my eyes were closed)* I relaxed as my tookus played. Man, she really knew that piano... better than Ella Fitzgerald I'm saying. That tune drowned out the Clapton's ringing telephone, with me stuck between piano keys— eyes sealed tight. I mean my little girl really WAS playing. I couldn't believe it. Not only stuck between the keys— eyes shut. I was numb dumbstruck between the keys.

How about that? All that time and a musician was in my genes. Cause I know it wasn't none of Tigga's genes. About the closest that woman came to anything mildly creative was the night I crowned her, as a band played.

Anyhow, and back to my tookus, she had me so stoked *(taking after me)* batting them pretty bright eyes like butterflies and moving her curled upper lip ever so slightly as her small dainty fingers glided kindly across the keys. I ended up missing the whole call between Paula and June.

Listen, Ella hadn't played like this when she was at her best, hundreds of years before my tookus was born. And despite not knowing where my snookums was before coming to June, it wasn't no way to ignore the irony in the fact she actually was playing one of Ella's songs, and not just any one of Ella's songs, but my tookums was playing *'Cry Me A River.'*

Oh, do let me be first to alert the reading public; I cried a river that afternoon, crooning hard enough to part the two oceans and insert a third one—Cummins Ocean.

I swear, my gorgeous gem ripped her daddy's heart out on that one. Couldn't tell me apart from the universe. My little bittums was in her world softly swaying on the bench, eyes closed at intervals, and little mouth going as her fingers pranced over the keys. Sounded like she could have been singing to Tigga, because every word in the lyric fit what any child abandoned by her decrepit mother would sing. It just broke my heart. God! It broke my heart. I was cooked, sand-baked and sun-fried, turn me over, I was a celestial collage overdone.

24

"Sweetie, are you all ready for our big day tomorrow?" June asked as energetic as she could for a call that didn't seem to go well. She was talking about moving. She and Eric had the house packed and were an airplane flight away from leaving much ugliness behind. To include the ugly call with Paula that I missed.

Quickly I zipped through June to check on things. While I wouldn't have been able to relive the entire conversation, I would have gotten a basic assessment of the situation.

The call really irked June, though she didn't reveal why. Mush was the most I got out of the assessment.

"Un hun..." I heard my little operatic pianist hum. She didn't understand the concept of moving...as in the great distance she was about to travel.

"Well let's—"

"—Are you taking me to go see my friend Reba, like you said you was, before we cut outta dis place?" My little innocent nookums abruptly asked, sharply and boldly blatant, interrupting June.

But WoW. That sure gave me a jolt. I never heard my precious buttons talk like that. She wasn't a fresh mouth like that friend of hers. Just as sweet as a Georgia peach.

On the fly, goaded by fatherly instinct, I zipped through snookums too—to see what triggered that little outburst. Lord help the wayward cell, or mass, if it had invaded my tookum's body like Tigga had. See, with Tigga

I couldn't do much about her... at the moment anyway. But anything else, and it was on!

Lord Jesus Super Star Christ, I got in there to now find Reba convalescing in a comatose state, lying just north of my tookum's thorax pipe!

This was the first time I had to gather some other enuis. And enuis, in case no one knows this term, means I had some ethereal cell research to do; except I was real short on time. You know how long it takes them scholars to look into things. Well I didn't have that kind of time to play around with. My looking into things had to be done and finished quicker; like within that split cell-busting second I saw Reba all laid up on my child's thorax pipe.

I zipped over to them Briggs' house quick and in a hell of a scurry. I didn't know what I'd find, but then this was how research sort of works...for those pressed on time in my state.

It was a Friday, and early, around 9-10am, so no one was in there but them deadbeat uncles and cousins lying all around the cellar. I poked around in Reba's room for a hot minute, looking for clues. I don't know what clues, but will refer to them as clues since I didn't know what in the hell I was looking for.

I did figure, since it was Friday and all, that the lot of this empty house was probably down at the welfare center. People in this hood call it the Cheddar Stop, but I call it a slop house, where a few thousand of them trollop through a building guarded by a guard posted right there at the door, one hand on a radio and the other pornishly fondling a worn out nightstick and huge ring of keys. The dollar-an-hour Rent-a-Cop was standing adjacent a sign written in big black bold letters on a blatant white background—MAXIMUM OCCUPANCY 150.

Don't ask me. I presume none of them can read, to include the workers and guard. Granny and about fifteen of them jokers in her clan sure enough were crammed in that place, like suspected, stuffed in a corner, sustained by hundreds of carbon copies like themselves, all waiting *'to get paid.'*

I zipped up on them making plans, like clockwork, for the windfall they preyed on every Friday.

"Granny, don't worry, when we get done here ya'll go on to the hospital and I'll put some money down on layaway and meet ya'll up there later," Irene said, code talk for rip-off.

Granny only nodded, sadly, staring off into a space so condensed I needed a magnifying glass to see through. Of course, with what I had in mind, I didn't have time to be thinking about what Granny was seeing. She was used to Irene running off with the welfare loot, which could only mean Reba must've been in the hospital...since she was nowhere in the Cheddar Shop.

I zapped along, racing ahead of the Cheddars' lot to beat them getting to the hospital. Sure enough I found Reba, laying in a spot called the Cusp. Now, for those in the real world, she actually was laying in a hospital bed. Yeah, poor little thing had ripped and ran herself into a state of botched delirium. Her chart hanging on the bed said *(in coded medical speak)* she was a breath away from death. Tore me up because I knew just how she got there. Without snooping in on what doctors were saying, I knew she missed my baby terribly. That wild child was dying of human loneliness.

It must've been then, when I asked the ICON with the iron voice to help me understand how Reba could be in the hospital and in my snookums at the same time. That's how I learned about the Cusp. It's a rather peaceful state between living in the real world and heaven...or hell.

Well, to spare us all of the extra fluff ironing out that talk, and cutting straight to the chase, I squeezed off the grapevine that the Cusp is located closer to earth than upward. In other words, Reba could pull through.

This was where I had to go through another learning curve. Cells and masses and other ethereal beings, I could handle. Living entities on the *'cusp'* of dying, whose outcomes I cared about, had to be studied up on and proceeded with caution. This however was a case-by-case operation. Every situation was different.

So here was the deal with Reba. She was hanging on this thin thread in a really precarious spot. Actually a really beautiful spot, despite having slit her wrists. All she had to say was, *'I'm ready'* and the ICON *(or I)* would have carried her on out of my snookums and on her way... to heaven... or hell. And by the way, all children go straight to heaven, unless they specifically specify otherwise, which is rare of course, so there is no need to worry about her suffering needlessly.

And yet I had a real problem here. Because Reba had traded blood with my child, or whatever the hell she'd done, she, like Tigga held precious real estate in my pearl. She could invade my snookum's body and do some real damage, or end up living inside my tookus forever, the one fear that had me spiraling *OUT OF MY MOTHER-FUCKING MIND!!!*

I know this stuff confuses most lay minds in the real world, especially those who read religious books, or subscribe to other sacrilegious principles. Trust me. I'm confused! Like I said before. I'm learning on the fly. These are not my rules, but the laws of the ethereal world. And yet, like it or not, right or wrong, I couldn't have Reba laid up on my child's voice pipe.

The good news is, while I'm a helicopting, perhaps over-protective daddy, I'm not a cruel cell. I love Reba, in that pitying way, wishing she was born into a better lot. I even cried *(so too speak)* upon arriving at the hospital and seeing her laid up the way she was. She not only loved my daughter, but she saved my child's life far as I'm concerned. That's why I'm almost as dedicated to ensuring her well-being as well. I wanted her to continue living in the real world, and yet all I'm saying is I couldn't let her take my cuddle bear down that raggedy road she lived on.

Now, what could happen, and ultimately did happen, was I blew x, y, and t-plus cells into her dilapidated
veins and woke her the hell up...suddenly wanting to live!
Doing this was great, and yeah, so pat 'ole dad here on
the back for his fast dexterous thinking, even if I saw far
ahead. This wasn't going to be the end of my dealings with
Miss Reba. I was going to have to keep her wanting to live,
and her mind off my snookums and off her thorax pipe.

25

My work was cut out and my to-do list growing like cob-web fiber. Every waking cell I saw extra pieces to a puzzle coming in that didn't exactly go with the picture. It started making me cogitate on how, or when my essence might die. In case you're wondering, although cells can die, or be killed, a cell also can live forever. Fool around and don't get too cocky, but stay lucky, *and like me* be smart, and I could hang around forever. This was my aim.

June and Eric packed up my snookums and as a family the three of them flew first class out West. I smiled, cell-style smiling, all the way. This all happened in a knick of time because Reba came out of her bad state to have some recollection of where my snookums lived.

Over there on Corky Valley, where the Clapton's *used to* live, Reba almost found a way to get over there; three or four neighborhoods over. But it didn't happen, and definitely wasn't happening now. My snookums had moved 3000-miles West! Good *'f'ing'* riddance *(in Briggs language)*...so says her daddy!

While the Clapton's were getting all situated with my sweet tookums, I zapped on over to see how I could get Reba situated. After-all, I really wanted her to come out of this bad situation...*somewhat upright.*

I zapped back over to that Unfit Social Services agent, LOW-retta; remember her?, and got to cooking up things in her office.

Let's face it. These people really did need real work to tend to. And what better cause to boost their gridlocked brains, than by ensuring all of their literature on '*helping poor families,*' shined.

First thing in the morning I got in there. I knew this was the time where I could recruit the best soldiers. This here should be a nice pointer for anyone who doesn't know where to look for superstars who will go the extra mile. Let me tell you where they are. They're the first ones who arrive to work. Those are your diamond's-in-the-ruff *(as it's said).* Your superstars. They'll bend over backwards, forwards, sideways, and march down to city hall, *on foot if necessary,* to snitch on slackers.

Charmaine Goodwill was in the office. It was 10:02am; and despite every government office in every city, state, and country code for that matter, opening at 7am, no later than 8, Charmaine was the only soul in the office when I got there.

So much for graduates who left graduate school full of hope to lance the ills off society. When they found out the work called for rubbing elbows with this under-class mix, they started showing up to work later and later. It's an odd surprise they showed up at all anymore. Guess there's still one more thesis waiting to be written.

I hopped on in Charmaine and got to plucking her feathers right away. It wasn't too hard to tell it was going to be easy stressing this woman up. Aside from her getting in there at the break of dawn, all bright and bushy-tail early, she looked refreshed and wide awake; like a pep squad leader...for a church—the single grandmother's ministry.

A quick dip inside of her, just to check things out before I continued assuming, I wasn't inside but a hot pink second before one of them old negro church spirituals hit me square in the mug and cast me the hell out of there.

Don't take this the wrong way, but I'd gone in up from beneath her, and not through her feet, why I say in a *hot pink* second I was backed out of there. And just to note; the soles of Charmaine's feet were ashy gray. Her Southernmost point playing the old Negro spiritual on a damaged set of drums weren't.

Charmaine was going to be easy riling up. My only hope was she was effective too. I didn't want to be spending too much time on this thing. I wanted Reba as comfortable as possible, as quickly as possible.

I start egging on Mrs. *I ain't been widda man since my last one passed on...17 years ago,* right away.

"Yeah, that's right...that's right...look at that score," I was telling Charmaine, zipping back and forth across an eclectic span of forehead. *"What's it read? Zero to thirty, don't it? Aren't you tired of seeing it? Aren't you tired of always losing?"*

In case you're wondering, Charmaine started working for Social Services 10 years after her last one left home. She was thirty-seven, and that was thirty years ago. She came on board with *'put welfare back to work program.'* Add that all up, like I did, it meant she was sixty-seven.

I don't care how nobody sees it, 67 is too damn old to be losing every case to LOW-retta's outlook, especially since she had so much more experience with these type people. She used to be *one of them!* For thirty-seven years for Christ's sake!

Charmaine narrowed her eyes, took in quite a bit of air, and exhaled deeply. She was just about ready. All I had to do was pull one of them hairs, at the nape of her neck, just after nudging her to open one more email...of course the latest case coming in...Reba Briggs—possible neglect, molestation, abuse, and suicide attempt.

"Think back," I told Charmaine, poking her in the back. *"Go back to when you were a kid, and think about what you went through. This is this child. This child is you!"*

Then I pulled that one plug of hair at the nape of her neck. She flew out of the chair. Came up out of it so forcefully that part of the chair came up with her. She had to shake it loose to storm over to a file cabinet, open it, rifle through it, angrily, and snatch a thick batch of papers in a folder out, slamming the drawer shut afterwards.

"Look at the photo," I was telling Charmaine, just as high-rolling LOW-retta strutted in; white wool Ann Taylor throw thrown over her shoulders, sharp hipster bell-bottoms following every curve on her body. Couldn't tell her nothing, with that jewelry spitting sparks at the cake of make-up and perfumes following her every move.

This was pay raise stuff me and Charmaine was seeing strut in near to the lunch hour. The whole damn country was cutting back and openly conserving on the extras, and here this heffa rolled in like she'd just stolen the Duchess of Wales rug and crown.

"Have you seen this," Charmaine ask Loretta.

But the heffa didn't even look. She strutted on by, curling up her upper lip and waving a hand. "Put it on my desk. I'll have to look at it later. I'm about to jump on a conference call," she said, headed to her office.

'Oh, like the hell you are,' I said, and Charmaine echoed.

"Loretta, Reba Briggs is in the hospital," Charmaine said, sort of giving Loretta one last chance to get her act together. "She tried to commit suicide..." she added, now watching the back of Loretta almost at her office. One more step and the heffa would have been inside, closing the door.

"Put it on—" *—and I slammed the damn door.* Had the high-fluting dame moved another fraction of an inch and the door would've hit her smack in the face.

Loretta snatched around to look at Charmaine. "Who's in my office?" she asked, too surprised to notice Charmaine gathering her hat, coat, and purse. "Did you just see—"

—and Charmaine was gone.

Part Three

26

It should be no secret why I did, and was doing, all of this for my snookums. My efforts stretched beyond my love for a child I neglected and abandoned. I'm not going to lie, I had my sights on redeeming myself from my past shallow ways by teaching assholes like I used to be, not to be a jerk like I used to be.

After humoring myself listening to Charmaine whip up on 13 office workers working out of a department LOW-retta reported to...singing some church hymnals that had every one of them praying, I headed out west.

It was a funny thing too. While Reba was getting adopted, the argumentative career imploding way, June and Eric were wended up in a tight nappable discussion of their own.

"I just think it was a little insensitive of you to go behind my back trying to dig up dirt on that child," June hissed at Eric, moving around a king-size bed karate chopping a spread to tuck the ends beneath the mattress.

"I'm sorry honey," Eric said, standing apologetically out of June's way, backed up against the door. "I just wanted to make sure she's really ours," he said.

'Oh, she's really yours,' I wanted to pump into his punk head, even though the pansy didn't deserve this wrath. I mean, I somewhat did want to know where my snookums had been during those 8 years while I was going through my transition.

June stopped with the tucking and snapped to an upright position. "Well, when were you going to tell me!"

"Well...Well..." stuttered the little wuss. He stalled trying to answer, miffed about why Mel had Paula look into the matter anyway. He knew she and June talked a lot, and just what happened, was likely to happen. That damn jealous ass Paula ran her mouth.

A soft knock at the door saved the puss. He stepped aside to let my little tookums poke her head in.

"Auntie June, can I go outside and play wif deese kids?"

These kids!?! What kids!?! It was 10-O Dear at night!

Like a tender-loving mother June rushed right over to my sweet noodles, brushing by the puss. "Oh honey, it's a little late to be outside," she said, which I only caught the tail end of; since I—*the loving daddy I was*—was already out in the dark, whizzing up and down a lonely cul'de sac, looking for these kids my angel must've seen.

Weren't no kids outside, not unless she was speaking of these two vulgar creodonts I caught across the lane necking. They weren't making out in a full-on humping romp, but the girl, likely in her late teens, lay pressed against *(I'm gonna guess)* a long-haired boy, slobbering on her neck. Nobody don't need to see that, especially not my precious tookums. So I hissed at a nearby cat, which took off with a squealing screech.

The girl screamed, throwing one long leg at a time over the hood of the car, leaving the long-haired slobber slobbering against the window.

"Aww, it was just a cat," he said laughing at her.

"Well, I don't like it out here. Feels kind of creepy," she replied, reaching for the slobber's hand to climb down off the hood. "Let's go—"

I didn't hear the rest of the exchange. I was on my way back in the house to make sure it also wasn't Tigga trying to strum up trouble for my tookums. I'll say. It was a pain in the rear, *if only I had a real one*, worrying about all the ways Tigga could influence my nookums. Actually, it was a pain in the tosh just being a father. I don't know how

I would've dealt with all of this had I been in a man standing on two legs, armed with only two fists. Just another reason, being that things were what they were, to be grateful things weren't worse!

"Look Eric, I apologize for getting bent out of shape about this whole thing. I just wished you'd talk things over like that with me first," June said, after steering my little angel to play on her laptop.

"Well, I'm sorry too," Eric sheepishly replied. "I certainly didn't want to upset you," explained the puss, rubbing his teary eyes. For the next life of me I'd be trying to guess how he handled being chief editor for Pinecroft for all those years. Like what did he do? Hang out reading and typing and corresponding beneath his desk!?!

27

Turned out, that girl I saw, her name was Rachel and she was only a year and a half older than my Cuttie bear. Ask me, she looked a whole lot older than my snookums. My little girl actually looked like a little girl. She could easily be mistaken for 7 or 8; not like that almost woman I saw necking on the family station wagon the other night.

When June and my tookums walked in the Washington's house, Rachel was wearing gold eye-shadow, and her eyes had been penciled around—heavily. She must've thought she was cute, or trying her darnedest to get cute, with that long large nose shaped like a fat man's thumb. She had long dark blonde hair too, except her skin was splotched with them adolescent pink polka dots. But the part I couldn't get by was how much taller than my tookums she was. Looked like the Sears Tower leaning over my mink minkus.

After all we'd been through, my nookums and me, and it was plain hard to believe my peaches was almost eleven. How other parents do it, I have no earthly clue. They don't have half the powers I do, and I was in there hanging on to my last wit end nerve cell trying to digest what I was seeing.

Rachel's mother was gorgeous however. I was thinking about paying her fine ass self a visit later on that night, until I flickered by a picture of her and some Harry Belafonte looking character dressed in a tux and smiling at her, sitting on the mantel. Yeah, I'm no homewrecker.

"I really appreciate your having Caitlyn over," June

said to Mrs. Washington. "We should be back in an hour or so."

"Oh, anytime," Mrs. Washington replied, with her fine ass self, exposing a deep set of dimples. "Rachel and I are just so excited that it is you guys who moved in that house."

'*I was too,*' I whittled inside. 'I just wasn't excited that it was her fresh pot daughter who lived across the street!'

The last thing I needed, or wanted to deal with, was more horse-radish. Gosh, this has to be hard for any normal parent. But then I couldn't expect June and Eric to take my lovems with them. They were meeting a Stephan and Marge, two of the supposed top genealogists in the world. Eric, bless his soft heart, laid down 10,000 pretty copper coins for this private research into my snookums. I was impressed with his snoop-scooping skills, trudging up these people in my hindsight, even if there was no doubt it was going to be a wasted trip.

But I got a grip and made the hard choice to leave my child with a necker, to meet two top Roots swindlers. I mean, if these folks names alone don't sound creepy, wait until you get a load of the rest of this supernatural visit.

First off, before I even got the chance to be all the way spooked out, I had to listen to Eric telling June, and just as honest-faced too, that these cons had linked a strand of hair back to the Tao Dynasty. '*Really? The Tao Dynasty?*'

Let me tell all of you gullible DNA believers right now, the science is bogus. There is no such thing! Every living soul, from beetle juice to cranberry juice, contains markers that cross-reference the other. Yes! Every one of us can be linked to the dreaded monkeys in Planet of the Apes. Read this and weep!

Just let me catch the fool pulling a strand of hair out of my snookums head and handing it over to these people. I'll pull their string and link it straight to hell, too.

So, I crossed my hope cells and rode shotgun style with Eric and June, all three of us sitting up front, hoping I didn't have to shred any other living souls apart that afternoon. We pulled up to what turned out to be a five-story, ca-boodles out of the noodles, gorgeous mansion these Glovers' people lived in. Damning proof they had swindled many with the Roots business.

I bet June was thinking she could've brought tookus with them and let her hang out in that *'dream come true'* library. The mansion was huge, so huge that my tookus could have easily stayed in the same room where we met without hearing the discussion, and that's even if we'd been shouting at each other to the top of our lungs.

A small man who looked like he needed two hands and many prayers to pull one strand of hair out of anyone's head, led us to an intimate corner in this massive library. Turned out this was Stephan.

"We were expecting Caitlyn to join us," smiled the feeble character calling himself Stephan, guestering at an empty chair were it was planned my tookus would sit.

"Oh, she's spending the day with a friend," June said, only partially telling the truth. Rachel hardly could be counted as my tookum's friend this early. That determination would be decided upon my return.

"How nice, she must be an outgoing little girl to have made friends already," said Stephan, waving over a servant bringing tea to this stuffy gathering. "So, how long have you guys been here?"

"A week," Eric replied, looking up and around as I was doing at that moment, marveling the most amazing library I'd seen in my life.

Most rooms have four walls, built like the typical square, but this room was shaped like an octagon. It was one of these futuristic digs, cryptically built, with the disguised walls not inclusive of the eight visible ones...and all, of course, paid for by the hair-pulling Roots business.

From the outside I thought... 12th century mental

prison. You know...the gray cobblestone walls, rounded corners, five stories high, and about fifteen windows a person would have to flatten out, sideways, and make like a rat to fit through. I honestly lost my social graces fizzing around this stretch of home. That's how I missed most of the opening dialogue.

I was rapt up in this awestruck stupefaction, fizzing up and down 15-foot-high walls when I heard...

"...hmmm...that's funny, that's what we called our daughter...Tigga."

I spun around, like a Cagney who lost Lacey, and shouted *'you called who what!?!'*

Now wait a minute, let's organize a few details here. First, no one heard me. These people can pull all the hairs they want, and lay them side by side on as many microscopes as they could find and link, and still, unless they died and went to hell, they'd never hear, or see me. So there, let that be your number one.

As for two, only one person in the universe had that ugly name! Now, given I never met Tigga's people, I didn't know these Glover's from a gnat, not that knowing, or not knowing them meant much. Tigga hated her folks, why I never met them. But I was curious... and thus while the Glover's hum-drummed through a husky list of clients they supposedly helped discover their roots; Tina Simms *(a famous dancer)*, and Jack Olson *(a black belt karate master)*, I fizzed through that camp like dogs dig up bones.

With my BA-hind, *if I had one*, up in the attic doing a little research of my own, the Glovers continued on rekindling their crimes; apparently schmoozing June and Eric drinking this swine, chasing down bullshit over ice-cubes. I gotta say...the minutia sharks get away with nowadays is worse than the shit sharks get away with.

Nevertheless, I was in the attic all of a few seconds when it came to me, *'I might be a CSI immortal...'*, but I for damn sure was no Colombo!

Coughing and gagging from the little bit of dust I

kicked up in the attic, I returned to the discussion in the middle of Stephan's golf-clubbing, teeing off more successes in the hair-pulling research business.

"Mallory Gilroy was astonished by our discoveries of her ancestry, going back to King Arthur's lineage," said Stephan ever so proudly. "It landed us a PBS program now going in its 7th season," he added.

'*Now tell me...*' who in the hell is Mallory Gilroy? And while you're looking that up, look up King Arthur too. I wanted to domino pimp smack all three of them, sitting there effecting high society mannerisms, speaking in non-lay terms I couldn't make heads or tails out of, and neither could they. Like how many King Arthur's are there anyway!?! Wasn't it thousands of them? And thousands more knockoffs?

And I know, what is the price of discovery when here I am, hovered between this theoretical theatrical textbook talk trying to knock off that who shot John at which preparatory school, to figure out what happened to my princess before the Briggs took her in.

So I had to. At the tail end of what was supposed to be a consultation visit, I zipped into June's head and got her to leafing through possible scenarios of how she would ask the question I nagged her not to leave the house without asking.

"If you don't mind me asking," June started, just after the Glover's had concluded that my snookums would be a very interesting subject to look into *(and I'll get back to that subject-labeling after I get through all of this genealogy hogwash)*, "did you say you named your daughter Tigga?"

Stephan reached for his left ear and began tugging it, vigorously, as if cuing Marge to answer just how she did. "No, I said we called our daughter Tigga," she replied, like a well rehearsed charlatan would do.

I didn't have a comeback, and so neither did June, thus the meeting ended there, at least for the four of them it did. 'Cause it sure as hell didn't end there for me.

28

As Eric pulled off the Glover's plantation, with June in the passenger seat looking deflated, I rifled around that luscious farm looking for *hidden* photos. I mined floorboards, drawers, shelves, closets, beneath beds, inside barns...and in some very tightly packed smelly places. That heffa told me some convoluted story about escaping a royal palace with wazoo crillos *(money)*, but I didn't believe her then and now... I smelled her!!! These swindlers were no more royals than they had given her lying ass one red cent. But Jupiter be my witness, Tigga had been on this damn farm!

While hightailing it around the mansion, poking into these Glover's business, I was so one-focused I forgot about my little muffin and how she might've been fairing with the defective Barbie Doll. My antennas were dialed to its top notch wanting proof these unlikely royals may have parented that woman I should've cut loose after our first moon trip! And I know, my dumb shallow ass should have known this from the start, and definitely shouldn't be talking like this now that I have my snookums.

Except here's the deal; I can't change what is, or might now be! I was thinking these swindles needed more looking into. From my purview these death baits were trying real hard to get themselves really killed. *And I'll be a mother blue damn!* No sooner than that notion crossed my dome did a small pill box, secured by a pink ribbon, tucked under a swathe of lacy extra large WHITE bloomers... or maybe shower caps, or how about parachutes, tell me exactly what was inside!

Sure enough, I was right. Inside the pill box was a photo of Tigga, when she was two, according to notes on the back. Looked just like how I imagined a miniature wannabe beauty queen would look. Gutted eyes, blank stare, ruffles galore and pissy grin standing next to a chunky boy, probably her brother, noted only as Stanley.

Man. I hated her more, shaking my head *(of course if I had one),* looking at poor Stanley standing there holding his breath, trying to keep as much of his guts as possible inside that loud purple-checkered suit. It may as well have been me...20 years later on our wedding day. Ugh!

At any rate, I erased the image of Tigga—*at two*—and hurried to hear what the Glover's were chewing on.

"I never trusted those two, and now I really don't," Marge was saying when I popped in on them.

"Yeah," Stephan agreed, "I feel somethings not quite right here either..."

'Yeah! How about this!?! It's called BUSTED!' Good thing I was there. This is the kind of shit, had I not heard it, could've set me back trying to figure out what was going on. But aah! I caught their asses, and was going to make sure whatever they were trying to pull off wasn't going to get pulled off. *I'll tell ya'. Idiots never cease to amaze me!*

"...we can always cancel the contract, of course less our twenty percent finders fee," says the hen Marge.

"But these folks seem too desperate to disappoint," Stephan smugly chuckled as if June and wimpy Eric, and thus my snookums deserved to be swindled.

Well, swindle this... *'if this chap and his mate thought for one of their future sleepless nights I'd let them rest in holy peace with my child's future sitting in one of their hedge funds, they had another corrupt thought a fucking coming!'*

These grand larcenist had some nerve. I gave a cradle less about the research at this point. Grandparents or not, I saw no point for these people to be entangled any further in my poo bears story. Like where could I find the next in quality genealogists?

29

Let me get one thing straight, before someone assumes I'm some sort of over-protective jerk for a father. I certainly am over-protective, and I am a jerk too! But let's not get this twisted. I'm a cell no different than any other highly competitive mortal that likes to win. Only difference is, I'm winning for my child! Now let that sink in.

Just because I assumed Rachel wasn't a suitable playmate for my snookums, after seeing her hootchy-cooing with that boy, didn't mean I was right, even if I was, though I'll tell you about that one a stretch later.

Same goes for the swindlers. Just because they acted like thieves, didn't mean they were, which they were; and I'll tell you about that one a stretch later too!

My problem was something I hadn't considered since waking up after my transition. I need accessories... cohorts...allies...accomplices...co-conspirators...aka, some damn good gullible friends.

I met Cook, who, all be damned, used to hang out with me when we judged together. The jigga *(that's slang for gigolo)* was inside my tookus. Now, I know what er'body might be thinking, because I almost sure did, but I didn't lose my cool then and there. As already expressed, I try not going inside my snookums just for what almost went down, but my tookus had been saying things that got me worrying about what was going on inside her.

Rachel was over to the house this day—it was a Saturday; and they were in snookums room looking at all of her things. Of course June had splurged on my girl. She had one of anything a child in this day and age could ever want, and not that that fine ass mother of Rachel's hadn't gone overboard in buying her sexpot everything she could want too.

But Rachel was one of them spoiled-rotten Valley air-heads who flitted around nosing in my tookums spoils trying to make sure she hadn't been outdid. My cuddlems wasn't hip to these type peoples ways yet, though she did have Tigga in her, which I got to wondering about when I heard tookus say, "we should just cut her!"

I was dozing at the moment, not entirely indebted to the girly chit-chat, trying my darnedest to let my little snookus be a little girl, even if I wasn't happy about this Rachel friendship business. I was just comfortable enough knowing that at least June wouldn't let my tookus stray too far off the behavior map, or go anywhere with that wild made-up Barbie. I really liked this part about June. Although she didn't have any children of her own, she had motherly instincts, and knew a thing or two about reading and rearing children. So far, she read Rachel like the bad book she was and kept a motherly listening eye turned on whenever Rachel was around.

But she hadn't heard this chit-chat, and really, neither had I because I was like, *'cut who?,'* and just like that skipped up and flew inside my tookus.

Got inside and went straight down to where I last saw Tigga. There she was, just like before, a crumbled over mess of gook, even messier than before. Looked like she was really in a losing battle with her judgment, cowered and withered up the way she was. She was so bad off she couldn't speak.

But that's how I noticed another mass, a new mass, a lot healthier mass, on the other side of Tigga...sort of poking her...you know... as if it was trying to rouse her.

"Stop that! Leave her alone," I shouted over Tigga at the mass."

"Who you," the mass said back, lifting up looking

like a ghost trying to stick its neck out.

"I'm her ex-husband. Who you?"

"Cook," replied the mass.

"Who?" At first I didn't hear him.

"Cook," the mass repeated.

"Cook who?" I asked again, meanwhile me, I'm stalling, trying to get a clear range shot to do away with this Cook. And yeah, I know I elaborated on how you can blast a mass and it end up exploding all over the place. But here's some new noncontroversial intel since added to my knowledge base. A straight aim at its nuclei nodule can clean take a mass out. Like ZAPPO! And this Cook would be gone forever. No one would miss his ass.

But I let Cook explain himself, while I sharpened my rationalization skills. Yeah, I was going for the kill shot; a clean erasure no one alive or dead would ever know existed. If Cook was who I thought he was, I didn't like him then, and definitely didn't like him now.

"Aww dude," the mass said *'all cool like.'* "Act like you know," it laughed, trying to *'f' with my head.*

"Act like I know what?" I asked anyway. It sounded like Charles Cinderella Cook... the dunce I used to judge with, when both of us were raking in beauties... like stoking coals over fire. We used to poke 'em all, ashes to hot rods, creating elaborate spreadsheets and setting up office pools to chart which one we were getting next. I was far ahead of Cindy *(I called him),* by about 249 subtleties to his so-so mix of 11 scuds. You had to know how to move in and out, which all too ironic was just before I buckled and married Tigga. Like damn!

"Boyyyyyyy," he mocked me. "You betta' recognize! You don't remember me!?!"

And so it really was him. "Aww man," I laughed too, "what the hell you doing in here?"

"You cheated," he said. "You knew I was on that! You knew I was on your girl first!"

Ok. Forget the obvious discrepancy here. "Tigga?"

I *all the same* asked surprised. And I really was. Tigga hated Cindy. She wanted no parts of him. He was too short for one, and too chunky around the face, neck and middle for the other. His lips were blubbery too, and his tongue way too juicy. Plus, he was loud, causing all of this clunkiness to get extra clunky, which of all ugly amenities, he had the nerve to laugh at the baboons, donkeys, and ugly ducklings he got stuck with. We called him booga too, and none too affectionately either, behind his back.

No wonder why Tigga had smeared all the way down to a chromosome. Gosh, her luck was getting worse and worse. Too bad she didn't know how to rise up. And apparently Cindy was the same old slow Mo-joe himself. I mean, like DAYYAM! Tigga's drone must've had a hella' stank code on it if she attracted joka'! Like WOW!!!

"Yeah dude, Tigga," Cindy said, laughing in that derisively loud raggedy yowl I hadn't forgotten. "You kidnapped my lady and took off for them islands so I couldn't catch up with ya'll. How'd you get her to go? What'd you do dawg? Drug her? Hit her over the head with a pipe, packed her up in a suitcase and stashed her in the baggage compartment?"

"Nawl dude..." I humored him back. "She told me your feet stunk and she wanted to get as far away from the smell as possible. So I took her to Maldives."

"Hahaha," Cindy laughed. "Aww dawg, you cold. You know you ain't right." And then he paused... "so, what you doin' in here, trying to block me again?"

And this was where the problem came in. Where the controversary ensued. Proof right here in the pudding, Cindy definitely wasn't up to no good, but he also was a long shot from doing any harm. Just another dud wandering around adding extra fluff to life, nothing I needed to hip him on, however. What he didn't know wasn't none my loss. Actually, it was all my gain. He didn't need to know he was helping my baby live. Tigga wasn't ever going to rise for that funky foot fool.

"You got that right mo'," I chuckled like old times. "Fussy said you was here, so I came to see for myself."

Fussy was another one of the judges. Frank King; a straight-up practical guy with halitosis. The women loved everything about Frank, but his stanky mouth.

"So, how you find Tigga? How you get in here?" That's all I was really trying to figure out.

"Aww dude, one of them chop-sticks told me. Holly," he said. "She killed herself riding one of them jet skis, on Hobo Lake a few years back. She told me Tigga got butchered up in a back alley, getting an abortion."

Now remember when I said I didn't know much about the politics behind wars in the ethereal world. Well, here's another example.

"Whad?" I murmured, more surprised about Holly dying, than hearing this rumor about Tigga getting hacked up in a back alley. Holly was one gorgeous lay. Her stuff used to smell, and taste, like cinnamon. Back in the day that's who I used to always go see for my morning break-fasts ...before I started dating Tigga heavily, of course.

"Yeah dude," Cindy went on, my silence inviting him to keep lying. "I bumped into her waitin' in line to get in. She was number 726, and I was 729...so you see, we had to talk over heads...none I knew though, so nobody but me knows she's here," he wryly chuckled. "Well, at least not nobody down here..."

"Umm," I hummed, trying not to hip this fool to what I knew. I had already lied about Fussy. Last I knew, that man was still alive. I just wanted him to keep talking about this waiting in line...and of course Holly. Nothing too shattering, but educational all around.

Last thing I wanted to do was let a stupid man know I was stupid too. Plus, I wanted his ugly ass to stay just where his ugly ass was, for as long as his ugly ass could, so that Tigga would have few incentives to rise up. The longer she remained weak, the better.

The important tidbit I figured out, but didn't like,

apparently my snookums needed some part of her mother. I just didn't want her having too much. So Tigga needed to stay put. Eventually when my snookums got a little older, depending on how things looked, I could then usher Tigga on out of there, just not now.

"So, ya'll still talk," I slipped in, trying to keep him talking on more cell layout. I passed these fools all the time and paid none of what they were doing, or saying, any mind. Coming down the other way so very few got to come, it looked like a waste of time dealing with them. But apparently not; not if it meant having to trust leaving this fool inside my tookus. I was trying very hard not to hurt nobody else.

"Naw," he said, dipping a lobe that looked all healthy and rejuvenated, possibly from the excitement of finally running into someone he could shoot the shit with.

"Don't any of us down here talk much," he admitted. "You the first one I ran into who's said more than two words. Shit...I been trying to talk to Tigga for a whole week and she's only said two words..."

"Oh, what's that?" I asked.

"Go away..." he sadly replied.

30

So, what did I learn about all this cell activity. Well, for one; I learned Cindy's ugly ass didn't get in. He got to the pearly gate and must've been turned away, banished over to the super Hell highway. What a damn shame. I don't know if Holly got in either, with her fine cinnamon smelling ass. I didn't ask, and Cindy didn't say.

But I also learned that some highly unorthodox crappola was going on behind my back. Must've been, otherwise Holly wouldn't have known about Tigga in a back alley. And true too, like most rumors, Holly could've mixed stuff up. A lot of pinecones rattled around in her jellybean too. I figured that out one day when I heard her trying to count change back from a quarter. I bet she mistook our trip to see that facelift shrink as a back alley baby abortion. That was one special girl. It's too bad, but not really all that surprising to hear about her jet skis smacking a tree. I could easily see how something like that would happen to her. She was one of them ones who you couldn't trust anything she said she saw.

I left Cindy telling him I was dipping out to go find some bubbles. A beer run was always the best way to skip off from him. No matter how many times I used the line, he never caught on. I'd catch up to him the next day, or the following week, saying the same old thing I said the other hundreds of times I pulled this exit alibi.

"Aww chump, why you didn't tell me you were hanging out with Holly?" That would make him feel all big, putting this big ass lying grin on his ugly mug, talking about how she had his tongue all twisted, or something as ludicrous, given I had been the one out with Holly.

The good thing was, I didn't have to worry much about leaving him alone like that and possibly messing things up for my tookus. All it took was something bothering her, and I'd know just where to look, and of course be there in a flash, which speaking of...I zipped out of her just in time to find June sitting beside her on the bed, talking.

"...But honey, why would you talk like that? Why would you want to cut anyone?" June asked my tookums.

Oh Lawd have mercy, now what? What done happened to my jewel while I was away? Someone had to be bothering her for her to want to do something like this.

"...Cause, Rachel said she didn't like her," my little jewel answered just as sweet as maple pancake syrup.

All right, let's break here and get things straight. It wasn't none my concern why my tookus would want to cut someone. There were plenty reasons why.

Shit, lots of times I wanted to cut someone. One time I wanted to take my blade and just go down a long line of 'em. Matter of fact, I wanted to run up and down an aisle with my blade. That's right, I thought about cutting some fools before; a whole bunch of fools if we're looking for an exact count.

While I was a judge, when I was judging beauty, I was at a conference one time listening to this joker talking about how no one cared about what was going on inside the body, only the outside. That speech ticked me the fuck off because even though I was shallow and all, I hated all them sons-of-bitches sitting around nodding their heads up and down, agreeing with this bullshit. Deep down I always wanted to do right, but messages like this got my thinking all hay-wired. That's how I ended up hooked up with Tigga in the first place, though I can't deny we didn't make a lovely child.

"Well, what did Rachel say about why she doesn't like Sara," June asked when I got back to their talk.

"She said she thinks she's cute," my cuddlems replied.

"That's no reason not to like someone," June said.

My cuddly cuddlems sat there quiet. She was thinking deeply about the matter. Both her and I knew there was every reason not to like someone who thought they were cute. It was fucking annoying, that's why! They'll irk the fuck out of you with them snobby looks, going along with shit, nodding along cause nothing else is inside them.

"Mrs. Washington and I are very concerned about this," June said—just as I took a flying leap to the ceiling. I barely missed busting my lobe and getting splattered up there. I could've easily been on my way back to the gates.

What the—wasn't like nobody got hurt! Though, I piped down when my cuddlems started speaking.

"...But Rachel said that stuff on her FB page, and she put them pictures up there too," my sweet tookus said. "I don't even know who that girl is..."

Hang on here, as I collect myself to righteously distribute a lil barbarity over the matter. First off, Mrs. Washington is cute and all, but don't think for an inth of a second I won't fizz by there and straighten her cute hinny out to fit ugly, cause you know I fucking will.

Did that cutie pie really believe her hideous gremlin was innocent in all this? I didn't see that polka dot Barbie, laying all over station wagons to let Neanderthals slobber all over her, in my tookus's room with a laptop of her own. No! She had to have commandeered my tookus's laptop to taunt that child, *cute Sara,* because I know good and well my little titan didn't. My tookus didn't know anything about an FB before Rachel got to stirring up all of this hate. No one showed her. And I do know this as a fact. I am her father. A father who is not only involved very much so in his child's life, but a father who has special powers; powers that can tell when someone needs to be shown just how special my powers are.

Secondly, serves Rachel right. Let's face it. Rachel just wasn't my tookus's speed. My tookus showed her she didn't play around posting silly comments on FB pages or whatever the hell they called them walls. Tookus was the real McCoy, taught by the best—the realest of the Mc-Coy's—them damn Briggs. That's right. She was something like her daddy, too.

To Mrs. Washington's good fortune, and Rachel's too, June decided to keep my sweet cuddly bear away from that rift-raft. I overheard her talking with Eric about it, as he was deep in thought drafting another letter to the two swindlers still trying to hang onto my sweet noodles education fund... just where I was headed next!

31

I got a lead on where my sweetums had been just prior to when I saw her on the schoolyard. Actually, before I catch myself in a lie I need to go on and get it over with, and give credit where credit is due.

Eric got this lead. Yep, it was him. His determined, stubborn wussy self was a pen wielding maniac on paper. On one of my routine checks I caught the swindling Glovers whole faces pressed into them hand-scratched letters and digital contracts they drafted...trying their damnedest to etch out a win on keeping funds that clearly did NOT belong to them!

While I was busy trying to see into that Rachel friendship; figuring out who said and did what, and to see how *cute* Sara was involved in it all, plus untwine what the cutie pie Mrs. Washington had said to June based on what her troll had told her, Eric was knuckles to paper begging for his dimes back. So I can't harp on the 'ole puss in boots too much, even if it was Mel who I think was most instrumental in *'getting the goods'*. Of course we all know with that man knotted up in this stink, it was gonna get 'Godfather' crazy if 'ole soft pants didn't have his way.

At any rate, turned out my lil tuggums had walked off from Grand Mercy Hospital...and they tried to cover their tracks...just like June suspected.

"I really appreciate your taking the time to do this, hun," June said to Eric, walking up behind him sitting at his desk, to wrap her arms around his neck. She gently kissed him on the cheek, and then in the ear. "I hope you're satisfied that she belongs with us...someone who can look after her and be concerned if she ever walked off."

Eric sighed deeply. "I am," he gingerly admitted, before taking in another deep painful sigh. "I just feel there's more to our little girl that someone is going through great lengths to hide."

"But what," June asked lifting up, now frowning, losing the sentimental guise.

Really, truth was, all three of us, *for various reasons,* clamored to know where our darling came from. Eric's was more by habit...being that editorial nuisance he was. No chief editor ever looked the other way on stories of this caliber. It was *kind of* the same for June. Teachers, by nature, cared deeply for children. In her mind... *and yep, I overheard her talking to Paula about her feelings,* she wanted to see the person or persons prosecuted for abandoning our child. Of course then, everyone must appreciate why I did... and didn't want too much sniffing around.

Although I don't recall exactly when, but around the same time June got all mushy with the wuss, I heard her talking with Paula in the next room—the bathroom.

"I can't believe it," I heard her whispering. "Someone left that child in the hospital and didn't even care after she walked off!?!"

"But how do you know Caitlyn is that same kid?" Paula asked. And in case you're wondering, yep, I hopped on the phone line soon as I heard the whispering.

"DNA," June sighed flatly. "Plus, there's a photo of her, taken when she arrived at the hospital. It matches her school photo."

"Oh dear..." Paula gasped.

"I know," June seethed, hissing her words. "I'm so angry about this I don't know what to do!"

"I do," Paula muttered back, no emotion invested in her tone whatsoever. "Sue them! I would sue the pants off them. You probably could end up owning that place. I'm sure you and Eric could use the money."

"Yeah, but who wants the headache?"

"Huh?" Ambition aside, Paula had a lot of rocks mixed up in her scrabble too.

"...Sick people need a place to go to—"

"—why should you care," Paula broke in, screaming to the near top of her lungs. Almost like to have blasted me off the line she was so damn fired up. "Hell! If they can't keep up with patients, then the patients are better off somewhere else anyway!"

"Yeah, but Caitlyn is safe now. What if there's more to this story and we end up losing her?" June managed to get out before Paula cut her off again.

Damn what the rest of Paula said. I definitely got June, and most certainly saw her point. It wasn't so much as things *could* get messy. Things positively WOULD get incredibly disheveled if curiosities got out of hand. Let's face it. Some battles are best won by not fighting them to begin with.

That damn Paula.

32

My sweetums was in her bedroom, plopped up on her nice fluffy pink comforter lying on her tummy and feet kicked up, just typing away on her laptop while all this conversation was taking place. She was being a little girl, doing what any nice little sweet girl at her age, and goodness, would be doing—browsing the latest fashions on the high-end apparel websites.

I love my darling. I love her so much I don't know if I've accurately or precisely explained in generous enough detail, how far I will drive this motherfucking planet out of this motherfucking solar system to ensure my snookums has a reasonable chance to enjoy a quality life. Just to look at her little eyes fluttering every time she saw a new, bigger, and better image pop up on screen made me gloat even harder. There's nothing in the world I won't do, or see to it she has, if that's what her little innocent heart desires. Nothing. Not even those $579 pink sneakers with the lacy bowties she's smiling at, despite knowing next year she will have outgrown them, and tossed them to the back of her closet.

I sift inside of her as she prepares for bed. That's where I've been hanging out, for 20-30 minutes, before turning in myself. I've been going in there to chat with my chum Cindy, just to get things off my chest, which this night is particularly heavy given Paula and June's chat.

"So, how you holding up over there dude?" I asked Cindy. Each night he's been looking worse and worse. I can't help wonder why he doesn't move on. It's not like

Tigga will ever give him a second of hope. She hasn't lifted up yet. She's not even a clump anymore. There's just an outline shaped in the lump that used to be her, with a flicker of glitter in the center that when looked at really hard, pulsates ever so faintly. My snookums must have obsoleted the one measly job she had left.

"Aww man, it's okay. Just taking it easy," Cindy said, sounding bad as he looked.

"Yeah, I hear ya'," I quietly chuckled, trying to match his glumness. "I keep thinking about them days when we were living large. Every night was a party," I laughed a little more livelier. "Hey, remember when we used to—"

"—aww dude, don't go there," Cindy stopped me. "I don't want to remember them days. It's probably what got us here; why we didn't get in."

Sheeeit...I did get in, but I can't let him know this. Instead I yawned and sighed, "yeah, I guess you're right," masking my heavy heart covering a general good feeling, to spiral into a glum mood to match his.

"So, you never told me. Where exactly are you going to get those bubbles you never bring back...and why do you keep coming back," he groaned. "...To check up on us?" he wryly and very sarcastically added.

I guess 'ole Cindy finally got me huh? Talk about late in the house though, given I never ever told Cindy a whole lot. But make no mistake about it, old hanging partner or not, this fool would learn more than he ever wanted to know if he started some mess in here. I'd take him out for sure. He'd end up in worse shape than that puddle he was still drooling over.

"Just checking out things," I said anyway. "Trying to see if I can catch up to anyone I know."

"Guess you haven't found anyone, huh?"

"Naw...seems like everyone else made it in..."

"...Yeah, same here," sighed Cook.

33

June may have been reluctant to report the hospital for letting my snookums walk off and then covering it up, but not Paula. That woman was persistent. She was not letting this thing go.

She took her looking for a lead self, straight up to the hospital to get answers, while my tookus was living large in her new life, practicing her elbow swing with her new tennis instructor Gary.

So, while my tookums was good and settled, and living her best life, I took the liberty to see what Paula was up to. Sure enough I found her, right in Grand Mercy's children's ward.

Now, before I get into what all happened, let me emphasize; Paula is a fast woman. She's fast as a Jag going downhill with no breaks. She had to have done hundreds, if not millions to billions of these skits getting a story. That's part of her job. She either has to get a good lead to feed to her boss—Mel, *and I don't have to remind you how Mel is,* or she has to get that story to build onto her own ego.

Long story sweetened, her and June's relationship grew out of their father's philandering. They met during weekend visits with their sex addict father. Not that I'm roasting the guy...*like who am I to disparage anyone for committing such faux pas...*yet facts first. The dude had so many crumb snatchers that June often had to share court ordered visitations with his other *mistakes.*

At any rate, Paula and June's bond was built around this dysfunction. Being the more *'successful'* career-wise, of the entire *'half-sibling'* brood, their connection was deeper, yet in no way to be construed they were utterly close. Namely, due to Paula's drive to be on top getting what she saw as the better job, flashing more money, driving luxury cars, wearing designer garb, living in the top zip codes...basically having it all, which included ensuring her name was at the helm of published top stories, she could be insanely motivated...alas jealous.

June wasn't all that thrilled by Paula's drive, thus all that follows falls appropriately in line with how things should have fallen...Paula driving her outrageous silver Jaguar, with the black and silver zebra patterned suede-felt convertible top, right up to the hospital, and parking it in the emergency entrance. Someone tried to stop her, but this was Paula, the self-appointed queen taught not to take NO for an answer.

Paula had planned the skit out, which only took her a day and a half to draft, flush, and run with. I know this because I overheard June telling her about my tookus walking off from that miserable hospital. Really, June should've known better than to feed a career editorialist, and dubious sister like her, a lead like this. This type person has no boundaries and a limited understanding of *'this might not be your day.'*

It furthermore must be drilled in, I don't think very fast, very well. Oh, a thought'll shoot out of me like a rocket, but just like a rocket it'll gouge a hole in whatever it infiltrates, big enough to sit mother earth in. Yet, every one of you reading this must know how much I really love my tookus. I love my tookus so much that her daddy will shoot ten rockets off at once if it means keeping her out of harms way.

The way I saw it, and the way June as well saw it, a story like this blowing up threatened my angel's safety, comfort and future. From thrill-seekers, to opportunist, to outright haters would crawl from the bowels of iniquity to take advantage of my snookum's situation.

Just thinking out loud here, a story like this blowing up would draw grifters from their Harvard law books and Grisham novels and Nancy Grace programs, slobbering with giddy excitement to hear gavels of the Supreme Court magnitude crush my darling's life, all while ignoring money-mules running off with loot rightfully belonging to her. And I mean EVERY SINGLE TRILLION belonged to my sweet tookus!

I only wanted June...and Eric *(who I'm only adding out of bare obligation, considering he and June came as a unit)*, caring for my child. They are who I CHOSE, and who my snookums is used to. She loves them, and I don't want this caring relationship interrupted...not even for one day in court. There's no point in having to go through all of that minutia so that a judge, who drives a jazzy car like Paula's, will have me to contend with, to rule on matters the way I see fit. What's the point in going through all those motions, at the risk of many people getting really hurt, to after all, see things my way? I am her daddy, and as her daddy I know what is best for my tookus.

I come on scene *(at the hospital)*, as Paula was asking to speak to the head nurse on duty. It's about 11am, so I suspect this head nurse will be a higher-end head nurse, instead of a nurse in training working graveyard.

Out comes a woman who couldn't have been no more than 20; 21 max, holding a clipboard up to her chestplate. Young as I know she is, she still looks beat.

Now, I'm just hovering at this point. I don't know who I will have to jump inside. I'm feeling things out to be ready to jump when the time calls for it.

"I'm Head Nurse Andrea," the young woman said.

"Hello Andrea, I'm Paula Broaddus, chief editor for Mel Gallagher," and she flashed her editorial badge, which even from the distance I saw it, *her flashing it as if she was head of the FBI*, it indeed looked official.

Andrea saw what I saw too. Her eyes glowered and then settled.

"Is there somewhere where we can talk," Paula asked the surprised woman, questioning not only what an investigator wanted with her, but who was Mel?

"Sure," replied Andrea, quickly turning around to lean over the reception desk and whisper a super big chunk of words to the receptionist witnessing the exchange.

"We can talk in here," Andrea said to Paula, when she was done whispering. She stepped aside, literally two steps in a right-direction slide, into a prep room where she snatched a curtain close after Paula stepped inside.

Curtain closed and Andrea stood there, staring at Paula, as if asking what is it you want?

Paula quickly took note of the room, *knowing her*, expecting that they would talk in a room more receivable, something like where they held conferences at Pinecroft; plush conference rooms garnished with melodramatic wood furnishings and black leather high-back matching corporate chairs.

In one suave move Paula slipped a notepad out of her large hobo bag and flipped it open to an earmarked page. "Where were you, Tuesday, May 7?" she asked.

Andrea's expression hadn't changed. She stood crisply still, staring at Paula as if she was stuck in a stand up shower... being electrocuted.

I hovered between the two, staring too. I still was trying to figure out where Paula was going and what I was going to do about where she was going. I was thinking fast, though very poorly.

The curtain snatched open, abruptly and force-fully), and in stepped one tall, aerobics-thick, husky voice Pediatrics Head Director, Princess Mean. *(No kidding, that was her name!)*

"You needed to see me," Princess boomed in her husky voice, looking left to right, from Andrea to Paula.

Clearly this Mean woman was speaking to Andrea, though *'we all'* stared for a moment. Andrea at Paula who stared hostility at the uninvited *(according to her)*, interruption, who glared back at her, as I stared at them all. A five-second stare-down was what we had going on, before Paula answered.

"I'm trying to find out who was working here on May 7th...Tuesday," Paula said, though not as abrasive as she had asked Andrea.

"What's it to you?" Princess threw back.

Paula caught her breath, swallowed hard, looked down at the floor, rocked on one heel, seeming to think *'how dare this wild beast question me,'* as she lightly scratched the nape of her neck, grinning *(inwardly)*, and clearing her throat before replying, "I'm here on behalf of Mel. He wants to talk to anyone who worked May, 7th, 20—" she said, looking Princess dead in the eye, before being abruptly cut off.

"—Who's Mel?" Princess asked with attitude. And before Paula could part her lips, she added, "and who are you!?!"

"Oh," Paula shuffled, thrusting one hand out towards Princess who stood with her arms fixed firmly to her side. "I'm Paula Bro—"

"—Paula, any inquiries you have regarding this hospital, or our department, should be directed to our Internal Affairs office," firmly stated Princess.

"Well—" Paula stammered, as I jockeyed into position. "I thought you might—"

"—Paula, excuse us. We are very busy. Children are very ill here and—"

"—and walking off while you and your treacherous staff cover it up," Paula quickly snapped before they, Princess and Andrea, were able to clear the curtain.

"What did you say," Princess sneered, pivoting to face Paula in this slow, deathly spin.

And Paula had the gumption to answer. "I said you and your staff are neglecting these children, letting them walk off and then covering it up," she hissed back.

Here's where, if I had ears...and hands... both my

hands would have been pressed *tightly* against the side of my head. Sounded like Princess blew a whistle directly down my eardrum. Gosh, that hurt. It was easy to jump inside Paula after that.

I moved directly to her head, as I heard her rattling off a mousy terse spiel to security officers who rushed to the ward to have her removed from the floor.

Eventually we made it to the entrance; the emergency entrance where her jazzy jag was about 4½ feet raised off the ground, hooked up to a tow truck.

There was more yelling, and threats of a law suit, which I'd estimate everyone in the hospital who had at least one good ear heard. Among Paula's chief complaints; neglect, abuse, missing child, a cover-up, a pending lawsuit, and double that pending lawsuit for recklessly mishandling her precious jag trying to illegally tow it.

I said to Paula, as she sat in her jag, now with two pebble-size dents in its fender, stewing. *"Paula"* I implored, *"calm down. You didn't expect to waltz in there and have those people fall at your feet begging forgiveness did you? They are going to fight you tooth and nail; and all the way, you better believe it. You're going to need some winning power to come out on top of this one... this time,"* I said.

Honest to goodness that was all I said and did. I swear I didn't put no other thoughts in her head, other than what all I just laid out. Paula, as you may very well be aware of, is a very fast thinker, and likes to stay on top. I could've never come up with, at least not in that reckless spur of the moment, a plan of attack so outrageous. She said and did all the rest on her own swift discerning.

34

I'm not even going to go through what all Paula did, and didn't do, since no one was hurt. That's the important part. No one got hurt. Now, there may have been a few bruised feelings. In fact there were quite a few bruised feelings, commencing the moment Paula first approached Andrea, insinuating that she and her boss, Princess, were running a foul department. Shoe on the other foot, Paula herself, wouldn't want to be approached that way, and I'm saying this as a father who could've lost his daughter due to the hospital's hypothesized negligence.

It didn't take long for the same security officers, Luther and Magnettus, who ushered Paula out the first time, to defer the incident report they were texting to their boss, Lou Gu, on the first incident, to swing back by and haul Paula off for what would be the culminating incident.

Wearing light blue scrubs—nurse's issue, she was taken to a secure room where she was restrained, and she claimed, handcuffed, searched, and unlawfully, without reading so much as one right, spitefully questioned.

"Paula, what in the hell is going on," Mel asked very, very concerned. And he had every reason to be. She shelled out his name nearly every time someone asked her a question. To count, he received 69 voicemails, aside from the 29 messages she left. Lou Gu's message was the most disconcerting. He said Paula was being detained for attempted kidnapping.

"They're mad Mel. I'm over here trying to get a lead on a story and they're mad."

"Who's mad?" Mel really was confused. These were not his instructions, though whatever his instructions were, he no longer recalled.

"The hospital," Paula said, "The hospital that let that little girl walk off and tried to cover it up."

"What hospital," Mel asked bewildered. He still was lost. Had no clue what Paula was talking about.

"Eric's adopted daughter," she explained, not sure of much herself. During her detainment she'd been tossed and tussled around quite a bit.

'Eric's adopted daughter,' Mel mouthed, as if trying to assemble a giant jigsaw puzzle. He definitely didn't recall having such a conversation...with anyone, period!

"The hospital," Paula said, "The hospital that let that little girl walk off and tried to cover it up."

"What hospital," Mel asked, his eyes lit like fizzing firecrackers. Paula had parceled out his name like Jehovah Witnesses passing out Awake! flyers.

"Eric's adopted daughter," she continued, shaken herself now. Mel could be scary if he felt double-crossed!

"Eric's adopted daughter,' Mel muttered.

"Yeah," Paula piped in. "Remember when you told me to see what I could find out? Well, it turns out *they* lost the kid, and then tried to cover it—"

"—Paula," Mel abruptly cut her off. "Where are you!?!" He knew damn well he never instructed her to kidnap no kid. Whatever else she babbled could wait. This story could finish Pinecroft.

"—Look, stay there," he seethed, chewing up the rest of Paula's meely explanation. He slammed down the receiver and I took off. I wanted to stay with Mel, if nothing more than to follow the man's ire, but this was not the time to be giggling and gloating. Things started poppin'!

35

I jumped off the call between Mel and Paula to hang out with Princess Mean—Pediatrics Head Director at the hospital of Grand Mercy. The story had hit the airwaves... just as Paula intended.

Pinecroft was talking. The Glovers were talking. Teachers at Princeton were talking. June and Eric were talking. Everybody was talking. But none more so than the staff at Grand Mercy Hospital. That's why I got over there first. There was no way I could lay low now. The ducks were out and wild geese running afoul and loose.

I caught up with Princess in her office. It wasn't quite four, but she was packing up as if she was about to leave for the day. A young assistant looking woman stopped by asking Princess if she needed anything *else*. Glumly Princess shook her head no, thanking the woman as she backed out of the office. Her phone rang, but she looked at the caller ID and didn't answer it. Quarter after 4 she was all packed up, briefcase in one hand, a jacket thrown over her arm, purse hanging from her shoulder, and head held high she marched by a reception area where all eyes were on her as she turned neither left nor right heading straight for the exit.

'*Oh shit.*' Her ass must've gotten fired.

Inside her car, or Hummer, smelled a little musty. Like a gym locker room tidied up by a linen scent squirting from a deodorizer every 10 minutes or so. As I watched her driving with one hand I figured it was how she got them great biceps. From the gym. 'Ole girl had some big 'ole cornbread and biscuit arms!

The car stopped in front of a home I wouldn't take for a place where someone driving a Hummer (Class III) would live. It wasn't a bad neighborhood or anything, just a little too neighborly for an SUV as large. A few of the houses on the block did have paved driveways and an attached garage, but nothing that would fit a Hummer. She couldn't even park properly on the street. Cars driving by could barely squeeze pass. Each one that finally made it by gave her a dirty look, or the finger, or both.

A few minutes later a guy jogged out of a house, down the driveway, and up to the vehicle. He hopped in, and she sped off. Had I been in the vehicle, in a physical way, I would've been shaken up. Definitely was no kosher vibe I was getting from these two on this ride.

"So, do you know the kid she was talking about," the guy asked as calmly as asking the time.

"Don't have a clue," Princess smoothly replied, using that large arm to navigate turning a corner.

"Somebody's gotta know who she's talking about, right?" the guy continued, probing in this arcane hollowly tone. Sounded like this fool was about to get hisself hurt referring to my snookums like a slab of meat.

"I'm going to meet with Rose and them tomorrow," Princess said.

Who Rose is I have no clue.

"So, what are you going to tell them?"

"Do me a favor and roll your window down," ordered Princess, as I swiveled around looking for a reason she would break in with such a request.

Driving with one hand and reaching down in the console between the seat, Princess pulled up a container. I tried to figure out what might be in the container, but it was covered by a lid. I'd have to slip inside to know for sure, but didn't want to miss anything. These two characters were acting far too suspicious for my comfort to move or look anywhere.

"When I get on the beltway can you dump that for me? I've been meaning to empty it ever since this morning," she said, chuckling a little.

The guy looked at her, as if to say *'why don't you dump it,'* but ultimately did as instructed.

My quandary, however, was deciding if I should high-tail it out the window with the contents about to be dumped, or stay with this strange colloquy. I almost jumped, until I saw ashes, a heap of them billowing by the window. *'Awl hell, I'd be forever trying to read through them ashes,'* I muttered as a cloud of thick gray dust flew behind the vehicle. *'I'm not trying to instigate here, inflaming this part in the story with harbinger hunches, but the dust had the quality of a leg. A human leg. Just saying...'*

"When you get a chance," Princess went on, "you should get the kids set up with Christmas accounts...or just figure out something to do with the money," she said waving a hand as if it didn't matter what he decided to do with this money.

He kept quiet, and so did she, for the eerie ten minutes it took to reach another home. Princess never said the guy's name, but he was thin, small and elderly; likely in his late 60's or early 70's. He also had hairy knuckles and wrinkly skin, and walked in a leaning forward folded over position, with his head down. Yeah, this old hound had been pounded on for a long time, about good and due to be taken behind a barn.

'Ole collard greens and tata' salad muscle mama drove on. No farewell. And no idea what that rendezvous was all about. It was as if the hamburger *'Mean'* flipper knew I was in her ride!

36

I was back at square one, though not for long. As stated, the airwaves were lit. So, I checked in on my priority first. My one and only concern. My baby tookums.

Got in the house to find the three of them eating dinner; (My snookums, June, and Eric). My boo was just a swinging her little legs beneath the table, happy as the sweet pea she was, humming to herself and smiling as if she saw me enter the room. This day June had her hair parted down the center and two large yellow ribbons on each part, letting her soft brown tresses fall along her cheeks. I won't lie to you. She looked just like an angel.

June and Eric didn't look so happy however. They sat at the table eating in relative silence. Aside from silverware clinking against their plates, and my snookums soft hum, the room was otherwise silent.

June cleared the table, turning to my tookus before she ran off with her little happy self, asking if she completed her homeschool work.

"Yes..." she sang. "I'm going to work on a book report now," she said.

"What book report?" June asked frowning.

"Oh, it's a surprise," my precious love said. "You don't know who it is I'm writing about. I read about him on some chick's blog," my tookus continued. "He was orphaned like me. His people left him like mines did me, and he got teased a lot too. Only he was born in some place called Nova Scotia ...in 1939," she grinned. "He a real old head, who only types all his books out..."

I was floored to hear my sweet innocent lamb's voice, something I honestly paid little attention to until now. I think June was surprised too. This was the most either of us ever heard our child articulate. And I mean smart stuff, too. I was cooked meat I was so overdone and blown away.

"What's the name of his book," June said, drawing out her words as if afraid to ask, "who is he?"

See, you have to understand, although snookums did talk, and laughed and giggled, and behaved like most school-aged girls, she was a reluctant socializer. She preferred being in her own world, after getting used to being alone so often. Rarely did she express more than common phrases most young kids did.

"Road to Entebbe," my tookus answered like nothing. "His name is Zoloft. I can't pronounce his last name though," she said, again like nothing.

"That's great, Caitlyn. I can't wait to read the book report you're working on," June replied mesmerized.

Snookums slid over to June, across the kitchen linoleum, breaking her slide like a skier comes to a stop. "When I finish do you think Uncle Eric can publish it for me," my tookus excitedly clamored.

I could see it written across June's face. She didn't want to disappoint my tookus, but she wasn't going to lie to her either. "Well, first you'll have to finish it, then we'll ask," she said, smiling as if she could see tookus's entire future ahead. By the smile it looked mighty bright.

Later that evening, while my snookums was in her room typing her cute little heart out, June was in the next room she shared with Eric, speaking in a tone where I sat on her upper lip to hear.

"Honey," she started, slipping into a negligee as I struggled to stay on her lip. Yeah, that was tough. Almost lost my balance and slipped straight down! Man! I would've seen it ALL! Oh, okay. So most of it. Well, let's just say enough of it that could've ruined things for us ALL.

That woman has a gorgeous taut tan posterior. Ahem... caught a glimpse in the mirror.

"I hope you know I'm not angry with you about all that's happened," she quietly said, easing over to Eric who had turned away from his monitor to face her.

I mean just knowing that putz was facing all of this loveliness, sleepy weepy-eyed, made me dislike him even more. But hey. I'm not like that. I respect the loser...and their relationship, though it was pure torture hearing his drivel. "I'm sorry about all of this too," he babbled. "This isn't what I had in mind either."

Oh Jesus! What a lollipop! Like, do I even need to repeat myself!?! The fruitcake was an editorial specialist! He sensationalized stories for a living. It was in his...and all his Pinecroft cronies' blood...to include, and especially the top dawg! His BOSS Mel! So, why would he not think asking these top sensationalists to dig into my tookus' past wouldn't get duplicitous?

Of course, I didn't think things would go this extra mile. I was running raggedy as it was. Now this fool had me running raggedy-ER!

The sad sap stared blurry-eyed through the floor-boards as June ignored his guilt-ridden guise and changed the topic. "Do you know what she asked tonight?"

She was smiling softly, as if grazing over my tookus' words. Whatever she had heard...or knew about Paula's shakedown/upset was since forgotten...and forgiven. The dumb-bell now in the clear.

The stooge looked up. "Who?" he asked, looking as if Paula's name was going to fall off her tongue. He saw the news broadcast, but Mel hadn't confirmed the story. That convo would be the Tell-All.

"Caitlyn," June said.

"Oh," and his complexion turned a shade lighter, though it was so dark inside him night looked brighter.

"She wants to write a book report, and wants you to publish it."

"Caitlyn?" Eric asked. "A book report," he asked more perplexed.

"Yes darling," June said sliding in his lap. "I could hardly believe it myself. But did you know she's also reading Road to Entebbe?"

Oh my goodness. I forgot not to look! *I think I just saw one of June's boobs. I swallowed hard—Sorry. Just sayin'...*

Next I noticed Eric, looking more flummoxed than usual. From his recall Zoloft wrote biblical prose. "There's no way a child who speaks 'street lit' can even read an advanced book like that," he said.

Yep, started to insert myself here, but June beat me to it.

"Sounds a bit pre-judgy," she said. "I feel that little girl is special. I think she's going to surprise us all."

"Tell me something," the retired slow sleuth says out of a blue. "Have you ever asked her about her past?"

Whoooooooooa...

Obviously this fool hadn't learned a thing. He was a true life to form glutton for unstoppable punishment. The first of his kind I ever encountered. If he continued to pry more poignant details out of my sweet noodles, it could hurt her daddy's feelings, and get a whole lot more people very, very hurt. Now, no one wants that, do they?

"Well, I think we should sit her down and—"

"—No!" June damn near shouted. And good she did because I was a jerk away from shaking him inside out. He was so lucky to be married to this lovely woman.

"All I want you to do is sit down and read what she has written," June hissed. "You should have heard her this evening talking about that book."

Eric shook his head, and started to turn away, except I turned his wound up self back around.

'You look at your wife when she's speaking, I ordered. Do you want me to end up being the one she starts confiding in? I'll break up this union in a jiffy, pal. Just test me! Find out how in a jiffy I'll have you researching divorce attorneys!' I really didn't mean this, though it's exactly what I told him.

37

Thanks to June keeping my darling busy with the swimming, and tennis, and dance, the piano lessons, and you name it, she didn't know a thing about the wars erupting, coast to coast, over her. June had my tookus enrolled in every activity she could find.

I watched my precious darling climb into June's car with a gym bag thrown over her shoulder. They were headed to one of her athletic social meets. I hadn't caught which one, due to oversleeping, tired as I was after all of the ripping and zipping around dealing with crappola cooked up from Eric's wimpy cry to Mel. *I'll get to some of that clapped up crappola in a snap.*

Gratefully, at least Mrs. Washington *(from across the way)* wasn't a part of the crappola. June managed to keep my cuddly bear away from the fresh pot, only waving at her mother who waved back like she had a pinched nerve in her hand when they passed each other.

Good! While June mashed the gas taking my love bug to her social meet, I punched the accelerator fizzing back East to the epi-center of where the drama Eric had clapped up was in overdrive—Grand Mercy Hospital.

It was a kangaroo zoo when I fizzed through, starting in the grand entrance lobby.

"You need to get her over to Emergency," said a young desk clerk speaking to a wild-eye man pushing a lumpy figure crumpled over in a wheelchair.

I don't know what it was, but something told me to look back. I guess the lone wild-eye man pushing what looked like a cotton ragdoll in a wheelchair caught my attention. The figure didn't look natural. Skeletal limbs and knees knocked together with the feet turned inwards amused me. Oh, and the hair, that's what really got me. A mop of brown tresses flipped over the head hiding the wheelchair traveler's face had me thinking of Halloween. I think we were in the month of March!

Why this wild-eye person pushing the crumpled up emergency wasn't running, even if he had no clue to where, beat the devil out of me.

So I inspected, noticing the mink, the Coach bag and a car key ring off which a Jaguar charm dangled. Instantly I knew who I was looking at. Aww man! Last I saw of Paula she was tall, hourglass made, and not a bend in her ego. But who else but her would be flopped over in a wheelchair made by Rolls Royce!?!

Paula was hurt, though I spent zero more seconds guessing what her drama was all about. Flurries of cusps jetted around the hospital, but not one found the expert headliner worthy of giving a lift. I don't know. She looked ready for a ride to me, though I didn't have time to check her pulse. Far as I was concerned, she had done her part. Thank you Paula. You, My Lady, have done far too much.

I headed on up to the Children's ward, colliding head on into another spectacle of badgering sorts.

"All we're asking is for 5-minutes of Dr. Mean's time," said one journalist wearing a Herringbone checkered suit and red bowtie. "...I'm telling you, she wants to get her version out there first," he added.

"Dr. Mean is not speaking to the press at this time," replied a huffy woman sitting behind the reception desk.

"Well what time will she be speaking to the press," pressed Herringbone. "...When she's behind bars and no one cares what she has to say," he laughed.

As that exchange went into overtime, a second desk clerk leaned over the reception desk and pointed, fingertip to nose, right in a suit coat's face. "I don't care if you're here to visit a patient. If you're asking questions too, then you are trespassing!"

Leather-suit was a journalist too. I caught him on the sly slipping Herringbone the eye. He was one of them undercover reporters trying to dig up a scoop playing the played out good cop, bad cop. His act wasn't working on Rhodesia Smith though. She received her legal credentials off the street.

A third desk clerk, Minnie Mouse Kibbles, in a far right directionally opposite corner squealed, "help! Help! Somebody, I need help over here!"

But help came running from nowhere. Everybody I fizzed by needed help of one sort or the other. There wasn't enough help to cover one tile of floor space in all nine thousand nine hundred and seventy three square foot of space in the hospital.

A group of women huddled together, sat on the floor holding candles and chanting about overthrowing unskilled doctors and nurses, or anyone who handled so much as a bedpan. One lady wanted to get her cold dead hands around a Dr. Sworpatrick's neck. Apparently he never kept his word, always breaking their appointments. She also vented about whoever made the coffee she was left to drink while waiting. It made her sick to the stomach.

Others vented about wanting their children moved out of the hospital, ASAP! One parent had already taken matters into their hands, that's assuming the child with the tubes hanging from four or five drip bags belonged to this person, navigating a zig-zag path through throngs of chanting, suing parents of patients, using wheelchairs like weapons.

It was an open quagmire in the ward. A floodgate had been opened and emotions poured out. And why? Well, all because of my little sweet innocent tookus who at that moment was probably enjoying a sundae with June, just a licking ice-cream without a care in the world, while her daddy sought help too! I needed a real magician!!!

38

I got Cinderella. He wasn't a magician, not even close, but since I needed to be in many places at once, and being as though he was the only creature of my kind who talked my language, but didn't know apples from granola about what I was up to, I turned him into my *real* magician.

"Dawg, how you know about all this," Cindy asked with all of his tentacles shimmying out there. This meant he looked something like a ghost in a bag moving its arms and legs every which way.

"Look Cin, I don't have time to be doing a whole lot of explaining. You have to pay attention, or else you'll end up at the back of the line in hell," I explained.

See, the last time he was on the Causeway he got booted up to the front on account of a fight breaking out where he was positioned. And since he wasn't involved... scared as he was, he was able to avoid the drama. Of course he told me this one time when we were chatting, so don't take my word as gospel for any of it.

The point here, and what I realized after the fact, was I probably should've explained things before baiting Cindy out of my snookums. Or at least I should've told him the truth, you know...been more up front with him. See, I told him they were handing out tickets for first class seats on a flight going nonstop straight into heaven. After spending so much time talking with him I realized, despite his misplaced pitiless machismo talk, all he really wanted was to get into heaven. Don't ask how he got stuck in line, in hell. He is pretty dumb though. Just saying...

At any rate, I obviously made all this stuff up. Forget not having any pockets, I didn't have any hands! But if Cindy had a lick of sense, he would've known this.

"Aww dawg, looka here dawg," he excitedly got to clamoring when we got to the hospital, punching me with his tentacles to look at some social-like activity he found taking place behind a closed door; two fools necking if you want me to be precise.

Now this part is going to sound really strange, but many cells, *(Cindy a prime example)*, didn't know a lot about cell activity like I did. For instance; the hearse business. Hospitals harbored the biggest hearse enterprise of any business activity in the world. The necking Cindy saw in the closet was actually happening all around him, but of course he couldn't see shit. If he hadn't been sobbing over Tigga, waiting for her soggy ba-hind to lift up so he could get a little bit, he might've found out he could've been getting it everywhere, any time, from any source. As it stood, and how I came up with this ticket business, was learning about cells amoebing. *Ahem...having sex.*

See, when I first saw cells stuck together, I thought they were ziplining. But upon closer inspection I learned they were part of a hearse caravan, carrying lost souls to and from Hell...and on very rare occasions, the Pearly Gates. Neither required a ticket. Both were free trips; one a one-way, and the other an open-end way of travel for as long as the soul wanted to stand the heat.

Of course I didn't share any of this with Cindy, which was why he was out here in the hospital acting like we were at a damn concert or something, scalping tickets to get in on the ameboing. This boy is so damn dumb!

"Aww dawg..." he cried, when he finally realized how to tap into the slop going on inside this utility closet. "Look, look...she don't even see me," he gushed, slipping and sliding around with these mortals doing their thing.

I snatched Cindy up as he was about to go greaselining elsewhere. "Look Cindy! I'm serious dude! You've got to stay focused and do just like I say, or else you will end up at the back of the line in hell!" I repeated.

That time he heard me, but barely. He rolled his happy lot down to a smaller lurch and tried to remain attentive, though I caught his simple BA-hind stealing peeps around.

"Now, I want you to stay right here on this Purell bottle, and blow real hard every time you hear Cummins or Glover," I said looking the dizzy lumpy fool directly in the frontal lobe.

"Aww dawg, this shit is burning my lens, and it stinks to high hell...I don't think I can—"

"—Dude! You still want these tickets, or not!?!"

"Aww dawg, shucks," and he raised his tents to cover his lobe trying to ward off some of the alcohol scent.

Really, he didn't know how good he had it, me thinking to hide him in this iodine spot. I mean, in the ethereal world it looks busier than a million Chinas in a million Chinas. Well in a hospital, multiply that sighting times a few more millions. Hospitals are the metropolis of any type life one could ever imagine. But it would take centuries to explain every life form and its associated causes and activities.

So, to a simple BA-hind like Cook, you don't. But just know I placed him in a very secure safe spot, where provided his horny BA-hind stayed put, he wouldn't be at risk of being carried off by one of these hearse caravans, or worse, put at the back of the Causeway for pissing me off. Oh hell yeah, Daddy Cummins had some new juice. Tell you about it in a shake.

At any rate, what I did do before zipping off was twist his center lobe, something like twisting a pair of lips, so that when he blew I'd hear him. It was kind of funny. I looked back at the fool as I zipped off and saw him trying to speak. Looked like a constipated jellyfish. Sorry, but I had to laugh. I just hoped his simple BA-hind hadn't forgotten how to blow.

39

Got to room 431-A just as Grand Mercy's Internal Board of Investigations was in full swing. Fizzed in and found a front row *unoccupied* seat in the dead center of Princess Mean's next thought. And how convenient too. The large woman, much too pronounced for the chair she sat in, was pushed up to a microphone just about to speak into it.

'Throw yourself on the mercy of these good people,' I shouted like an avenging avatar *(whatever that is)* through Princess Mean's diaphanous psyche.

'Save yourself before you're uncovered and discovered!' I screamed like a Holy mad Emperor. I knew what an Emperor was, and certainly knew about being mad, but a Holy Mad Emperor I knew nothing of, and neither did I know anything about the operation she most assuredly was involved in.

Needless to point out, the thought surprised Mrs. Princess Mean. It was nothing near to what she was about to say. I heard her whisper, *"what?,"* before gurgling words not among her original plans to express.

"The child was given to Mr. Swinee Ottma," she garbled in a voice that came out awkward, as if she didn't know what in the hell she was talking about.

The gasps in the room played like one elongated bumpy crescendo. No one knew what in the hell she was talking about. As a matter of fact, I didn't know what had been asked. For all I knew, she could've been asked what she had for breakfast that morning. But did any of this stop me? Hell no, it didn't.

I had other business to attend to and didn't want to spend a lot of time farting around with this issue.

"He paid me 25-billion," Princess said, obviously at my instructions. "He took the child to live in a village in Burma... somewhere called Ragoon I believe..."

More gasps bounced along a crescendo of oohs and aahs. Feet shuffled and danced, and chairs scraped the wood floors, amid papers rustling. Then a fist came down. BAM! The fist hit a table hard.

"Let's get some order!" bellowed a judge.

"What in the hell are you saying," hissed a dude sitting beside Princess, directly in her ear.

"He said the child was his daughter's. She was trying to hide a pregnancy," Princess hissed back, clearly not used to being told she was wrong, even if she was unclear what I had her admitting to.

"What did she say..." asked a surprised witness, cut off by Princess's attorney demanding a break!

Like I said a few times before, I've never been a clever ad hoc last minute thinker. Whatever clicks in my soul is what clicks. This was what clicked when I saw the Princess at the mic, and it definitely worked like singing wings stretched from one part of earth to the other. Call 'em harking angels. You know the ones. They sing carols during Christmas...or lullabys to people afflicted by the blues, how Princess was described as she left the trial.

And just in case someone is lagging behind on just what happened here; first and unequivocally foremost, I DID NOT want no large scale investigation pointed at, or centered around my tookus. She was innocent, and didn't deserve to be harassed because greedy thrill seekers were looking for entertainment. And no, Princess wasn't seeking attention, but her honest testimony also wasn't going to drive attention away from my snookums. I had to *help* her. She can thank me later.

Now, back to the fool Cindy. His part in all of this was I needed him to be my ears and eyes in places where

I couldn't be at the same time. Yeah, that one lended to some of my long range thinking, which, like my quick thinking, I'm not great at either.

I zipped back to the Purell where I had the fool on the lookout, eager to get the juice on what was being said about the trial. Given how I helped Princess bungle her deposition, I expected the gossip to be gushing at fire hydrant levels. Obtuse as Cindy was, this was something he really was good at. Every time I talked to that boy he had a story about someone or something he'd heard or seen. Now, it wasn't always reliable gossip, but storytell that boy could do! That's all I needed him to do, given it was my job to root out the narratives that conflicted with my interest, and SHUT THEM DOWN!

But Cindy never whistled. After the investigation in 431-A abruptly adjourned, and everybody spilled out of the conference room dazed, I got back to the Purell station to find his simple BA-hind GONE!

Part Four

40

Ok, so all wasn't totally lost. Wasn't like Cindy's help was by any means an integral piece to my planning, poor as it was. But he sure could have spared me from running ragged. By the time I got back West, and I wasn't gone all that long, I caught wind that things had settled to a breathable degree. It still wasn't all honky dory, but workable enough that I didn't feel as if I had hauled my BE-hind around for nothing. But wait until I catch that damn knucklehead! *Ahem...if he hadn't succumbed to the Purell and wasn't back in hell.* Hahaha!

But tell me something. How does a loving daddy be gone for such a short time, less than 24-hours by my estimates, leaving my sweet virtuous lamb's innocence in tact, talking about writing books, playing a piano better than the maestro Ella, loving sports, and last seen climbing into a car with a Power Puffs gym bag thrown over her shoulder, having not once mentioned an attraction in boys, or dating, or anything of the sort, suddenly, like over one *'Daddy Curtis watch your mouth'* night, acquire a palate for such unsavory characters? How!?! Why!?! And since when!?!

Let me say this, *as if I really need to...* I am a man. Well, at least I was once a man. I was a boy too. I know what us male creatures think at various stages of our being. We think tag the girl, get the girl, hump the girl, and then find an innocent girl no one has tagged, got, or humped, and marry her. This punk I saw trying to tag my snookums in the gym, who she was giggling at, and light-heartedly trying to dodge, was one-hundred percent trying to tag the very wrong girl!

Where was June, *'I vowed to know.'* And *'punk! If you put your filthy, crusty BA-hind claws on my...'* ump! And the fool tripped and fell.

"Aah! Shit!," he cried. He wasn't hurt. Nothing on the fool broke. His important ligaments were still in working order and attached, even if the fall embarrassed him with all the kids laughing.

"Oh my goodness, are you okay Donny?" asked a mother who came running to his aid. Two other adults who hadn't been properly supervising these children came running along too. June, admittedly and unfortunately, was one of the two.

The kid got up, not a bad looking kid either, but a rusty BE-hind boy just the same, who had nothing but unsavory intentions for a little girl who happened to belong to a father who knew his type. They were all alike; clean-cut, decent home, two-parents, and two-car garages with the maids, butlers, cooks, and the whole kit and caboodle to boot. None of this loot mattered. BEING A BOY WAS ALL THAT MATTERED!

This did get me to thinking however. *Oh boy.* After all I'd done to avoid a near catastrophe, and it still wasn't clear-cut over, but I had this hurdle left to clear.

What was a man like me, with all of my fatherly bearings in proper order, to do? Jeeze! Looking after a princess was not easy.

Later that evening I nestled on the pillow beside my snookums and saw *(at a minimum)* damn near seventy years of hard work ahead of me. Like my ancestors told me, there'd never be a day when I'd be able to enjoy a cold beer without my child on my mind. Thank Moses I only had one, though I'm not complaining. The more I think about things, the more I realize, I loved my *new* life!

'Daddy loves you,' I whispered to my tookus.

I don't know if she heard me, but you should've

seen her. She gave me the prettiest smile. I didn't have no need to dip inside her this night, since Cindy had skipped off for grayer pastures, which speaking of...

...you know what that fool BA-hind told me when I next saw him!?! That silly strings for brains told me, "Aww dude...I searched every scrap of paper in that ward and wasn't nothing written on any of them scraps with either Grovis or Clovis!"

Man! He was so lucky he was in that hearse!

Look, I realize I don't use the best English. I cuss a lot and lean on using Ebonics when I'm stressed, but I know damn fucking well he never heard me tell him to search damn scraps of paper!

You know... it's why...and how...he ended up just where he is. At first I thought a neurotic cell had carried him off. Or that maybe he got disoriented from the alcohol scent and by fate ended up accidentally in the palm of someone's hand, getting mixed in the Purell where...yeah, unfortunately...he then would've vanished without a trace.

Still, me being the guy I am, a *big time user* haha... I managed to lure him out of the hearse line by flashing a halo...basically a circle that to him probably looked like ameboing. Dumb ass.

Once free and a safe distance away...and after I *(of course)* knocked him around a bit, *(his stupid ass thought he was gettin' some)*, we fizzed back over to the hospital. This time I took it easy on him, hooking him up with slicksters *(basically panhandlers)* selling spit bits *(something like flyers)* to new lost souls, *code for hotties*, coming to the hospital.

This chore was specifically suited for his simple ass. He could be a hustler, showboat and snitch rolled in one...all the things he ever wanted to be but never was.

Sad part was, I had him covering an entrance where generally healthy specimens attached to earth bound bodies entered the hospital *(mostly during visiting hours)* to visit the heaven...and hell bound souls. He only needed to be able to tell the difference, or be able to comprehend the

Moral Code of Ethics After-life Handbook. So, I guess we all can uncross our fingers now, since hoping that will happen is a wasted hope.

I don't really fault him. The poor dumb ass can't help not knowing what he don't know. I just did my best to keep him busy until I needed him again. He was happy as a bandit. Thought he had it made. And he was a BOY. Hopefully his fool self didn't wend up in another hearse, or worse, back in hell. But if he did. Oh Well...

Of course a few checks later, after checking on a few things...like old flames *(as in Ethel...Omega...Laticia and the likes)*, I swung back by to check on Cindy before heading back West.

I asked 'ole tip toes Cinderella if he'd heard anything and he gives me this long ass incredible story.

"Aww dude...man, I slipped down to the celly *(morgue)* and found a whole bunch of jellies *(women)* down there. All the jellies you can dream up is down there," he grinned like a sputtering comet *(another term for a star falling out of the sky)*. "I can't believe you held out on a brotha' like that dawg..."

I almost left the plug spooling in his slobber, except something told me to inquire further. "...Oh, yeah..." I said like I was interested...and he was telling me something new. Though I hadn't yet been to the celly, *as if I needed to witness more death,* I for damn sure had seen enough repugnance and morbidity.

"Where's that?" I asked, feigning irritation. Tip toes liked thinking he had one up on me.

"The basement," he said like I should know. "Man, down there in the celly where all the honies a man could ever hope for hang out!"

"What in the hell were you doing in the morgue, when I specifically told you to hang out here!?!"

"Aww dawg, I'm here now," he exclaimed. "But it ain't nothing happening out here! You know this stud don't do duds in scrubs..."

I hovered there for a sec, watching the ala'king hustler gettin' played right in front of the both of us. Two hotties wearing their presence up front, *(meaning they were letting us know they were females...willing, ready and able for sex)*, were making a game out of setting off the sensors that kept opening and closing the automatic doors.

Did I say this fool was not only close to his final days. Well, let me update that. He also is a prime prop for embarrassment.

I interrupted the hotties game, smacking the doors shut on them. Squish! And YUCK!!! The mess they made getting squashed in the doors required a team of mortals, wash rags, and buckets of piping hot steamy soapy water.

"Why'd you do that," Slow Mo' asked.

"Do what," I innocently asked.

"Why you crush my hope?"

"Look dude, just think... THAT COULD BE YOU!"

Of course I knew this warning wasn't going to do nothing for a lobe stuffed with air. Like I've already laid out, we were some forgetful simple creatures of habit. We don't give a rat's tail about everlasting hell...until we get there and find out we can no longer roam. Cindy, especially, was no different. After the yucky mess, and the clean up, he continued to act like he was in gold-mine heaven. He wasn't phased in the least. And that, my friends, is the quickest, most reliable, and very verifiable way to slip up on the Causeway and stay forever. Perhaps, and just maybe, in twisted logic this is the pimp to envy?

41

Finally got back West to find my snookums and June in the kitchen eating breakfast. Ever since my little girl started talking about wanting to write, she's been a talkative little thing. She was sitting at the table just a swinging her little legs and talking her little head off in that super thin voice of hers. June looked on, just as captivated and ingratiated as ever, every so often asking a question to encourage her on. Only thing missing was that Eric, which I bee-lined straight to his corner of the house where he hung out damn near 24-hours every damn day!

Found him up there on a Skype call. Looked at the screen and saw Mel's big 'ole moon pie filling the intsy-wintzy little square box.

"Paul," Mel heavily sighed, turning away from the camera to provide a pug-dog profile of himself. "...Pal, I don't know what to make of these recent developments, but buddy," and the pug profile turned to look back at the camera, though not directly into it, again sighing, even heavier. "I think if you plow on, you just might have your-self one heck of a story."

First off, who the hell was Paul? I moved up close to the screen trying to see if I could see through this box, to figure out who all else was on the Skype call.

I even zipped in nano seconds to where Mel sat, in his office, where wasn't no one in there but him. I also zipped on the node this call traveled on and found no Paul there either.

There were two others, unbeknownst to either Mel

or Eric, on the call. But ones name was Joe, and the other Goleb. Both worked for the FBI. At this point I could only assume, *'Lord Have Mercy, Mel's done already and really forgotten his chief editor's name!'*

Wasn't no real incriminating, or worthwhile information debunked in this call. Both men having been in the business knew these calls were free range to anyone who wanted to tap into the conversation. Mel was just signing off, discreetly, to his end of the deal. There wasn't no mention of Paula, but I knew what was up. Mel was apologizing for putting her on the case. Just to think, he was about to make her chief editor. Well, all that changed. Paula lost that slot, and her old job to go along with it.

'You bean dip head,' I said all up in Eric's noggin', *'didn't your wife already tell you to leave it alone! Do you want to see your family ripped apart? Cause I can assure you, if June loses my—'* and I caught myself here, stumbling trying to recall the name June gave my snookums. "Caitlyn," I picked up with, *'yeah, if June loses Caitlyn, you are toast buddy!'*

The thing was, and I realized it the moment I said it, but Eric was just another guy—a typical man. Well, not A-typical man, like one of the Cinderella A-types, or yeah...the A-type man I used to be, but he had the man bits that encouraged him to chase after loose threads like A-type men chased after skirts.

So, could I really blame him?

Oh, the hell yes I could, and did! My tookus was in the middle of his meddling. I also realized June really didn't need him for a husband, even if I wasn't all too fond of breaking up *somewhat* happy homes. In fact, I hadn't broken up a happy one yet. And still, as the story goes, I had to *curtail* the meddling.

<h1 style="text-align:center">42</h1>

Eric, though, proved to be a hard nut to crack. Harder than I could've ever imagined. A part of what made it so tough to crack this nut was because I didn't want to hurt my tookus or June. Otherwise, I would've flipped this chump over in the Pacific like flicking a booga off a finger.

But I had my sweet pea and June to consider. They saw the computer goof as more than a booga. And more startling, to my overwhelmed wits end, my snookums now wanted the booga-crusher to publish her book!

I tried talking to June, but couldn't think of how to put it in a way that would make sense side-stepping Eric to have the book published. Initially, and quite honestly, and only because I hadn't read my snookums manuscript, I thought June would read what my tookus wrote and rub some buttery motherly words on, that would convince my little girl to keep plugging away at it.

But that backfired and shot straight to the moon as I never expected June would drop her manuscript smack flat abracadabra on top of Eric's desk.

"Look at this," June said way too excited to even hope my snookums words weren't already a best-seller.

Eric picked up the pack of papers and started reading. I saw him quench his eyes, zeroing in on the small typed font with the curly-cues my darling liked to use. This was one of the reasons I hadn't already read her work.

My tugga bear just typed so darn tiny, and way too fast, and used too many curly letters for her daddy to keep up. I used to watch her in the bedroom, lying on her belly, always smiling and grinning, and typing a mile a minute. But I was too bone-tired to read what she was typing. So long as she didn't have one of those i-Chat sessions open, or so long as my senses didn't pick up any other sinister dealings, then that was the one time I left her to enjoy a little privacy while I slept.

But now she had completed the thing, and June loved it, and was standing behind Eric smiling wider than Main Street, bouncing like a pro-baller cheerleader.

Soon as I saw this, I jumped on the page, reading along with him. Actually, I read far faster than Eric. I'm what can be called a champion of speed-reading; one of the powers I have...of course, once my antennas are raised. I was at the end before Eric turned the first page.

Oh man! And I'm not saying this because she is my little darling tookus, but my snookums is a writer! And more so than a writer, she is one heck of a storyteller. I see why June was so excited. We'd been running around pulling all types of grass from our BA-hinds, and here my tookus knew all along where she came from. I loved her version!

Eric was going to be greased, cooked, fried, and overdone as me when he got to that end. Wasn't no way he could turn down this manuscript. I liked how she never gave away the secret she claimed had been in a lockbox. And was thrilled past the last galaxy that only she and I, and maybe one other person knew what she really was saying.

Oh, please do believe this, my tookus had her A Best-seller here, and this was coming from a loving daddy who'd never in his life read a best-seller. That's because there can only be one best-seller known to all existence. This one was it!

Ten pages along Eric slowly looked up at June, startled. "Are you sure she wrote this," he whispered in a sultry tone, as this piece truly was no ordinary master-piece. This work outdid his own. Like I said. This was IT!

"Yes, she did hun. I believe her. But you have to read it all the way through," June trembled, wringing her hands. "Sounds like it could be true...in a fantasy way."

Of course it was true! And of course I followed up my private celebration with a personalized lyric of my own, harmonizing the occasion by hopping inside Eric's head.

'Yes nit-wit!
How ya' like her now!?!'
and I danced a few notes on the left side of his head.
'You thought you was it;
the shit,
but now the girl street lit
done made a solid hit
one up on yo' wit, it's legit!
You know damn well it is it!
So sit!'

I tapped another number on the right side of his head, moonwalking to get there, dropping street rhymes, dope lines and f bombs.

Eric grabbed his head and whimpered, "Ugh... Think I've got a headache."

"Oh hun, should I bring you some Aleve?"

'Yeah, go on and get the chump a pill. He'll be all right by the time you get back. I'm stepping out now,' I laughed, kicking him in the side of the head like shutting a car door closed *(with my foot)* as I stepped out.

"Aah," he moaned as June ran off to get him a pill.

43

It was a whole new ballgame I was now playing. My tookus started bonding with Eric over this book. Instead of loafing off to his corner of the world, he hung out at the dinner table longer, asking my snookums questions she was always eager to answer. She believed in her uncle Eric. He was going to publish her story. Make it into a real book like Zoloft's book June had taken her out to look high and low for, until she held her own copy in her hands.

You know I wanted to, but I couldn't challenge this type bond. Just like that Eric had stolen a piece of my tookus's heart. A big piece in fact, at least while the book deal was on the table. I couldn't interrupt the relationship; the two of them talking for hours sometimes, about twists and turns in story plots, and character development and what have you. Sometimes a real man just has to man up and accept things he doesn't like.

But trust me herein, I watched Eric's eyes and hands very, very, very closely during this period. Any shady business at all, and there'd be no reason to doubt, uncle Eric was going bye-bye. I would recycle him myself.

So far the glib man was playing on the up and up. He was showing himself to be a real mentor for my snookums. And June, too, she looked a lot brighter herself.

Almost a month had passed since my little genius's story garnered the love and attention, and admiration of both June and Eric; both of them reading the story from beginning to end. I even heard Eric tell June, "It's quite impressive." My snookums had written over 81,000 words.

"Can you imagine her having that kind of imagination...and dedication, to write in such detail about an infant being born with three eyes and no mouth?" June asked, still surfing a euphoric trance.

Eric shirked his eyes, staring deep into his monitor, at nothing. My snookums story was open and facing him, but he was staring off beyond that Word document.

"Yeah, I'm still trying to figure it out," he replied, peering hard beyond the screen that faced him. "How she could write a story so well, tying up all of the ends as if it really happened," he mechanically uttered, slowly climbing out of a deep space when another thought must've clicked. He swung around to face June. "Hey...do you know how long she's been working on this story?"

June laid the magazine she'd been reading in bed, down in her lap, to look up at the ceiling and think back. "Umm...I'm not sure. It had to be over a year ago she said she was going to write it."

Eric sucked his teeth and shook his head. "That's got to be impossible," he said turning back around to face his MAC. "There's no way," he muttered to himself.

"Do you think she might've found this story somewhere online and downloaded it?" June asked, doubting my tookus's credibility that she had written this story all on her own, too.

Eric continued quietly staring into the monitor, rubbing his head, as he slowly moved the cursor, blindly advancing a few pages. "But I've typed over a hundred key phrases and nothing is coming up," he said comatosely.

June picked up the magazine, smiling. "I always knew there was something special about that little girl," she shrugged. "I sensed it the first time I met her," she said nonchalantly returning to the article she'd been reading.

"That's it!" Eric exclaimed, leaping out of the chair and throwing his hands in the air. "It's the friend in the story!" he cried out. "That's who knows what's in the lockbox! Do you recall her name..."

June slammed the magazine down in her lap and abruptly dropped her smile. "Oh hun, NO, please! Let's not put more into what's already there," she said more in plea than anger.

Eric rushed over to the bed, as if moving closer would convince June to understand his reasoning. "But can't you see we have to substantiate this story? No one's going to believe a thirteen year old girl wrote this...this..." and he rubbed the nape of his neck trying to fish up a word that would describe my tookus's best-seller.

'Ut...'fraid I gotta stop ya' there buddy,' I said lifting up off his pillow where I was kicked back listening to the two of them going at it. *'You of all persons should realize your snooping days are long past over.'* I definitely wasn't gonna let him risk stirring up more minutia over validating whether or not my snookum's story was real or not. My ass was tired...and not in any shape to get back on any treadmills any time soon.

I was just about to hop in his head and untangle a few ventricles, if that was the problem, except June spoke up before I revved up my fiz.

"Eric, hun, honestly!" she retorted. "You promised not to do anything that might jeopardize Caitlyn's future. Let's just let readers enjoy the imaginary story for what it is...and not entice them into digging up dir—"

"—no hun," Eric pleaded, hopping up on his knees to straddle his wife. "This will just be so that our own personal curiosities are settled—"

"—Do you mean yours or mines?" June said pushing him back. "Because my curiosity is fine!"

"June, I promise not to make any trouble," Eric babbled. "You have to understand, as an acquiring editor it is irresponsible not to thoroughly investigate stories we get, namely stories that we perceive will receive a lot of attention, and raise a lot of suspicions with that attention."

'Yeah, bud...I get your point, but you're going to have to respect mines and your wife's point too,' I said. *'You know how*

it goes buddy. Some things you're going to have to go with the flow and make shit up.'

I hopped out of Eric and watched June stare at him like the absolute imbecile I stared at as well. This was a man we were looking at; a brand of a creed that had a hard head, and had no inclinations I could have him spend an eternity in hell.

'Let him do it,' I tried to tell June. *'No matter what you say he's going to do it anyway, because that's what hard head men do.'*

But June shot back, "I would think after what happened with Paula, you learned your lesson! But I guess I was wrong," she near screamed. "Looks like you won't get enough until one of these scoops breaks up our family!" And with that June was off. She swung her legs by Eric, almost kicking him in the face, saved by him ducking out of the way. She stormed into the bathroom slamming the door behind her.

Now that was one beautiful tirade. I wished Eric could've seen me laughing in his face. *'She told you dweep!'* I laughed so hard and so loud my tookus appeared in the doorway asking if they were getting a divorce.

That sort of seared the laughing. Like I said, I hadn't split up a happy home before, and I certainly didn't want my sweet pea's happiness interrupted now.

44

I suspected Tigga might've lived after I transitioned. But almost croaked stumbling upon the possibility that vane gold digger kept our child, working on her until something happened. I'm not sure what that something was, and my tookus didn't seem to know either, *(at least not according to her story)*, but whatever it was, was how she ended up in Grand Mercy, where she was not treated very well.

The fascinating part for me, was her retelling the visit with her grandparents; the swindlers whose name she didn't spell out. She however described that dungeon they lived in to a tee! Hahaha!!! Though I was glad my tookus had the perspicacity not to use real names, even if I'm not sure it was done intentionally.

I also, didn't care to know what was in this lockbox, what happened to be the core of the story—the part that dealt with the third eye, and the secret(s) it contained. I liked using my imagination speculating on this so-called secret, and if Eric's comprehension skills were worth a nickel, he *as well* wouldn't want the mystery unravelled. But then you know how men are; like the adventurous child who prods a rattlesnake with a stick, just to see what it'll do. *'I'm telling you...MALE specimens have heads thick and dense as rocks!'*

And yet what *(literally)* had me up against a fence and wound in a tight knot were my vanishing powers. It started after re-reading my tookus's book, shortly after that night June and Eric got into the argument over investigating my sweet pea's book.

I couldn't get June to say a word I was telling her, and the other night when I laid beside my tookus, she opened her eyes and looked directly at me and said, "Daddy! I see you peeking at me. It's time for you to sleep in your own bed!"

I was crushed. C-R-U-S-H-E-D. Mushed, mashed potatoes, ashes to damn dust, speared, spooled, refinished, spit shined, done and finished I was totally crushed. For days I fizzed around in this whacked upside the head mummy state.

Had my snookums really saw me? Or was she imagining me? Not too long after, we *(me and my tookus)* slept in separate rooms, like June and Eric who started sleeping apart. June slept in her room; Eric ended up on the sofa. And me, I tossed and turned in a crevice of the drapes in the bathroom, unable to clear my conscience.

'Oh God, could that judgment Tigga got now be coming after me?'

After a week or so of this tossing and turning I woke up one morning to hear my little munchkin's squeal. "Uncle Eric! Where you going dude...looking sharp as all get out?" she teased.

'Wow, my precious bottoms really was growing up.' I didn't know how to interpret this little bit of sass, except to feel more of this mushing and mashing sensation. Maybe that's why my powers had withered. As my tookus grew, perhaps it was in the computation that I shrink.

"I'm going to get this little puppy shined up darling," Eric said patting his briefcase. "And get us some tour dates lined up so that we can show off our rising star," he smiled, kissing her on the jaw, ignoring June's cold glare.

I swear that man was so lucky to be standing so close to my cuddly teddy bear. I was a last resort away from using my remaining powers to take him D-O-W-N!

He walked over to June, who had her arms folded across her chest, and started to kiss her jaw, except she turned the other way. Surely she was as pissed as I was.

"Look hun," Eric started, *'lying through his coffee stained teeth.'* "I promise I'm just going to meet with our publishing group and nothing else. I won't even tell them who wrote the story, okay?"

"Unt un," my snookums spoke up. "I want my name on the cover like Zoloft's...in big letters too!" she cheesed like normal, oblivious to the hostility in the room.

"Oh, don't you worry my little buttons, we're going to make sure your name is nice and big on that cover," he smiled down at her, touching the tip of her nose with his finger.

'Ugh! My little buttons,' I snarled. It took everything in me not to fold him over like a piece of laundry. It would've been nice to stuff him in a drawer too. I know June would've liked to see that happen, but then my cuddlems was there. I didn't want to have to deal with seeing her tear up over her uncle Eric getting doubled over the way I planned to fold him.

"Yeah! But it's got to say Cuttie Brown!" my snookums squealed, to June's unmistakable gasp.

45

Soon as Eric hopped in the car, on his way to the airport, I flew right behind him. The guy was heading East...*I was sure*...to meet with them Pinecroft troublemakers low on lassitude. No telling what this next meeting was going to entail, except the strangest thing happened. Instead of feeling my power waning, I fizzed off and got as far as the desert to discover I had NO power AT ALL. I plummeted flat splat to Earth, landing in hot-ass sand, and not a damn thing else but sun, heat and bugs.

Thinking I might've needed more rest, as I'd been fizzing recklessly for a while, I tried a few hours later. But I really had ZERO power. Desperate and dearly concerned I managed to crawl beneath a rock. That's where I bumped into a turd. I'm not sure what protoplasm left it but was confident no one was coming back for it. To my good fortune there were a few maggots inside which...sssh...yes I did, I sucked the life out of one for pinching me. True, I only did it because I was pissed, but that sweet juice got my ass back to the crib!

Let me tell you. I was lucky! The Kalamazoo River was just up ahead and it was full of mosquitos—big, fat, sloppy red suckers nastier than a porn fest in a barnyard. Skeetas mate like nobodies business and them jokers don't ever die. They only duplicate. And don't get stranded and stuck inside one, like what could've happened to me. It's the fastest one-way trip—through—hell.

I got back with no issues; my power returning to almost like normal, except I couldn't slip into my poo bear like normal. I was going inside of her to check on things, to make sure wasn't anything amiss, but I'll be damn...I couldn't get in. My tookus had blocked me!

I knew something was way off track at this point. I mean, Eric was with them Pinecroft instigators doing what only the Lord could guess what, my power was shrinking, and I couldn't check on my snookums to make sure none of this was somehow connected.

I paced all night trying to figure out the problem and what to do next. Maybe I was reaching the end of my lifespan, though according to cell metabiology, unless we're ill, which I didn't feel sick, we had no end date, something like a skeeta.

With the little power I had left, thinking hard on what a man in my position might do, something Cindy said suddenly came to me. At four in the AM I hitched a ride to the hospital, and headed straight for the morgue.

Soon as I reached the bottom level the first thing I sensed was grayness, the same grayness most humans see in areas as dark. Reminded me of old black and white films that didn't play with sound.

I fizzed up and down a few corridors, on each trip feeling sicker and sicker, seemingly connected to the heavy gray saddness. I started to abandon the visit. This was one time when I thought this was it for me. Cannons filled my orb with desperate ideas, urging me to abandon my life and hand over my weapons. But I didn't have any weapons, the only reason I also kept thinking something was 'f'ing with me.

Right about then I heard it. At first it sounded like a lot of wailing and moaning—funeral type noise. It just sounded sad, and bad, so sad and bad I stopped my fiz and braced myself for what I expected to find beneath this baseboard where the entrance was shielded by a large dust bush.

Standing there at the dust bush, debating about whether I really wanted to enter, a group of catty chatty cells came up behind me using plenty of vulgar language talking about "hey there daddy, you wanna party with us?"

I turned around and saw at least 20 of the most exposed cells, with all of their presence hanging out there, doing poses more lurid and vulgar than I'd ever seen in any of my lives. And let me tell you...I used to judge beauty. I've been to a lot of striptease shows, turned pornographic. I do know vulgar, and am no drip dweeb about sex.

"Excuse me," I said, you know...about to hold my position. That's one thing I learned that applies to all life. Don't ever let 'em see you sweat, cause they'll sweat you 'til you're pure (I).

"Excuse you!" one of them shouted. "Now, Daddy either come party with us or get the hell out of the way. You're cock blocking here, you know!"

I turned back around to get another look at the dust bush and was about to turn back around when those hussies ambushed me! That mossy one shoved me through the dust bush giving me no time to fully consent.

It all hit me at once. This was a party...a fairly live party once I got inside. There weren't any strobe lights or anything like that, but about twenty to thirty bands played at once and the AO was packed and stacked full of my kind of life. That meaning...everyone in there was more or less my type species. Their essences filled the AO.

The only problem was everyone was engaged in a social exchange of varying sorts, everyone but me.

"Welcome," a beautiful velvety luscious voice flanking me on the right greeted.

I turned to face the sexy voice and was repulsed on sight. The beautiful voice looked like a hairless tarantula with about five dozen eyes and no legs. I'm guessing that in its other life that thing got zapped by some pretty repellent RAID. Gosh that voice looked so awful. But I am a man, so I did try to peep it's presence, which by the way, what I mean by presence is *mating sex*. This one was the plus sign, a female, as the voice hinted, just not my type of female. I had to pass, even if Luscious wasn't going to let me give up on her so easily.

"Hey dude, so you finally decided to come hang out with ebbs more your age," Cindy laughed, drunk as a funky coon, surprising me approaching on my left.

"Man, what the hell did you drink? You smell like a skunk!" I didn't know whether I was more horrified of his odor or the fact I was in a morgue, in the vicinity of a fool with no luck.

"Aww dude..." Cindy chuckled, as I stepped aside, bumping into Luscious who left me no breathing space. This was not my type party. I felt invaded by repulsion.

"We got us a spot over there in the corner. Why don't you join us," Cindy said, fumigating a wide circumference of AO around me.

"Or, you can always come and hang out with me," purred Luscious, emitting an odor slightly less repulsive than Cindy. And I realize my descriptions aren't the best ever described, but all I ask is that you picture a hairless bug covered in RAID with no legs and smelling like fried hair and baked blood. Would you want to talk to it? Date it? Sleep with it? Go any fucking where with it!?!

I will admit though, I was feeling a little horny, and with them god-awful smells circling my orb I started feeling a power that made me feel like I could uphold heaven. That's when I thought about my baby girl.

"Come on dude, come on over here and chill with us a bit... and get a little taste of this juice..." Cindy said, blurring my vision. He looked far worse than he smelled, with all that gook hanging off him. But I followed him still, over to a cruddy little corner where we had to crawl under another baseboard to enter an even livelier party than the one I just left.

Everyone was drinking the juice, loaded and toasted, laughing and lip-smacking, as ten more bands played at once, smelling up the AO so awfully rotten that the whole room smelled nice.

But no sooner than I got to the bar, did I lose sight of Cindy. I wended up flanking two scholarly types, holding drinks and talking.

"Hello, I'm Smarty. How do you do this evening," said the shorter cell emitting quite a bit of light, *(obviously his smarts).* He extended a tentacle towards me for shaking, which I shook.

"And I'm Maurice," said the taller egg-shape dim-lit one, also extending a tentacle for shaking.

"Great to meet you guys," I grinned greedily. I've always been a social butterfly. At this point I would yap it up with *'almost'* anyone. These two were about the best I'd come across... *thus far.*

"And you are?" asked the egg lobe.

"Oh, oh...I'm Curt," I stammered.

"So, when's your flight?"

'Flight?' I must've looked perplexed because the stump Smarty broke it down for me. "When's your trip scheduled," he asked.

"Oh...oh...yeah that," I stammered more. "Ugh... well, I didn't make my reservations yet. I'm just hanging," I replied.

"Oh," said the egg lobe, raising a tentacle.

"Aah yeah," I chuckled awkwardly, thinking as fast as I could without making a complete fool of my slow thinking self. "I like it down here," I said.

"You do," asked Smarty, now perplexed himself.

"Yes, I do Mart," I repeated, only less spineless.

"Smarty is fine," Smarty said.

I ignored him though. "Say, you fellas don't find it better to be more mobile?"

They both exchanged that look before Smarty spoke up. "Ugh, Curk—"

"—Curt," I interrupted him as well. "That's Curt with a 'T' on the end, not 'K'." I started to add more, to make a joke of the matter, except these two looked fresh out of humility.

These nim-whits seemed to have already tallied up they were *'getting in'*. That's how scholarly types think; no different than mortals. They calculate 24/7 because they have no use for reason. All those such and such's on the other side of the baseboard chewing up their nails and pacing up and down walls, to them, were the aggregated sum of those who missed the boat by not getting a good education. *'And yeah, I did forget to mention there were many of these types attending this live wild death party'*. The only reason I didn't mention them was for the same reason the scholars thought themselves so above the rest that they excluded the rest from their 24/7 calculations. They weren't important to the equation. Haha. What a hoot.

But, seriously... Have you ever been assaulted by ten bands playing at once? That could drive anyone up a wall, even if I realized most of the soul's I saw crying and crawling walls were the ones not anxious about transitioning. They had unfinished business left, which the last soul you want to be near was one leaving unfinished business.

I already knew all this stuff; it wasn't a critical assessment in need of more analyzing. It was freaking obvious, the same obvious as why humans walk up right and should continue to do so. Greatfully the scholar's weren't among those climbing the walls, and as such, they were crockpots full of perfect entertainment.

"Ugh, yeah Curk," Smarty went on, amused by his charm at continuing to slight me, "looks to us as if you're the only one grounded," and he burst out laughing, joined by his eggy fuddy-buddy chum Maurice—the lobe.

Damn! He got me there. I probably was the only one, out of all these outward bound souls, with principles.

"So?" I said anyway.

"So, it means we don't like it down here," said the little smelly guy. "We've already lived a good life, and now we have first class tickets for a one-way trip where we won't ever have to be concerned about another retirement plan."

"Yeah, I see your point," I said, trying to keep this chat as amicable as possible. I could tell they wanted me to kick their asses—badly.

"Yeah, and we see yours too," Marty continued, with the shoe-shine wit. "We're just glad we're not on the end of it!"

"Man, that's too bad," I said, feeling not one bit sorry for these assholes. I hoped to hell that gate was padlocked, and a For Sale sign up when they got there, not without mention, Cook must've sold all these fools on them tickets I sold him on, and they bought it. My man Cook, and oh man, now that shit was the real hoot!

"No, it's not," the smart aleck shoe-shine kit threw at my side. "It's only too bad that you think it's too bad," he said, once more laughing to a strenuous chorus of hard 'hahahaha's.

As a kid I used to go out of my way to spare the life of creatures like these, but these two took everything inside of me not to want to squish like bed bugs.

'Hahaha,' the laughter chorused on, "He wants to squish us like bed bugs but can't," the teary egg Maurice laughed as they both turned and walked off.

I stood there watching the two coffin heads for a minute, when this slim goodie slid beside me. "If you drink a little of this juice, you won't be so transparent," the slim goodie coyly slipped beneath my thin skin.

Of course I recoiled. It was going to take some getting used to that smell. Slim goodies' scent was about ten times worse than Cook's.

"Oh, it smells bad, but it gives you power," the slim goodie said.

46

And that's how I got my power back...well, some of it. So I owe Cinderella *'Cindy'* Cook one. Instead of sticking him at the back of a line, I'll try slipping him somewhere in the middle. Haha! *'You know I'm kidding right?'*

Main point is realizing I don't know everything. Although I'm pretty smart on many things, I can be a guessing nimrod at times too. Still, and regardless, I shouldn't have lost power like that.

I had to stay away from my snookums for a few days, and that was pretty rough. But when I heard them scoffing about the smell in the house and looking for ways to kill it, I got out of the house and slept in a tree just outside of her bedroom window. By the time I eased back into the house, Eric had returned, forcing me to play catch-up.

He walked in the house, little linen suit wrinkled as if he slept all five days in it, and laid his briefcase on the table like he'd lost all his quarters in a slot machine.

My tookus was upstairs in the bedroom, probably typing up another brilliant story. Only June was in the kitchen when he walked in. She was standing at the sink peeling vegetables, with her back facing him.

"So how'd everything work out," she softly asked.

"Aah," he sighed. "I think I retired at the right time," he said, slumping in a chair and heavily throwing an arm up on the table beside the briefcase.

June continued quietly chopping vegetables, keeping her back to him, only slightly turning in a diagonal position so as not to be so offensive.

I could see her face. It looked like she'd forgiven him, though she looked pissed too.

"Well, aren't you going to tell me you told me so," he sighed when his wussed-up apologetic tone went nowhere.

"Tell you so about what," she replied, scooping a handful of vegetables off the cutting board and dumping them into a boiling pot of water.

"...Tell me I shouldn't have gone," he said staring into the table. I wanted to jump inside his head at this point, to get a lead on what was going on, but having just fizzed into the house myself, I was concerned about fizzing up that god-awful odor, or worse, finding out all of my powers hadn't been restored and end up stuck in that putz's head! Imagine that shit. Being trapped inside a wuss. Nothing could be worse. Well, that's except for getting trapped inside a mosquito. Skeetas have to be the absolute last thing to get trapped inside.

June continued on with her chores, preparing one of her gourmet meals, as if Eric wasn't in the room.

"Sweetie, her family moved out of the state," he said, as if this would clear up the fact he ignored her plea.

"Oh! So you did go on and tried to pry into her past anyway!" June hissed spinning around, clutching a large ten-inch chopping knife.

"No June, I did not," Eric said like the yanky doodle yodle he was. "I would never do that to you... or to us. You were 100% right. I would have never forgiven myself had I gone against your wishes and messed up what we have. You and Caitlyn mean the world to me right now," he said out of a puppy-dog look that told me he meant it.

June let her shoulders drop as she gently laid the knife on the drain board, exchanging the dragon guise for a kitten ensemble. She walked over to him and dropped to her knees, taking his hands into hers.

'Oh Lord,' I thought, 'do I really have to witness this?' It's a bitch having to be subjected to witnessing folks make up all lovey-dovey right in front of you when you don't have anyone. I was too glad to hear my snookums coming down the stairs squealing, "Uncle Eric! Uncle Eric! Did they like my story!?!"

June stood up and moved aside, letting my peaches push her way between them to wrap her dainty arms around her Uncle Eric. *Damn. I don't think I'll ever get used to her loving that guy!*

"So what did they say?" she beamed, bright eyes staring up into his face. *Yeah, I hated this part too.*

But my peaches is just like her daddy. We might see out of rose petal lens, but we get straight to the point.

"Darling, they loved your story. You are going to be the next big superstar," Eric said, smiling down on my tookus, brushing her bangs away from her eyes. "Everyone is going to want your autograph."

"What's that? What's an autograph," my snookums asked.

Eric and June exchanged a quick glance. I wasn't sure what to make of it, but settled down when I saw them grow them warm smiles again, turning them back onto my peach.

47

Okay, so I found out I couldn't slip inside my snookums any more. And I also found out Eric was the biggest poker face liar I'd ever known! *(More on the poker face later).*

I was more wrapped up with my tookus not wanting me inside her; a major disappointment that had me feeling quite low.

I know I said earlier, how I didn't like going inside her for fear of exploding, but I misassessed some intel. Then I was a real rookie about the after life, spooling my thoughts off willy-nilly. I assumed I knew how to handle myself when traveling in and out of humans, especially when it came to my darling daughter. But here's the thing.

I could get inside June and Eric okay, except who'd want to be inside them with the way they'd been carrying on? All that lovey-dovey talk—kissing and necking got me ill. I'm not sure how I may have dealt with one of Eric's necks sneaking up on me from behind while I was inside his wife trying to figure things out. He might end up short one less neck, which reminds me, I need to take that rant back. I actually learned something else about us cells, but more on that to come.

The horror of my snookums growing up, I guess... was a lot for this daddy to bear. I tried once more to slip inside of her while she was asleep, easing in right around the back of her knees, where I was sure she wouldn't see me. But clear as day I heard her say, "daddy, no! I told you I can take care of myself now!" And she shook her leg, shaking me off of her, almost mushing me in the process.

I was so ashamed...and hurt. That night I zipped off to a tree to sleep, where I've been sleeping every night. I'm too afraid to even go in the house now, though I do, hanging out in odd places like bookcases, between books, or underneath rugs, and behind portraits and whatnot.

So far *(save for what I didn't know, but know now)* things generally have been on the up and up copacetic. My snookums is a happy little camper, excited about the attention June and Eric have been pouring over her and her story. And I am... well you probably know how I feel about the matter.

It was another day of book stuff, this time my darling jewel and June were driving to meet the woman who'd be designing the book cover. June was driving, while my snookums sat in the passenger seat, and I hung upside down, suspended from the interior light fixture. A spinning day it was. Just gorgeous. Not a cloud in the sky. Sunshine as far as common eyesight could see, and then my tookus spoke up.

"I change my mind," she suddenly said. "I don't want my story to have no title. I just want my name on the front cover."

June smiled, and briefly glanced over at my tookus. "Honey, every book must have a title. You don't like Lock Box anymore?"

"It's all right...I just don't want it on my cover," my tookus said.

"Well I'm not sure it can be published without a title," June said. "Every book has to have a title."

"Not mines," my sweetums smacked back. *Now tell me if she is not the best example of a budding entrepreneurial.* Not even a teenager all the way, and already she has that individualist spirit. A girl like my little peach can go a long ways I beamed, despite casting her daddy aside.

"Let's think about it a while more," June said, pulling up in a driveway facing a modestly rambling white home.

I hopped out of the car with my snookums and June, and waited for the owner to open the door. It took a minute, which gave me and my little tookus more than we needed to stare at these garnishings decorating that giant storm door.

Yes, holy mackerel! This wasn't an average storm door. This storm door was one grand piece of artwork. I'm saying parades hadn't cleared all of Main Streets *(and I'm talking 4th of July parades),* but yet this lady had Christmas wreaths, hollies, mistletoes, bells, yarn, and just name it, sculpted to this door. Never in any life have I witnessed decor *(something that's supposed to be calming, and peaceful, and generally beautiful),* culminate into a hectic homemade suicidal combustion of nomadic art.

Mackerel made from straw was glued to the door, *(Elmer's glue)*what made *holy* mackerel my initial choice of explaining what me and my tookus...and of course June too, faced. I only excluded June because she was smiling. My tookus and I weren't. We had the same expression. Ill!

A porcupine helped open the door. Yes, the door handle—and again, holy mackerel! Moccasins framed the doormat—I mean, do we ALL agree? Get the point? Must I describe more...like the summery sea-shells', the noisy wind chimes, and the loose goose that I'm going to take a wild guess speculating was a *'Mistletoe?'* Whoever this door belonged to had to be a piece of work. Only unusual people with uncontrollable bursts of resentful energy and creativity live behind doors like this.

And sure enough, the love of my future opened the door, WIDE, as wide as her smile, and girth and mirth combined. She left no room to spare. We barely squoze by. And yes, that would include me too.

"Hello June," she sang, sounding like a sheet of music when she moved, pushing the storm door *'with all those trappings'* outwards. "And you must be Caitlyn," she crooned, looking down on my snookums as she invited them inside.

"I'm Iris Simpson," said the woman of many women, once we were all inside. And don't think I hadn't counted all these women in this one. There was a woman on each arm, one beneath her chin, a few wrapped around her ankles, three or four on each knee—respectively, and too many to count hanging around her posterior. She was a lot of woman, tripling in effect when considering her bubbly personality. She could pass for a jolly Santa if only she had a white beard.

What I'm saying is, She Was Gorgeous! Rarely do you run into women of this caliber. Someone who can fill a room and all you notice is how much there is to love.

"You have a lovely place," June said looking up and down and all around, marveling the room where she and my tookus were led.

I mean, if I thought that storm door challenged my vision, then this said nothing compared to what was going on in the room where Iris claimed her most prolific visuals took place.

Not a square inch of wall space was forsaken. Novelties of many originations ensconced every margin of space. Long corridors of walls, and shelves, mantles, the ceiling and floors...just anything with a hard surface were hidden by one-of-a-kind attractions. Paisley print doilies trussed up armrests and the back of the chairs. An elaborate tea party was taking place in two corners of the room—a Cabbage Patch/Raggedy Ann doll tea party that being. There was so much going on in Iris's creative space that everyone's voice sounded heavier, like several octaves up a musical scale heavier.

"Thank you," said Iris. "Why don't you both have a seat," and in the next breath she asked, "would either of you like a cup of tea?" Instantly I looked over at those dolls, one of them holding a porcelain cup sewn to her cloth hand.

"No thank you," June politely declined, *and I could tell,* trying her darnedest to keep that womderful smile in place without screwing up her face. Every time she turned her head a furrow between her brows blossomed.

"Are you sure," Iris asked, pausing midway before continuing her swishy sway headed to the kitchen. Oh man, I loved her sway...each cheek I imagined taking an hour to sway. That's how long this vision was going to stay with me. That meaning, each time I pictured that apple moving, I was going to be seeing each cheek roam up, and then down, an hour at a time.

"It's no bother," Iris added. "I've ordered lunch for us. It should arrive in a few minutes."

It was at that moment, watching Iris turn and swish those heavenly hocks, that I decided she was the woman for me. An ass that great, and that large, I imagined backing up to personally serve me lunch on. I would eat like a King forever.

I don't believe I've ever fallen in love like this. And sure, like most, I've fallen in lust before, many times over, but never in love, where I wanted to skirt beneath that smock and play in that wide range of field until my heart was content.

"So Caitlyn, are you planning on writing a sequel?" Iris asked, returning with a tray of tea, despite June's weak decline.

My snookums looked over at June. She didn't know what a sequel meant.

"Oh, we haven't gotten that far yet," June answered for my peach, before looking over to my snookums to explain what a sequel meant.

My tookus giggled and reached for a cup of tea off the tray. It was the prettiest sight to watch. June had her dressed in a navy sailor dress, tam and all. She looked just like a little princess reaching for the tea with the daintiest little fingers, one that wore a gold pinky ring with a heart hanging off of it.

"Well, this is a great story," Iris said, picking up a copy of the manuscript she had lying on the coffee table.

"I've never read anything so imaginary and realistic at the same time. It definitely reads like a story that should have a sequel."

My snookums carefully sat her cup on the coaster June placed in front of her and bounced once to sit back on the sofa. "I would have to find something to write about first," she said to Iris.

"Well, you don't want to tell your readers what's in the lockbox?" Iris asked.

48

I must confess. I started spending most of my nights over at Iris's house after this visit. Might as well. It sure beat sleeping in trees. Too many crazies out in the open. I kept waking up fighting off everything from wind, to simple black BA-hind bugs thinking I wouldn't knock out their guts if they tried eating me alive.

It was the same thing when I slept inside, away from my snookums. Not being able to nestle up next to her left me open to crazies in the house too. One night a silver worm had gotten hold of my BA-hind and ate me whole. I woke up inside what I first mistook for a pocket. But I knew I hadn't jumped in any coat closet, or clothes hamper. Well, let me put it like this; that silverworm had eighteen legs when it got me, nine on each side, likely thinking it had consumed a delicious meal, but when I got done coming out of it, it ended up with only nine legs, on one side. Yes sirree, you better believe it! I know I'm tasty but I sure did split the son-of-gun right down the middle leaving it with half of everything; nine legs, one eye, and half a head. Hahaha!

Point being; I wanted to be hugged by warmth, and something that could love me back *(not saying I ever used my snookums for this purpose),* but putting all the tapioca on a plate and leaving nothing untouched, Iris was some kind of warm and loving inside; not just outside.

First off, I liked the woman from the start. The way she talked with my snookums, and had read her story, and loved her story. After June and my little writing tiger left, I hung around just to see what she really was up to. You know how some people are. They'll smile up in your face, and throw dirt behind your back.

Well, not Iris. Soon as they left she called a dude named Harry. "I think I just met a prodigy," she said. "This little girl Caitlyn Clapton is even more fascinating and amazing in person," she went on speaking God's gospel unscripted truth.

I didn't bother to hop on the line because I didn't give a damn what this Harry fella thought. I did kind of care who he was, but by then I had swelled so severely that I had to get quick and in a hurry inside Iris. I mean, you must understand, I hadn't taken care of my manly business in quite some time.

I wasn't in there but a burning hot flash when I felt all this shaking and gyrating, and then heard all of this laughing. It was a lot of movable parts inside Iris, slabs of walls that weren't easy moving aside. So I poked the upper part of me out of her to hear what she found so funny.

"Woo, Harry...I'ma have to let you go. I've got something cooking on the stove," she said, all the while gyrating like jello.

Thing was, she was standing in her garden, watering grass, not to mention, she'd just eaten with June and my snookums, which the entire meal had been catered. Wasn't nothing cooking on the stove, at least not then.

I ducked back inside and started punching slabs aside. *'Get out of my way! Get out of my way!'* I punched, until I had made my way to a real juicy spot...you know... the spot where I longed to be. It smelled vinegary and like Dove soap, and felt like a warm bubble bath.

'Ooo, mama mia you sure feel good,' I cooed, taking my good sweet time to enjoy this bubbly bath, when that fierce shaking started happening again. I didn't peek out that time. It would've taken too long to find my way back. Plus some things were happening to me, I hardly wanted interrupted.

The ferocious shaking got more intense. I felt and heard a tumulus eruption headed directly towards me... as if I was in a tunnel and an ocean was coming through.

I didn't have much time to muse on all of this, in fact, it was right after this surmising when I was suddenly and quite violently discharged from a cavity that I couldn't make heads or tails where I'd been ejected from. I saw a string, or maybe a rope, which I had the great dexterity to catch onto as this kind of jovial tide went racing by.

It took a minute or two for things to subside, but soon as I was sure the coast was clear, I swung back inside and hopped back in the tub. And it happened again, this shaking and quaking building up to tsunami force gales flushed me right back out. On that one I flew across the room, landing on a parlor curtain. I looked over, and don't ask how, but somehow Iris was laid back on the stove, legs spread as wide apart as they could go, and were flailing in the air. And her hair was on fire!

It was wild! And for sure crazy. I didn't know what the hell to do, except to fizz into a bag of flour sitting on the counter. It burst open. Flour flew everywhere, dousing out the fire and calming Iris down too. Yeah, it was wicked wild, but hella fun! Hahahaha!!!

And oh, this covers that *'more to come...'*

49

Seeing Iris didn't get me so out of sorts that I neglected my fatherly duties. My snookums may have thought of herself as a grown young woman, but I was still her daddy, and I didn't. I still had a job to do and wasn't neglecting it until I decided her coast was clear...or hell froze over...whichever occurred first!

"I just got a letter from Pinecroft," Eric started, holding his forehead in the palm of his head, finally coming clean with his lying self. "They rejected Caitlyn's book."

"What," June gasped, as I was about to take off. *'They did what!?!'* I screeched so loud I distinctly saw two eyes dart up from the paper Eric gazed down at.

"They said the story was too farfetched, and there was no way they could find an audience for an author as young," Eric whispered, deeply troubled by the letter his elbows rested on.

"Is that what they wrote in the letter," June sighed, disbelieving what she was hearing.

Eric pulled himself up, like climbing out of mud and turned around to face June. "No, they sent a standard rejection letter," he sighed deeply. "But I talked with Mel last night. I think they're salty about that whole ordeal with losing Paula over some of this," he said.

"But what the hell does any of that have to do with a great story," June fumed.

'My point exactly!' No wonder snobby publishers were running fast downhill. They were turning down great literature to chase an almighty buck. Evidently they didn't

know whose daddy they were messing with. I'd show them a snobby almighty buck!

Look, I'd been out there in the limelight. I know what the game is all about. Everybody selling funk chasing the dollar. It didn't matter if the model had not a scruple in her head, and had mass-killed her whole damn family; uncles, aunts, grandparents, the whole clan. So long as she was gorgeous they'd prop her scruple-less BA-hind up on a runway and run with her looks while the loot was hot. And when she, or the loot dried up, they'd dig up her family secrets and sell it to the nearest tabloid.

It never stopped. All of us in the business figured out how to make a buck, from the agents that wiped her slate clean to get her up on the runway, to the judges like me who screwed her, to the grand finnally...crackpot dime a dozen lawyers who milked the legal system until it was bone dry. But what was the benefit to society in all of this? What did it teach any of us? That crime pays!

'Oh, yeah..what was I thinking!?! Crime does pay!'

I headed to Pinecroft to find a few executives so we could enjoy a good old-fashioned crime spree. I couldn't let my snookums be disappointed like that. She was going to be so broken up when she heard this, and no way was I about to let ANYONE break her heart!

I had just gotten airborne when we crossed paths, me and Cindy. He was hooked up to one of those hearse caravans; this one carried a bunch of honies on each side and a gaggle riding shotgun. Jet streaming behind was that god-awful familiar odor, creating a tremendous smelly wake. Blew my ass off my glide slope, instantly!

Knocked off my flight plan and tumbling beneath the caravan I looked up and caught sight of that gown of gook I last remembered Tigga wearing, exfoliating. Under other circumstances I would've really been pissed but *'All be damn,'* I chuckled instead. Cinderella finally won one. He must've gotten Tigga out of my tookus, and not without mention, escaped my payback wrath.

It was a huge relief knowing Tigga wasn't inside my peach any more. Perhaps it was how I got locked out. Fortunately June and Eric were being responsible parents taking good care of my tookums, namely making sure she ate right and didn't entertain the wrong company. Just this small comfort slowed my roll, and kept me from getting bent out of shape about the wake altering my flight path.

Instead of the collision course I had in mind for Pinecroft, for dissing my bookums' story, I headed instead to my big girl's house.

Yeah, I needed to slow up, and stop jumping to conclusions. And like, what was better than killing several birds with one stone? To all the haters, my girl was connected. So, 'F' Pinecroft. And I was about to get some...

...until I got to my girl's place and found Harry in the house. Now, I had never seen this wannabe gigolo before. I only heard them talking on the phone. Far as I could tell, nothing too scandalous seemed to be going on. You know I would've stopped that baloney right away. But I hadn't entirely dismissed this relationship either. After all, he was a man... and you know how I feel about men.

"I just got off the phone with the child's mother," Iris was telling Harry when I got there. "The publisher doesn't want to publish the story, so she wants to cancel our agreement."

'Wait...Whatdt!!!'

"Big deal," Harry hohoho chuckled, looking like Santa off duty and out of uniform. "There's literally thousands of other publishing houses!"

'Ok, I liked this guy's way of thinking.'

"But her husband worked for a publishing giant," Iris sighed. "I think he was a senior editor."

"Umm...that doesn't make sense," said Harry.

"It certainly doesn't," Iris agreed. "His wife said the book was rejected because it's too farfetched."

"And that makes even less sense," Harry added.

"Tell me about it," Iris replied. "Something isn't

adding up here. Now I'm more intrigued."

"It'll pass," 'ole Harry said like passing gas. "I've got a 65-gig thumb drive full of intriguing stories..."

This accident risk, slated for an emergency trip to the hospital, was definitely treading unsafe territory. His 65 gigs paled in comparison to the ethereal devastation I could cause him for dissing my darling so carelessly!

Iris didn't respond to the Billy-goat who I now watched like a hawk, sitting on the rim of the glass he was drinking from; *more of Iris's famous ice-tea.*

And so that you have a good visual of what I faced; Harry was not that bad looking—that's if guys with oblong heads and wide hairy nostrils don't look bad. My problem with Harry was how comfortable he looked sitting on Iris's sofa, *talking shit* as far as I was concerned.

Slouched over and leaning to the side with an arm behind his head, he gingerly held the glass I was sitting on the rim of with the free hand...*pimpish-like*. I was glad his gut sat in his lap. Things may have gotten a lot uglier, a lot quicker if I looked down and caught sight of a form that could easily be mistaken for ...*a weapon.*

I know I shouldn't be so vengeful, but come on now. Fair is fair. I got there first. I didn't even know Iris all that well, but knew enough to know Harry had never made a move on her. That's what he was over there for.

I watched Iris show him the book design she'd been working on, while still sitting on the rim of his glass. He only had a few more swallows left to go.

"That's pretty cool," he said. "I like it..." and he picked up the glass he had sat on the coffee table. "Is it finished," he asked, taking a sip, nearly catching me with his top lip. What saved us from connecting then was on account of it being so slippery around the rim. I slid the opposite way of his lips.

"Just about," Iris said, leaning in to look at the design from a catty-corner incline. "I was waiting for them to send the back matter... before all this..." she sighed.

"...And the title, right?"

"Huh," she frowned before caching his drift. "Oh, yeah...yeah, well the little girl doesn't want a title on the cover, just this image."

"The little girl doesn't want a title on the cover," he huffed mockingly.

"Yes, didn't I tell you? The little girl is actually the author of this book."

"So," he muttered, bringing the glass to his lips. "What's a child know about how a book is made? Hell, writers old as me don't even get to make that decision," he snapped and sipped, this time swallowing me as I slipped around the rim of the glass directly into his mouth. *Oops.*

I tried to be nice though. I kicked around a few of his throat pipes and raked my bristles *(something like fingernails)* up and down over his tonsils. A doctor should've yanked them corroded things out a long time ago anyway.

"Aah," I heard him groan, which at this point I was going to hop on out of him. But something told me to hang tight.

"What's wrong," Iris asked.

"My throat feels scratchy. Say... what's in this tea?"

"Just lemons. It's fresh brewed herbal tea," she replied. "...You think you're allergic to lemons?"

Harry cleared his trake, making distressing scratchy noises. Sounded like a frog trying to clear its throat.

"No," he finally answered, coughing and trying to breathe at the same time. "Can you..." he huffed, puffed, wheezed and coughed, "...bring me a cup of water?"

"Sure," and Iris left his side to head to the kitchen, just when I was about to make my move too.

See, my plan was to catch Iris in the kitchen, alone. And I know it was a little risky. I wasn't sure if she would let me do all the things we did last time, with him there... but I wanted to give it a try. If anything, my aim was to be in a position where I could get Harry to back off if he made a move on Iris. Yes, I was thinking in the realms of major catastrophic sexual dysfunction damage.

But I didn't even get out of his throat before I caught this glimpse of her, the back of her, pouring him a glass of water, when I started to swell...and swell...and swell, and by the time Iris returned with the water, Harry was as blue in the face as Poppa Smurf! Hahaha!

It surprised me when Iris sucked me out of his throat though. I flew into her mouth with something like open arms while Harry gasped and panted. Eventually he collected himself and took his old snarky BA-hind home.

50

"You know hun, maybe we should give this publisher a chance," June was telling Eric after a phone chat with Iris. I only caught the tail end of it, on account of spending so much time in my new hot shugga-momma.

"This woman I hired to do the book design knows a friend who knows of a publisher that might work with us," June explained.

"Is it one of those do-it-yourself arrangements?" asked the fluff who had nothing!

"I haven't called them yet," June replied. "But have you heard of Lipton Press?"

"Lipton Press?" Eric asked surprised.

"Yes. Harry Roinken is one of their authors."

"Harry Roinken?" Eric asked even more surprised.

Meanwhile I'm like... *'oh God' NO*, please don't let it be Poppa Smurf.

"You've heard of them?" June asked.

"They were our number one enemy," replied the empty yoke.

"But were they repu—"

"—If you call them, just don't mention anything about my working for Pinecroft," Eric blurted.

"But I already did," June replied, looking worried again. "Will it make a big difference? Seems like it should give us an upper hand."

'Unlikely!' Pardon the interruption, but that was my thought, though June was asking all the right questions. It was just that dunce she married. I didn't even need to own

a backtracker *(a device that restores historical events)*. After witnessing Paula's handiwork, and already knowing Mel... plus knowing there was NO DOUBT Mel had him doing some shady shifty shit he 'F'd' up, June had better not use that hang nail for a reference.

"The thing is, I haven't broken the news to Caitlyn. She isn't asking too much about it anymore, but I'm sure she'll be disappointed if we can't make this happen for her," June sighed.

And that reminded me, I'd been so wrapped up sowing the fruits of my essence with my hot shugga mama that I hadn't been doting on my little princess like before. Of course I saw my snookums every day, and tucked her in with June and...*sometimes Eric*...at night, but I neglected little things such as checking over the writing she seemed to be doing outside of the activities June kept her involved in; piano lessons, and tennis, and swimming, and the homeschooling. June ran things pretty much routinely; what allowed me to slip off to be with Iris. If this were a real child-custody battle, I suppose June would be a little salty with me right about now.

I hate to dote on the details of our daily, almost hourly romp sessions, but to keep it short and sweet, me and Iris just about tore her cottage spread apart. There's now a great big gash above the spigot in her master bathroom, in the shower. The legs of one of her dining room chairs gave in too. She pushed it off to the side and has a doll sitting in it, making it off limits for guests. There also used to be a telephone on the wall... in the alcove between the kitchen and dining room. But that's no more... the operative word here being *used to be*. And of course she won't go near the stove when I'm inside her.

But don't take this wrong because we also talk. At least I think of it as talking. She probably wouldn't tell her friends about our late night talks, on account of not wanting to be thought of as creepy. You know how people are about the *hearing voices thing*. Well, it's ten times worse if you claim to talk back to this voice. Mortals didn't dig the clairvoyant thing. Immortals didn't either, but at least they didn't lose friendships over the matter.

"So, when are you going to introduce us to your friend," I overheard, after overhearing Iris's bragging about her *little man friend* she had to entertain. I knew she was speaking of me, since the only other male I ever heard her talking to was the prick who by no means was little.

"Oh no, this one is my secret," Iris chuckled. "He's not the type you take around your single friends until you are sure it's real."

"Well, I hope he's not only keeping you company at night cause that's a bad sign," said the friend.

"Well, it's a good sign for me because I like the vampire types," Iris threw back.

"Oool Iris, you naughty girl," cooed the friend.

I hopped off the line then. Hearing her talking about me like this got me all hot and horny. That night we broke her coffee table in half. I gave that voluptuous body of hers a rest after that. She needed time to get a construction crew in there to repair some of the damage we caused. And too, to be really honest, I wasn't in the best of shape. My BA-hind was –ussy-whipped tired! I had to find me a spot where I wouldn't be thinking the things that would get my jollies all riled up, and at the same time be warm and cozy too.

That's how I ended up lying on the bed, *out of sight of my tookums,* so she couldn't see me watching her.

It had to have been a good two weeks or more since I laid beside her and watched her like this...opening documents with those delicate dainty little tiny fingers, and those tigress pretty lashes flickering and fluttering, competing elegantly against those large dark magnetic mesmerizing angelic eyes, sparkling like diamonds set inside gold. Let me just say, this is a very beautiful little girl I'm describing here. She is perfect in every way, and I'm sure I love her way too much!

At any rate, this evening I wasn't so taken by this love that I wasn't paying attention to what she was typing. Lazily I came upon the passage... '*I love you Jeremy*'.

Jeremy? And I love you?

Who in the hell was Germy, I had no clue, but what I did know, '*the Devil was a LIE*'!

In Curtis T. Cummins' book germy was the damn antichrist. Now, you can take that bit of strap to the stock exchange and cash in your own best seller!

I inched closer to the screen, moving to a vantage point directly north of my snookums' line of vision, but behind the laptop where a maze of wireless lines blocked me from her view.

I think my tookus was trying to write poetry. The verses rhymed and were properly choreographed, but going by my understanding of poetry, when I read the lines back, they didn't sound all that poetic. Not one bit!

> *I love you Jeremy*
> *your mantra strut, your tight cute butt*
> *the way you brush your hair*
> *crush on me,*
> *licking them sweet wet lips,*
> *before parting my hips...*

Huh!?! 'The way who's parting whose motherfuckin' hips?' So, I read the fuck on, my androids standing higher and higher at each stanza. By the time I reached the word '*ooze,*' I was fizzing around the room so hysterically my snookums cried out, "Auntie June, Uncle Eric! There's a bumble bee in my room!"

Both of them came running, June dressed in a red satin camisole, and Eric wearing only briefs, covered by a partially opened robe.

"What's going on Caitlyn?" June asked looking around, up and down and back and forth. Eric just stood there looking.

"Something's in here buzzing. I think it's a bumble bee," my tookus said.

They'd never be able to see me, June and Eric that being, even if they looked their earnest. Only a microscope could see me, which first it would have to find me. I'm not 100% positive, but I have a feeling my tookus can see me, if I'm directly within her line of view. It seems to be more of a sensation however, but I also have a great sense it's tied with that lockbox she described in her book. I sometimes would like to know if this is true, but not at the expense of her being seen as a freak. She's been through enough already.

During my tookus's panic I took flight, hiding in a crevice of her curtains, at the top. The Priscilla curtains are pink, and I'm so microscopic as to be invisible, so there's no way I can be spotted by a human naked eye. But a fly swatter, which June grabbed from the utility closet in my snookums bathroom, could put me on that path like the one I saw Cinderella and the rest of them dead honies on.

"Hun, I think it's gone now," June said, Eric still standing there, looking like the Statue of Liberty, save for the pose...torch...and crown.

"Sweetie, why don't you turn the computer off and get in bed," June said.

"Unt un..." said my snookums. "I'm not sleeping with a bumble bee in my room."

"Tell you what," June said sliding on top of the bed next to my cuddlems. "How about we have a sleepover? If I hear that 'ole bumble bee in here farting around, I'll give him one of these," and she whipped the fly swatter across the air back and forth real hard, making my tookus laugh.

51

Let me spell this out for all the aunties and uncles, and infertile childless teachers and wannabe parents. It's next to impossible caring for, loving and raising children at the same time.

The latest incident involving my snookums was hardly a laughing matter. To all precious timing...and my good fortune, I got a grip on myself. Seeing her snuggled up to June and sleeping so soundly the way she was, I had no other choice but to let go. Didn't stop me from crying though. Oh, I shed enough tears to flood the Pacific and push the Atlantic off a map.

But just think about it, though. A fly swatter! A fucking fly swatter and two little frail arms was more comfort and protection than her daddy who could put Earth on a new rotation if I really wanted to. And yeah, I was locked out of my snookums, but that was only because she didn't want me in there and I was respecting her wish. Like I said, I didn't want to see her upset. She'd been through enough already.

But don't think my pity party carried on for days. The very next morning, after finding myself splat laid out in the carpet and being mashed by two tiny feet, I brushed myself off and fizzed over to my girl's house.

Yeah, must've been a curtain cleaning day for June because there I was raveled up in curtains beneath my snookums two little tiny feet. Instead of taking her time to take the curtains down as June had probably asked her to do, she snatched the whole damn thing off the windows;

rods, brackets, curtains and all...in one yank. But I'm not angry at her. I probably would've done the same thing when I was a kid.

So I fizzed on over to Iris's place to find her cleaning too. She had the music going and with that big BA-hind was swaying, dancing and vacuuming.

'Enjoy yourself...Enjoy yourself...' was the lyric that had that rump moving left and right, shaking both sides of her living room when I fizzed in.

"What are you so happy about," I whispered into her cheek, kissing her on the jaw.

'Enjoy yourself...' she hummed to 'The Jacksons' top hit, bouncing around not expecting me to tickle her where she's most ticklish.

"Oua!" she shrieked, and fell right in step with the lyric shaking more of that *'Enjoy Yourself'* jam.

I watched her for a while longer, actually enjoying myself, watching this beautiful woman shaking the entire house with her rocking behind. You had to see it, or maybe you can just picture it; the moon shaped like a heart dancing beside the sun at midnight, with stars *(those would be me)* bouncing up and down on each hump.

Nothing in the world could beat this visual. Not a thing. I fell asleep gazing at it, wishing there was some way I could marry it. I was ready to sign my life away to be with her vibe forever. Damn dying. We would never part company. Never. For this was what true eternal living was all about.

I woke up to a jewel studded silence, realizing that the moon was gone and the house had stopped vibrating.

"Iris," I called out, as one of her coo-coo clocks on the wall coo-cooed the time. *'It's noon, who's ya' daddy... time for some big ass lovin', who's ya' daddy...'*

—Damn coo-coo. I started to knock it off the wall ...smart ass coo-coo clock, but got a better idea.

"Oh, there you are," I said fizzing out on the sundeck, enjoying the beauty that faced me, trying to think of a way to entice her to get near that damn coo-coo clock. It was a little high up on the wall, but then Iris had a pretty good kick. I'd seen her kick that high.

"Oh, now don't come out here getting me started," she said with one knee raised and a book in her lap.

"Darling, I just wanna talk," I beeped in her ear. "I'm too whipped to start something like that." *A Great Dane lie. I was always ready.*

She took a sip from a frosty glass, smelling of the Daiquiri family, perching her kissable peach-plum lips and wrapping them around a helpless willowy thin straw.

"What is it you want now, Curtis?"

Yes, she knew my name, and who I was, even in my state. Like I mentioned, we'd talked, in depth, many, many times before. I found a way to connect with her, on that real level, fascinated to find out not only more about her, but curious to know about my snookums and the dealings involved in her book being published.

How well did she think the book would sell? Would it be enough money to build my snookums a decent trust fund? And what were any, or all of the pitfalls that could hurt my little treasure? Such as, who might be her competitors? Or enemies? I really wanted to know about those enemies. I planned to take them out before the ball got rolling.

These were things we mostly talked about, when she wasn't telling me how good I made her feel, and how blessed she felt finally meeting me, after years having to court men only known as Madam X. This was her secret identity when she worked upstairs on the third floor in a gentleman's club. During the day she moonlighted as a freelance editor, and graphic designer on the side of tele-marketing work.

All of these endeavors was how she purchased the large spread she lived in. But she never met the right man. Her size was held against her, except for when she worked in the gentleman's club, where clients stashed their *secrets* inside her voluptuous beauty. My girl loved some secrets

...and of course too, the first and only man *(that would be me)* who looked at her as more than a concubine.

I think I should mention before moving on, we broke a door that evening, tore it straight off all three hinges, indeed after Iris kicked that coo-coo off the wall. Well, she didn't quite kick the clock off the wall. She kicked the wall and it gave... in, thus the coo-coo caved in too, when it hit the floor.

'uck you daddy-O,' I think I heard it whine, clucking it's final words. I was so caught up in the swing of things I really didn't hear what that bird said. And after Iris stepped on it, not intentionally of course, but still...after she backed up on it with her ample potato heels, which as a side note I loved to nibble on, but after that... well, there wasn't nothing left to be heard at all after that.

All I have to add is, if June ever came back to visit, she would be so surprised at what shape the house was in. We laughed, Iris and me, all the time about how June had no earthly idea how this introduction to Caitlyn had changed her life...and home. Hahaha!

"I think it's time you and me started talking about a true marriage," I said to Iris.

She didn't hesitate, or choke on her drink, but rather cool as a cucumber sat the glass down and gently replied, "I would love that."

"You would!?!" I was the one surprised. I expected some rebuttal upfront. Something to the tune of, *'I can't marry a spirit.'* Or *'what would my friends say when they don't see anyone standing beside me at the altar?'* Or more to the point, what would her friends say period, about *carrying on with voices,* talking about a man they never once met, or would never see—anywhere?

But that rebuttal never came. Instead Iris sighed, "I don't expect to live much longer, Curtis. I know you avoid traveling near people's hearts, but there is a war going on in my heart threatening to send me on my way."

'Oh my God!' I shrieked inside. Out loud I asked

why she hadn't told me this. I could've helped; in mag-
nanimous ways, whether she wanted to roll out as one in
true everlasting eternity, or let me fix whatever was f'ing
with her heart... so we could continue as is. *You know me...*
Curtis T. Cummins had the power to heal, as well as... well
you know.

Iris was not only my lover, she was a savior, in
more ways than one. Thanks to her, June and Eric landed
a publishing deal for my snookums' book... without the
investigation. It still didn't help me respect Poppa Smurf
any more, but at least she had no romantic interest in him,
especially after she found out he couldn't satisfy her the
way I could...*ahem, thanks to you know who.* Haha!

"Look! Let me just handle this," I said jumping up
about to deal with the problem irking her heart. I wasn't
that selfish to let her transition. Much as I talked about our
forever, who really knew what our future held. I still didn't
know everything there was to know about this cell metabiology. I could come across a presence I liked better. You
know how men are...

But Iris freaked me out.

"No Curtis, don't," she said interrupting my sprint.
"Leave *them* alone. I think I'm ready."

52

I'm sorry, or actually I'm not sorry, but more like regretted I even asked Iris to marry me when I wasn't ready. I know she prophesized my snookums would be okay because she had loving parents to look after her... and yada, yada. Frankly, that forecast was far too damn shaky for my tastes. I had to be certain my snookums would be okay. Until such time, I was clearly not ready.

We didn't part company over it, Iris and me, at least not yet, because I, and this I do apologize for, strung her along... you know...like most men *(and some women)* who get cold feet do.

Almost a whole year had passed since asking Iris to marry me. The Fourth was right around the corner, when her storm door décor was about to look weird again. All that time I had been stringing her along with what heaven and hell was like, and all the rules needed to be followed to get in the one of our choice. You know it...I was stalling. So far there wasn't anyone I wanted to spend my eternity with, but her, and as such, felt obligated to lie my BEE-hind off, or risk her getting away.

One hot night after Iris had kicked two guardrail slats across the yard, just as I fizzed out of her, she looked down at me *(or towards where she sensed I was)*, and said, "Curtis, I know what you've been up to."

I was like, *'huh?'* just knowing I'd been caught.

"I know you've been in my heart, doing the Lord's work fighting my battle," she said in tears.

Look, I was shook up. What was she about to tell me?

I didn't answer. Iris wasn't the type that you could say just any old thing and she'd fall for it. Especially not after I told her all those details about heaven and hell. And especially not after all the lines I'd given her, stringing her along. And plus, adding on to this factor, was the fact that I INDEED had been inside her, dead center in the thick of her heart kicking much ass.

I already said it. I wasn't ready to go, and I didn't want to lose her, so that's just how I fought. I don't know who them fools inside of her were, or where they came from, much less did I even ask since I didn't fucking care, but I got all of them the hell on up out of there. Yes I did. I ran a hook straight through the entire line of them and flung 'em into her food track. From there I theorized they ended up rowing or back-stroking, or however things without a paddle paddled rugged straights, but I'm pretty sure they made it to the sewer.

"So, I guess you feel pretty good then," I replied when the silence got a little too uncomfortable.

"I do Curtis, and I thank you," she smiled, to my instant sigh of relief.

"I don't want you to be alarmed, but now that I feel so much better, I'm going to start working out at the gym," she said, now gazing up at the sky.

Tell me why this didn't sound good? Just like a woman. Fix 'em up and the first thing they want to do is go shopping...for a new man. But I'll tell you this, let me find out she's going to try to make do with that Poppa Smurf I redesigned. I'm still jealous...and I'll be much less nicer.

"Since I expect to be around for a while longer, I just might be able to find me a real man," she said.

I fucking new it! Not to say I didn't deserve it. But all be damn! I said the only thing I could say in such a heartbreaking moment.

"But Iris, I did it because I didn't want you to be in pain while we waited on our first class tickets." I said. *(Like gosh, how many times have these tickets come in handy)?*

"I know Curtis-bun," she started, the bun she used when she wanted me to see things her way. "It's just that I've been doing some thinking, and don't think I'm ready for that life."

Oh hell. I should've known. Once fickle humans start feeling better, next thing that happens is they start imagining they're invincible.

"Iris, you know it would hurt me deeply if you started seeing someone else," I said all choked up. See, I couldn't tell her what I was really thinking. And you know it. If Iris started fooling around with someone else, someone else was going to end up very, very hurt. She wasn't going to win this one, not unless I let her win.

53

We took a break at this point, me and Iris. And it was a civil break. She knew I still had left to deal with this Eric debacle he created. Remember my mention about the poker face liar I saw in him? Yeah, well I finally caught up with him, over at the Glovers, supposedly debriefing them for half the return of that ten grand he laid down.

I caught him a while back during mines and Iris's hot and heavy courting days, but let those visits drag out because my focus was a little haywire. Back then I was telling Iris I almost had the little fish when all I was doing was toying with all of them; Eric...the Glovers... and yeah, my hot shugga mama too.

But my misaligned focus aside, I was hipped to Eric and the Glover's little game; Eric thinking himself shrewd, catching one or the other Glover at home or on the phone, and pumping them for information instead of accepting 80% of the ten grand back. And instead of the Glovers writing Eric a check and being done with it all, they kept stalling, feeding the numskull half-ass leads. For sure things would've come to a head a whole lot sooner had I, of course, not been messing around with who I thought was my one and only main squeeze. MEN!

It was a little comical to be honest. Truthfully, Eric wasn't a wholly bad guy, and neither were the Glovers, or even I for that matter. *Greedy and liars maybe, but not toxic bad.* It's just that *they* happened to be toying with a little girl who had a daddy who wasn't about to let two fools play a game where my tookus was the pawn!

Anyways, my snookums book finally had a release date; Black Friday, just in time for holiday shoppers. The Glovers, and Pinecroft alike, heard about the book release date, giving 'ole Eric a lot more to prove. In his editorial ways he couldn't part from, he wanted this story as big as he could get it—the numskull he was, which I might as well point out this part too...since he wasn't the only numskull I was looking forward to recycling if necessary.

The day Iris and I decided to take this break I said, "Iris, honey, please don't do anything I wouldn't do." She didn't give me an answer, but before I left out I warned her that our break in no way would be an intermission in assuring her sexual needs would be taken care of.

I guess I really just needed a little time to deal with the possibility of her falling in love with another man. I never would hurt anyone I loved, but as for the crumb that stole her heart away from me, that would be another matter. It would gravely depend on my mood and how I saw things. A decent crumb might get my sympathy. But an indecent one...well, I'm sure you know my stance on punk-crumbs.

Back to Eric. This num-chuck weasel hadn't told June anything about his visits to the Glovers, or rather he flat out lied to June about the ten grand. He told her the Glovers had flown to Africa, and found the birth mother who died in a subsequent birth, and would release the info for an additional ten grand.

Of course June didn't want to pay ten grand more just to visit the village where there wouldn't be any way to interact with a deceased birth mother. And the phony-baloney picture he showed her was twice the insult. That person in the photo looked nothing like my snookums.

My tookus was a pretty little angel, with long golden-brown tresses and honey golden-brown complexion. The woman in the picture however, belonged to another set of angels. One that looked unrelated to Earth, and more native of Mars or Venus, or wherever ET hailed from.

I shook my innerlings the day Eric had the gall to show June that picture. I'm glad she noticed the difference, not that it was all that difficult.

But now the book was coming out and Pinecroft and the Glovers heard about it, along with Eric who notwitstanding wanted top dollar and attention on the book. Lipton, the publishers, were of course ecstatic. They didn't have to spend a dime on marketing. Eric was doing it all, telling June nothing about his libelous efforts.

"You might want to tell your lone sharks to tone it down if you don't want your daughter to deal with any long term backlash or controversary," Iris explained.

Now, we're all quite familiar with the backlash or controversary Iris referred to. As for the 'lone sharks,' that's an explanation best saved for another book. Short of it is, no one needed to know Eric *(and his misguided efforts)* spent ten grand to dig up my snookums' birth mother via the famous people-diggers—the Glovers.

But there the log-head was, dressed in one of his favorite Chino-American suits and unbeknownst to his wife, sitting in Four Seasons at the invite of the very people he'd been playing for a publicity plug, not knowing his egghead was the one being played.

"We really congratulate you on your daughter's book ranking in the top ten best pre-sellers," Stephan schmoozed, cutting an eye over at Marge who sat stiff as corn husk, staring through the dweeb's thin little summer blazer... at the exit.

"And yah," Stephan went on, "that was a pretty nice plug you gave us for our research efforts," he said.

The dweeb nodded, with his goofy self, nervous no doubt. I could see the curls at the nape of his neck starting to gel together.

At first I thought to help him out, knowing just what this pair was after, but thought he deserved to sweat a little more. Besides the fact he had no business being there, I didn't like that suit he was wearing.

"We were thinking," Stephan dragged on, taking his time getting to why he arranged the lunch-date, "maybe we can work out a royalty payment for our services."

And that's when the dweeb finally got it. I heard his simple BA-hind gasp.

"But...but..." he stammered, knowing that minutia he glammed up in interviews June knew nothing about, was all hogwash, being asked to pay for services that were never delivered. The swindlers hadn't even dug up any history, on the history he'd already lied to June about.

Simple BA-hind. What he ever did so well for Pinecroft was the greater mystery. But if these swindlers thought they were getting away Scott-free with my tookus' education fund, and her royalties, oh you better believe it, they were ahead of the rest writing their MOTHER FUCK-ING eulogy.

I jumped in Stephan's plate first, looking straight up at the punk-eyed shark. *'Go on toad,'* I taunted, *'go on and stick your fork in the bean sprout don going for broke!'* He did, and then stuck the fork in his mouth. Immediately he excused himself, headed for the restroom. One down, two small fish in a very shallow pond to go.

54

After Stephan's trip to the restroom, where he splashed his face with cold water and apparently tweaked his swindle in the process, I got busy tweaking mines.

And just to note, I didn't want to hurt the old toad. But that guy needed a *'coming to Jesus'* moment, while I pressed his wife to speak the hell up. She didn't want to go along with the scheme in the first place. She begged her simpleton toad to settle the money issue so they could move on to less troubled waters. But nooooooo, simpletons *one & two* wanted to play ball, like most *balls for brains* men. Now here we were. Juggling three balls!

"Every time I hear that man's voice or even get near him, or think about that child, I get a shortness of breath and feel this strange sensation," she told her ball.

Stephan looked at her, as if an odyssey suddenly occurred to him. "You shouldn't feel guilty. He owes us for using our name and blasting it everywhere," the tone deaf guy said.

"And you really believe it's worth all this," Marge barked, patting her chest trying to keep calm. *Yeah, I was inside her, gently tapping her heart.* But she also was having a problem exfoliating that Ad they drafted and posted online, to lure the nitwit *(ball two)* to them. That's what got all these balls in the air. Had not that Ad been posted, this story would be a lot shorter, and true too, my fair-minded self *(ball three)* less one MAJOR clue.

"I think it's worth whatever he's trying to hide," the tone deaf guy shot back.

"But it feels like we're about to make a deal with the devil," Marge replied through clinched teeth.

Whoa...whoa, whoa. While I WAS NOT the Devil, it sounded like Marge definitely was feeling them taps. It was one of my more easygoing tunes. *'Might wanna stop while you're ahead. Don't start none. Won't be none.'*

Stephan stared at Marge, sideways, and kind of cross-eyed. They weren't a chatty couple to begin with. I fizzed by their place a few times and never caught them engaged in discussion. They reminded me of a couple I saw in an Alfred Hitchcock movie. Morbidly weird. Like a science experiment, with the eerie music and low lights. It made me wonder about the catalyst that made these two decide to marry. Picturing them copulating was just out of the question. Hell, if Marge got chills thinking about my tookus, then I mummified each time I saw her laying on her back... and *'four eyes'* above her, humping.

And so as such, I didn't get what that cross-eyed look was all about, why I didn't want to hurt either of these people. Nothing seemed sweeter, and more appropriate than envisioning them one day reading their beautiful granddaughter's book...you know, after 'ole Stephan got through blackmailing the devil out of Eric...

Oh, I'm going to go on and admit it. This was a much more delightful karma.

55

Now, the other fool? Well he returned home sweatier than a shivering criminal watching a reenactment of his dumb BA-hind committing a crime playing out on a surveillance tape...in slow motion.

"Hun, what happened? What's wrong," June asked, seeing her husband so wet.

"Ugh...nothing," he quivered, shaking his head as if trying to shake off the entire lunch-date.

"Something did happen," June insisted. "Tell me what happened. Did you meet with them?"

She knew he was going to meet with the Glovers. She always knew when he was going to meet with them. She just didn't know why, or rather she didn't know the real reason why. So, of course the num-chuck couldn't tell her what had him dripping all over the damn kitchen floor. I had to hop in the num-skull and help him out, to prevent the fool from uttering something so banal I'd have to take him down to shut him up.

"I-I-I almost hit a deer," he whimpered.

And yeah, I know the lie was ridiculous, but then you had to consider who I was dealing with lickety split.

"Did you wreck the car," June wanted to know. Even this wouldn't have explained the amount of sweat wrapped around this dude's ankles. He had to be standing in at least an inch of body fluids.

But I left him on his own from here. I fizzed on out of him and hopped up on the windowsill to get my laugh on. I was ready. Showtime!

"No, the car's fine," Daffy Donald Duck Dick said. "I just think I hurt my back..." and "aah," the simpleton, with his bad-acting self, winced. Dumb ass didn't even realize he grabbed his neck when he winced. But then I guess the neck counts as a back, since they are connected. And I know. So were his feet, knees and elbows. Started to add his head, but I have my doubts about that one.

"Well, Marge just called," June said. "She wants all of us to meet about the book."

Both me and the redlined actor sat straight up on hearing this news, hurt back and all.

"For what?" the num-chuck asked so alarmed I saw all kinds of bells ringing in his eyes.

"I don't know. She just said about the book."

"What do you mean you don't know? Why would you agree to meet with someone and not know why?" said your anus, who had all of a sudden taken to pacing. Back and forth, back and forth. I watched him make ten laps. He was moving really fast, for a back to be hurting so bad.

"Who said I agreed?" June hit him back with.

'Ole your anus was stuck again, caught like a fat rat in a trap. So much for pinging him a good listener, and me too while I'm ribbing the fool. I was so far ahead of the dialogue, I already saw the four of them sitting in that co-pious library and that thin plot spooling around that vast space like tinsel draped around an astronomical clawfoot Spruce tree.

That fool was in trouble, and he knew it. June had only asked very basic simple questions he stumbled over. Sir your anus needed one of them diver oxygen tanks.

56

But then here's where I faltered. When would I determine my snookums was set and didn't need her daddy anymore? She already told me she could take care of herself, in so many words that is. She told me that when she locked me out. And unbelievably, which I can barely bring myself to think, my little tookus was a teen—officially. Can you believe that? She was calling herself a teenager.

Unbelievable.

This meant almost four years had passed since she left the Briggs, which as much as I despised that house, at times I wished for those years back. I guess I don't want my little girl to grow up.

At any rate, I was up on a party streamer June had strung up over the dining room to celebrate my tookus's book... and her sweet thirteenth birthday... observing.

Now, the book wasn't yet in print. My snookums had an advanced copy, which appeased her while a few legal and financial hurdles were cleared. So this party was sort of a symbolic celebration to keep the book dancing in my darling's mind.

Nevertheless, seeing my princess emerging from her bedroom freaked me OUT! *What the !$#! happened!?!*

OMG!!! My tookus's hair was combed to one side, held in place by a fancy clip, looking like a punk-rock rap diva from way back in the 70's! And with those glossy red lips and black four or five inch circles drawn around her eyes...drew my concentration straight to that outfit!

Oh lawd...that outfit!

Seeing MY CHILD, the child I brought into this life, dressed in a mini skirt hugging her little narrow BA-hind and a bra covered by ropes of gold chains, had me swinging like *George in the Jungle* from June's crystal chandeliers. On one swing my grip missed and I ended up severing a party streamer, falling into the cake. Climbing out of the frosting I cleared my lens to get a better look.

This wasn't the same child I saw that morning spooning Frosty Flakes in her mouth. This had to be somebody else's kid.

'*Noooooo...*' I howled in June's head after I was sure my lens were cleared and pried open. '*Where are the parents? Somebody do something! Take charge! Be an adult and cover up my child!*'

But June, and without doubt the anus weasel of the year, acted like my child was dressed perfectly normal. I mean, let's face it. That birth certificate Reba doctored up was a fake. It was no telling if my child was officially a teenager! We could be a whole three/four months off, or years for that matter.

"Caitlyn, your guests will be arriving shortly," June said. "Come help me get this streamer back up here." *Yeah, that was the streamer I severed.*

"Are you and Uncle Eric gonna hang around here when they get here," my child asked.

'*Oh Lord, dear Jesus, Father God of all mercy, please help Curtis T. Cummins, your best friend and child too, who has busted his tail to look after OUR child. I'm not like all those other parents who don't care, or have given up. I care! And damn it, I'm not giving—*'

—But I did. I believe the Iron voice sat my BA-hind down...by the baseboard where I could do the least damage and admit my job was done. Now, I have to admit it was hard. I am a MAN! And we ALL KNOW how hard a man's head is. In my case, my lobe seemed to be made of polytetrafluoroethylene—PTFE—Teflon; the stuff that's supposedly hard as nails.

I listened as June explained how they were going to entertain her friend's parents out on the terrace, where gratefully the Iron voice allowed me to hang out.

I was a mess though. At the rate I was fraying, staying indoors with my tookus and her friends was just not ideal. Everyone at this party could've been faced with an unscheduled, out of an amorphous invisible blue, off the National Weather radar, full blown severe emergencies.

So, I stayed out on the terrace doing what a typical daddy (and MAN) who doesn't want to lose his cool, does. Yes, I obeyed the Iron clad voice and hopped in a bottle of Yak. That's Cognac for the yuppity.

Parenting really is a bitch. That's what I thought on my first lap around the Yak bottle. By my last lap, I was so drunk I wasn't thinking at all. I climbed out of the bottle and hopped on the tip of a large fluffy snout, laughing in this parent's face for a minute before tickling some really pretty toes.

Oh man, you had to hear that woman's laugh. Her whistling shriek reminded me of Elton John's band in his Benny & the Jets' days, maybe minus a player or two. When she kicked me off, sending me hurdling beneath an armpit, I spit out the Speed Stick deodorant and got even busier; hanging on a tongue I caught stuck out there, and plucked a hair between a tightly packed cleavage. I pinched a BA-hind too. That one yelped and fanned me away, but oh man, you had to see the dirty looks she got.

The funniest though, was the senior of the bunch, a white-haired woman who wore red panties. She left the party early, zig-zagging to the door, which earned her a whole bunch of lacerated glares.

All in all, that party was a blast. I didn't disturb my tookus once. I let her enjoy her sweet 13th birthday party without her daddy's interference. Unfortunately June and Eric weren't as pleased.

"What in the devil was wrong with Kate," asked Eric. "It was like she had something up her skirt."

Yeah, she did. Me.

"I don't know," June replied. "I've never seen her like that," she muttered.

"And Amanda's mother, what was all that giggling about? Are you sure the food wasn't spiked?"

Dazed, June shook her head. "Yeah, she was weird too. I'm just glad we changed our mind about inviting the Glovers...it could've been really embarrassing."

57

...And yeah, to ensure the unlitigated success of my poo bear's book it was *yours truly* who orchestrated the final disconnect with the Glovers. Let's face it. The putz was not going to give up on his own!

I overheard Eric, the old practicing num-chuck he was, trying to pull another fast one while June was in the shower. "Umm...umm... My wife said you wanted to meet," he said, using 49 good seconds to make this point, and this was after a 2½-minute introduction. *Better not take any shyster points from this fella, huh?*

"Yes, we're still interested in meeting with you, and your wife and daughter," Marge flatly stated, clearly punctuating they were not interested in meeting with his simple BA-hind alone.

"Well, umm...the thing is, my wife and Caitlyn are going away...tomorrow...for a month," the simpleton lied, whispering like a dope.

"Oh," Marge said surprised. "June didn't indicate this when we spoke."

"Ugh yeah, ummm...well she must've forgotten," the fool continued with the *watch out I'm stupid* lie.

And before drawing out the rest of this birdbrained dialogue, let's clear up what made Marge super skeptical, aside from having personally spoken to June!

First of all, why was the moron whispering? And secondly, I was on the line!

"Well, that's mighty odd," Marge confirmed. "Your wife and Caitlyn are scheduled to meet with Mr. Sweeny next weekend...before the book's National tour launches."

'Ut oh, and wouldja' take a listen at that,' I laughed. The turtle was trapped like Scooby Doo using two stones to wiretap old news. He oughta been ashamed of himself. Even Cinderella wasn't this slow.

And what did the whipped untied shoelace come back with? "They do..." That's all the chump had. Like, whoa there smart whip. Don't blind us with your brights.

Look, if it weren't for my snookums and somewhat June, I would've gladly watched the fluff ball hang himself. But I had to stop this before too many people got hurt. It was killing me just listening to this.

"Yes, they do," Marge snipped, as I climbed into the dufus, so concerned about a guaranteed exit that I slipped in his ear. He rarely used that part of his body and on short notice happened to be the widest passage out.

But no sooner than I enter his barely used ear the first thing I hear is, "ArrrrrrrrrrggggggggHHHHHHH!!!"

'WT'—I hadn't even said...or done anything yet. Well, entering his ear may have tickled a bit, but there was no cause for that type yelling.

I know one thing though. He scared the YKW out of Marge, especially when the turtle dove screamed, "FUUUUUUCK YOOOUUUUUUU!"

I think he was talking about the tickle, though Marge must've assumed he was yelling at her. She ended the call *'abruptly'* and told 'ole Stephan she had cut that final check and was done with that shaky fluke headache.

58

Marge may have been done with Eric, and uninterested in any royalty payments, and Stephan willing to drop the matter for his wife's sake, but Mr. Sweeny was not.

That Mr. Sweeny, a major investor of the swindlers swindling business, and as well an integral investment principal at Lipton Press, let the Glovers know in direct communications they could NOT just walk away from this business opportunity... and would be at the Capital Grille as planned....and promised!

Oh man. Now things were about to get real. See what happens when you start shit for the sake of making loads of unearned money. Let me put it this way. I wasn't the only one sweatin' a lot.

Sweat, let me tell you, Eric did. After running out of excuses to dissuade this meeting, and laughing my *arse* off at this obtuse jingle bell, I got to shivering some too. Would any of these people ever stop!?! And what would it take to curb all of their curosities and let my snookums story be a success as is?

"Hun, I don't see no reason she can't meet some of these sponsors," June says, understandably puzzled by her nitwit's sweating about attending this meeting. She was *naively* under the impression Mr. Sweeny *just* wanted to meet the young prodigy of this incredible novel.

But the *short bus* regular passenger rubbed the back of his neck and walked away, returning 12½-minutes later talking about a producer pitching a movie deal. "Looks like this'll present a scheduling conflict," lied the nitwit.

June knew damn well the fool had no such commitment and flat out told him to change the date. Wasn't no way she was *'calling that woman back'*—again—when *(based on what he always said)* those possible movie deals rarely pan out.

Next he tried to get sick, something like two hours later, in sunny to be damned Pacific West, where temps all week, and the week before that week, stayed in the 80's. Problem here was he couldn't dredge up symptoms that would convince June he was coming down with a virus where she wouldn't race his ass to the hospital to get an official verdict.

But try he did...walking around the house wearing linty old sweaters, holding crumpled tissues, hacking and swiping at his nose every minute and a half. His symptoms cleared up when June told him she and my tookus would go without him. He got better real quick then.

And so now here I was, riding the steering wheel, sliding back and forth, laughing my BE-hind off at the failed rocket excuse-maker looking over one sweaty nose with two poppy eyes trying to get lost.

"Hun, I don't understand why are you in this lane when our exit is next?"

"Oh...oh...I thought we were going to the Grille in Ventura on Hersham Ave..."

Yeah, it was me talking... thinking as fast as I could to spare everyone!'

59

Here's the thing. It's true, something I'm learning and working on, but the Iron voice informed me that both mortals AND immortals must keep in check their own selfish impetuses. *Ahem, that would be me.* I can't always go around seeking revenge and persecuting those *'I'* believe deserve *it* because there's one more consequence to heaven and hell I omitted, and not unintentionally.

It's next to impossible to punish a deserving soul without hurting an innocent soul, often many innocents... such as my tookums, as what I'm currently experiencing. Besetting a blameless being, I, by default become a product of that upset.

Like, take Shirley, *and sssh,* Shirley was/is a booty call I'd been seeing on the side...you know...unbeknownst to my big gal. Long story for another venue. The point I'm getting at here is Shirley moved into an old dilapidated apartment trying to cut costs, and ended up getting into a nasty dispute with her landlord for turning off her heat and not living up to his promise to repaint the place.

Well... her mother, who lived with her, got ill, died, and for the next few weeks the fight was on between my side piece and this slum landlord. When I learned what was going on I was about to assist, except the mother who transitioned to hell, and from there the Causeway, eventually made her way back to deal with the landlord. That old bitter woman got all up in that man's head. She turned him batty as a fruitcake. Had him wielding axes and whatnot, fussing and swinging at anyone...or anything in front of him, from tenants to air. One night he got so dissorted that he burned the unit down...DOWN to the ground!

But this didn't end the war. The unhoused tenants and community of activists, plus family, friends and everyone who heard the story took sides. *BTW, I wasn't taking anyone's side.* I was just shocked to swing by the place, expecting to hook up with my side piece, only to find a big gutted hole in the block. I was pissed! Messed up all my plans, which speaking of all those affected, *that one little spat f'd up a lot of other lives.* Just on my annoyance alone, I broke up a half dozen relationships on account of my horny rampage. *Yeah, there were as well a couple of funerals resulting from my involvment.* And still, the whole point I'm stressing; Karma is a bitch!

As such, as much as I would've reveled in Eric's misery, this all encompassing meeting simply could not take place. June, and my tookus especially, plus me...*let's add in here,* would never recover from the scandal where this *'upmarket'* promotion looked headed.

Seriously! I brag a lot about selling tickets to the back of lines for anyone or thing tumultously crossing my path, but for the first time since my transition I really and truly wanted to make Eric disappear...FOR GOOD!

No matter how bad I needed a good laugh, I had to intervene.

Eric missed the exit, purposely of course, in which I used this time he circled the correct exit, to fizz ahead to the restaurant where the parties to this savagery were seated at a reserved table... waiting for the real star of this show—my sweet innocent snookums—who DID NOT deserve to be tabloid fodder.

Yeah, Stephan and Marge...*the DNA swindlers,* and Mr. Sweeny...*the money pimp,* plus two of his guests...Mr. Rosen and Angela Zwelwicky...*both media sluts,* and Karen Olney ...*CEO, Director and Senior Editor of Lipton Press* sat around one boxy table, dollar signs igniting their eyes, waiting on my peach.

Naturally, with this many *compelling* people sitting in one space, in such close proximity, blowing up the place occurred to me first. It was a lazy thought, but suitable for a desperate thinker. I had to be effective—quickly.

But see, I didn't. Instead, I flew in the kitchen. Why the kitchen, I haven't the faintest clue, but there I was, thinking fast, as fast as I could anyway, and acting faster when I saw it.

Beneath a rack of platters about to be hand carried out by servers were two of the largest rats on the planet. They were so large that cube size breadcrumbs were visible beneath their toenails. One was even holding down a brown roach with legs longer than many of the supermodels I used to judge. How they managed to fit beneath that rack without being noticed, I don't know. But there they were, and there I was, desperate.

The three of us spotted each other at the same time. A lot of humans don't know this, but rats have extra violent sensors in their eyes. And yes, I did mean extra VIOLENT sensors. It looks like a regular eye beneath a microscope, but it's not. At least to the rat it's not.

They looked at me, and I looked at them. "What in the hell are ya'll doing hiding beneath there," I said. "Don't you know you can have this whole joint to yourselves if you took your large fat ASSES out there and told those people to go HOME!?!"

They looked at each other, and I think said, *'Ump, you know...I think he's right.'*

Yeah, I haven't mastered rodent languages, but they got me...strutting off with their half devoured breadcrumbs, tripping one server right there at the swinging doors. Chef-bor-dar-de had just picked up a platter, off the rack they had been hiding beneath, when the trio got tangled up sending the platter, server, and food sailing across the dining room. It caused enough of a commotion to direct at least two-dozen eyes to look down at the floor. Easily the two well-fed rats running across the floor asking everyone to go home, were noticed.

Pandemonium ensued, my cue to get over to the table where the compelling scandal whoremongers were congregated... munching on bread and sipping water.

"Oh dear," one whispered to the other, all of them looking around trying to gage the commotion. "Wonder what's going on?"

'I'll tell you what's up,' I said to that inquiring one. *'You better cue your friends to get the hell up and out of here.'*

Marge was reluctant to move however, being a steward of the proper way to panic. But that was before one of the rats, *at my suggestion,* leaped into her lap. She ...and the others promptly left after that.

"Oh my goodness," June sighed. "I wonder what's going on," she asked no one in particular as they eased up to valet.

"I told you," my snookums said. "We should've told 'dem to meet us at Burger King. They got hamburgers deer too."

Now isn't she just precious? My tookus definitely don't have no stretched out of shape ego, and this is even with a best-seller in the works.

On cue Eric spoke up. "Darling, this doesn't look good. We better get out of here." And without waiting for a reply he took off, damn near catching the valet's sleeve in the door handle.

"But don't you think we should call—"

—But Eric wasn't waiting on a damn thing. He was halfway to the highway *(ahem... with my marching orders)* while June dug in her purse looking for her cellphone.

My tookus turned in her seat, looking out the back window with them *naturally* long adorable lashes, watching people spilling out of the restaurant. "I bet my daddy did dat," I heard my peach clear as the day say.

But June, dialing the Glovers, and Eric, consumed with *getting away,* hadn't heard her. But I heard her. I heard her clear as that day.

60

Obviously my tookus was experiencing a metabiology re-action. At least that's what I thought...which you already know about my thinking.

But here's the real 411. June obviously was going to continue reaching out to the Glovers *(Marge especially)*, because she knew something fishy was up with that clue-less husband of hers. I read her meter; suspicion written all over her heart. She thought his lying bad acting self was a two-timing cheat. So she reached out to Marge, try-ing to get to the bottom of the double-talk, but I blocked the call, reminding her of what mattered most. It was the one thing she ever wanted, and loved most. A child. My precious princess.

As for *the compellers*, they bickered back and forth for a few days, blaming and threatening each other about an incident that really was no one's fault. In the end they divvied their projected loot and cut ties. This meant Mr. Sweeny got all his quarters back, plus a cent on each book my snookums sold. Lipton Press also lost little, except that cent, *and don't worry*...already on it. *Be damned if they thought they were taking one red cent from my snookums pot!*

Those guests also lost little. No photo and tabloid headline for them, but no need to fret about them either. There were more than 8 billion mortals still living above soil; handy to be chased down, photographed, lied about, humiliated and devalued. I only saved one.

It was the Glovers who took a whooping on the balance sheet. WOW! Losing Mr. Sweeny as a client, and being forced to fork over his mils drove these two to the brink of divorce. I don't have to draw out this heated knock down, drag out argument. I'm sure this picture is crystal quality clear, even if I don't know what that damn Sweeny was all choked up around the collar about.

But see, EVERY FUCKING TIME, this is what happens when gluttony, stupidity and fucking with the wrong little girl ALL COLLIDE. Marge and Stephan should have never posted that Ad to lure that dumb ass, and his naive wife, to their door in the first place! Served them right.

Listen. I'm not a prestige type of guy, or soul. And neither was my tookus. Understood? We could care less if but one person, or if no one at all bought the book, so long as it was published professionally, and available in every format a book came in.

With that, I knew what I needed to do, leaving no time for fact checking and more figurings. I had to secure the lockbox if I didn't want June to end up a widow...and my tookus grieving the loss of her beloved Uncle Eric. For some reason I suspected that absolute dunce was NEVER going to quit on his own.

I hopped in Eric, quietly looking in that damn blue screen, and positioned myself beneath his last rib.

"May I have your attention? Everyone, may I please have your attention!?!"

I was talking in microbiology language, to what is called tike-cites. Translated in physical people talk, tike-cites are like a playground of children; normally harmless little cells easily distracted.

Tikes came at once and gathered around, looking something like sleepy guppies in the face.

"I want you all to go down to the souls of this man's feet and stay there until I get back, okay?"

"Un hun," they moaned like baby whales, floating down to the souls of Eric's feet.

And just so everyone is on board with what was going on here. The only time tike-cites got excited, doing more than loafing like stars floated in space, was when a cig-cite invaded a space in the body, or when a cell like me got to ushering them around.

Basically tikes acted something like people, where let's say an official news group announced a severe storm was on the way, and told everyone to run for their lives. Most people would run...whether there was a real threat or not. And they'd run following whoever was in front of them, whether the person was headed towards the storm, or away from it. In other words tikes don't reason, what renders them powerful in the senseless way regular people respond to panic.

Cig-cites, on the other hand, are aggressive and quite powerful. Folks, they are your cancer cells, usually traveling solo, what renders them less powerful than tikes.

Nonetheless, tikes main preoccupation were cigs. Like a weather news blast they were cued to react upon the presence of even one cig. And not that tike-cites were wholly knowledgeable of cigs, strolling around destroying internal organs because they felt like it, tikes were just so afraid of this very dangerous lot, that they would charge them on sight...and usually kill 'em.

Now, why would I want these tikes in a place where they were basically disabled?

Well...and you probably won't believe this. I really did care for the 'ole wuss. These tikes hanging out in the souls of Eric's feet would keep this bad actor off his feet. Hahaha!

See, the absence of these tikes would make Eric incredibly tired, just the way I wanted the puss in boots. While I was away I needed him off his feet, and his hands and mouth so tied up he couldn't think or speak.

"Honey, you look terrible," June said, turning over and seeing pink golf balls weighing down the wusses eyes.

"Ugh..." he moaned, turning away from her groaning, "I'll be alright. Just think I need a little more sleep."

'Oh, buddy...Let me serve YOU! Sleep comin' right up!'

June scrambled out of bed and hurried into her robe. "Let me get some tea going..." and her voice trailed off as she left the room. "Hope it isn't a flu bug. I might have to run to the store...I think we're out of Mucinex."

You know it wasn't a flu bug. He'll be fine. He's in good hands...or should I say...*good company?* Yeah, he'll be well enough that no hospital will admit him, and sick enough that no one will want to deal with him until...

...Well. Until I got back. Hahaha!

61

Not knowing how long I'd be gone, I made one final stop on my way out. I swung by Iris's place to get my loins in check, and just to see how she was doing—to be sure she was satisfied, and understood that in no way my absence meant she was free to hanky-pank! Yes, I was unsure and shaky about out future, but also still, greatly, in lust.

I fizzed in the house, and it was a late hour, something like two–three in the morning, expecting she would be in one of her creative rooms, creating like she normally did at that hour in the night.

'Umm…it's unusually dark and quiet in here,' I noted. One thing about Iris. She did not live in silence. If it wasn't her big behind humping around, it'd be something like that damn coo-coo clock, since departed.

I fizzed around, bumping into things, peeping in rooms on the bottom floor first, before hightailing it upstairs. She only went there to clean, sleep, or entertain me. This I fully knew, why I got a little anxious as I reached the top landing and saw no cleaning, and knew I wasn't *yet* entertaining her.

I had just reached the other side of her closed bedroom door when I heard raucous snoring. *'Ump…'* I mused for what could be a split sec. *'I'd never known or heard Iris snoring like jumbo jets falling to earth…engine-less.'*

Kicked in the bedroom door and there they lay, two huge lumps beneath one thin sheet—stuck together.

I yoked right up, funneling the vilest parts of me into an onion spin. And for you rubberneckers, no one wants to be near me when I'm in a viral spin. I work just like a tornado... only with a wider, but sharper epiccenter.

How dare you! I wailed, in this viral spin, pulling at flab inside a voluminous wally body. My lens were closed so I didn't know whether it was Iris, or who I slammed into. All I know, I was encased by fat doing all I could to rip apart these guts.

Suddenly it felt like I was on a boat, just a rocking, about to cap-size and turn over. But I grabbed hold of a bone and held on, kicking at everything coming near me.

'Fuck with this! Here, fuck with this,' I said swaying, kicking stuff left and right.

A gang of tikes got me though. They must've mistaken me for a cig with all the fuss I kicked up. By the time they realized it was me, seven or eight of them had hurled me into a swell of activity coming up from the South. I found myself wedge between broccoli and a piece of pork chop. It smelled awful.

Next thing I knew, I was flying out of the mouth of the body I jetted into, landing on a broad nose. Lights now on I saw the face of the nose I landed on; a yellow-bone complexioned woman who looked a lot like Iris, except she wasn't. This one had six or seven folds in her forehead. Iris only had three. Plus, this one had ashy coal gray eyes. Iris's eyes were steel black; leafy green when she was happy. And this one had a moustache! Definitely not Iris!

But the thing that got me, and I was thinking all of this in this frantic moment of *hollering and choking and crying and whatnot*...was that if Iris was STANDING in front of me... then who were...

...and that's when I turned around and it hit me. I'll be dern, I had made a terrible mistake.

Something like Santa's reindeer rhyme, it took not a flash to see two other bewildered eyes *(over to my left)* staring at me like agitating dishwater telling me to make like ghost buster and get the hell off this nose. I flew to the window and hid behind the drapes.

"Lord Zelda, what happened," Iris asked, bustling to the bed and leaning over what I came to realize was an unmoving loved one.

"I don't know," said Zelda, her eyes sudsy and still agitating, but on a slower cycle. "She must've had some kind of attack in her sleep."

It was a grisly scene; internal matter sprayed from the ceiling to the floor. My Iris tried to wake the woman anyway, wiping her face with the end of her gown and sheets, to perform CPR. *'Good grief, definitely won't have to be reminded—no more kisses for my kissy poo.'*

Albeit, in much noted seriousness it did occur to me I had to do something. I couldn't leave Iris's home as it was. That little *illogical* conniption I suffered could cost me dearly. Mistakes like this were unacceptable defenses. Taking an innocent life could get me banned from heaven, permanently.

As fast as I had zipped out of the woman and hid behind the curtains, I hightailed it right back to the scene of my crime, making sure not to utter a peep as I slipped back into the body I had been expelled out of.

'Anybody left in here?' I called out in what sounded like the bottom of an echo in an ocean of flesh.

'Nah Junior, they done just carried the soul on outta here,' said an old bent over derelict cell, picking what in human life would be called toes.

Derelict cells are like this. They hold an allegiance to no one or nothing and are the final destructive force to a body. Once their shelter corroded, the body dissolved and their essence moved on, setting up house in whatever life they came by next—be it man, mammal, rodent, insect...didn't matter.

'Listen pee, I got two first class tickets to the gateway if you do me a favor,' I said anyway. Note how I used the word *'gateway.'* That was to clear my conscience. This way there could be no claim I shafted a derelict dealer out of two tickets to heaven. You heard it. *I made no such promise.*

The derelict rose up, lighting up inside, and by god smiled! Ugh! The smile made me do a double-take, and then a triple-take. By Jesus no one would ever believe this joker had once been a human senator.

'You got two tickets, huh?' asked the distrusting…*and disgusting* old senator. *'Show 'em to me and I'll think about it,'* he said.

'Look, I don't have time for that,' I replied irritated. *'Like what the fuck!'* What did it matter to this out of luck A-hole if I was pulling its innerlings? Wasn't like it had anything better scheduled. But I guess it still had its delusional bartering ways, like I had my civil appeasing ways.

'…Damn imbecile still think he working over helpless voters in them damn community centers,' I muttered aloud. *'Don't even know elections are over for his ass!'*

'Put up, or shut up,' the prick said back.

So I put up. I kicked the A-hole out of the body, glad that this favor turned out easier than anticipated. *'Like geez, everybody wanna be swindlers.'* I was going to give the fool a pass to leave the body peacefully, but its attitude saved me the trouble. I just needed the AO cleared so that when I fizzed back with the soul there'd be no nonsense.

I caught up with the hearse carrying the woman's soul before Iris, or that dishwashing-eyed one, called in an official. Once officials throw sheets over humans it's usually over, since officials don't like being wrong.

Lucky for me though, the hearse had broken down. Yeah, they hadn't even cleared the top of the house. In fact, I had zipped almost 100,000 yards past them before I turned back on a hunch, expecting that something like this could've happened.

Those sad mo-joes was all underneath the caravan looking for what, I had no clue. I ended up with all kinds of time to highjack their cargo. And good I had this time because whoever that was in Iris's spare bedroom, she had a heavy ass soul. That woman must've sang on a gospel choir before all this.

I zipped back inside this giant mass of a woman with her soul in tack, and carefully laid it down. Within no time her generator—the heart muscle—cranked up, slowly giving me that sea-sickening rocking gyration.

'Let me get my BA-hind on out of here,' I said to myself, so tired I had forgotten all about sowing my loins with Iris, and definitely had forgotten about the derelict.

'Hey G! Hey G!' the derelict hollered as I poked my lobe out of the body, looking for the safest exit to avoid Iris seeing me. *'Where my tickets? Where my two first-class tickets to heaven you promised me, G!?!'*

62

Look, I won't even go through all the grubhub that went into locating Reba, but will promise that no one got *too much* hurt. The thing was, I was on a serious assignment to get that lockbox and close out this ball busting chapter of my transition. And in due tell...*almost* everyone prevailed.

When I caught up with Reba it was obvious that she had outgrown Charmaine who had taken her in. The child had one child, and one on the way, and thus had reunited with her family. They had moved into a house directly behind the one that burned to the ground *(the one my snookums lived in)*, after a series of back and forth moves that shepherd them from one relative to the next.

Assuming the above was the reason Charmaine eventually returned Reba to her people, trust me, I couldn't blame this social worker. The batch of Briggs Reba hailed from were beyond redemption.

I'm only thankful I figured out where little roughneck Reba kept the lockbox; *the secret my darling shared with her,* and what it was going to take to get it back. Damn! I'm such a nitwit. All that time... and trouble... it took figuring this out!

So now you're gonna have to trust me on what I needed to do to secure this box. As it stands, it's already been a pain in the rear explaining afterlife and how cells work. Just know it was going to be a delicate, hairy, dicey operation; one where...and oh well... we're already well disposed on my swift thinking capabilities.

This might sound real horrible, but the easiest way

to handle the situation would've been to simply get some stuff started right there where I found Reba, lounged up on Irene's favorite spot—the sofa, and grab the box while she was committed to whatever deadly brawl I managed to scrounge up.

As simple of an operation as this is to conceive, I do have scruples, and morals, and as well a plan to retire in absolute peace—heaven! In other words, it was not, and had never been my intention to willy-nilly see anyone hurt. I really like/d Reba. It would've crushed my soul to contribute to her, or her family's troubles. I really cared for these people. After all, they did look after my tookus, and cared for her with their best intentions. What I'm saying here is I owed these people too much to give them any more pain.

All that expressed, as usual I was a little desperate, and there was Reba watching a channel this TV stayed stuck on—TSDN—The Smack Down Network, airing one reality show after the next. When I fizzed in *Court Drama* was on, which had Reba up and down off the sofa.

"Smack that bitch down," she cheered when she was up, followed by silence when the defendant seemed to have heard her coaching.

That's when it came to me, watching Reba in this agitated up and down performance as swarms of kids ran in and out, throwing and breaking stuff cojointly, all while Granny yelled and hollered from upstairs downstairs at children tragically tearing the house apart. TSDN would be a noble vehicle to transport this lockbox on...*I thought.*

I watched Reba a while longer, glued to the TV as if she were a laser pointer. The only time she came off that sofa was when one of them claimants worked her last nerve, or one of the kids got between her laser and the TV.

It was sad, and then funny that them kids knew to roll on the floor when they passed the TV. If they didn't, either a sardine can or spoon would fly in that direction. Reba kept a collection of those tools nearby; can goods and eating utensils, *usually spoons*, just for this purpose.

"Stinky, go git me some more of dem' sardines," she yelled from the sofa, cans strewn all around her.

"But we ain't got nothin' left on da' card Re," a child of about six or seven replied.

"Boy, don't be actin' stupit. You know 'dey got a whole bunch of sardines at da' store! Go on over deer to 33rd Street. Dey got 'em all stacked up deer on da' shelf!" And then she happened to notice a kid standing in her line of view to the TV.

WHOOSH! And there went another can, and her shouting, "MOVE!"

The kid ducked just in time. Reba missed her by inches, only managing to put another chip in the TV. In fact, there were so many chips and cracks in the screen I didn't know how she was able to see the darn picture. But she did, and I know she did, because she rose up off the sofa each time she saw something on it she didn't like.

"What da'—" and there went another can, meeting its target—the TV, just before she yelled, "aww bitch, I should come down deer where you at and whup yo' ass! You know you ain't right!"

That's how I came up with the idea, and felt not an iota of guilt, shame or remorse about it. See, I still hadn't forgot what Granny laid on my mind. As horrid as Reba's life may have seemed, that girl saw herself a success. She was fine with her station in life; one of the few who true, woke up with her chest of troubles like most, but had no complaints. That sofa felt good to her BA-hind. Them shows kept her thoroughly entertained and chill...and her mind off changing this station. I'm saying Reba Briggs was living her best life!

63

Peaches Ludlow was at the reception desk when I arrived. Her nameplate, engraved on a shiny slate of gold, was proudly displayed on top of a polished mahogany desk facing a gorgeous atrium mixed of green marble, sparkling glass, and a spray of gargantuan foliage. Above Peaches Ludlow's head, also embossed on a large plate of gold, were letters spelling TSDN—The Smack Down Network.

Unannounced I breezed in and fizzed through the office gathering how best to orchestrate these people, in this lavishly buxom office, to do or say something that would get Reba up off that sofa, and down at this station, to say and do what I needed her to say and do. If all went swimmingly, my tookus would be set for life.

The people posing in the back offices were the bosses, upgrades of ghetto fabulous Peaches. They called the shots, wore the finest, and sat behind gold-plated nameplates too, but larger, with long names spelled out... some with double middle initials and important creds. People working in the building across the street could read Tim McGhee's plate, and the building sat on the other side of a three-lane divided boulevard...and the workers didn't even have to squint! His nameplate was so big it belonged on the building, rather than on the wall above his head. Man! *This was gonna be fun!*

"Tim, Swanney wanna switch Burlin'game's commercial with a legal app," said a thick shouldered woman wearing a lot of artwork...on her face. She kind of looked like Picasso's work. *(See the Weeping Woman).*

"Apps is hot right now, 'specially the legal apps," continued the weeping portrait. "I jus' gotta call on it," she said, looking like a tech-less hussy who couldn't tell the difference between an application, applicator ...or a first gen answering machine.

"A-ight boss lady...I got you," said a chocolate guy wearing a headset and dreds, and answering from across the hall, in a sawed-off boxed room.

'Listen at this', I sulked. *'Their kids and schools jacked up to all be damned while they're running around talking about legal apps?'* Legal app to do what? Sue somebody for a job? ...Or to get an education? Or how about jackin' somebody to get a clue!?!

It pissed me off. I had to fizz my BA-hind back up to the lovely Peaches to calm my hostilities. I looked on her desk, beneath her lunch where a medium size boat of fried chicken and Hush Puppies rested on a small stack of soiled crumpled papers. That's where I saw the greasy program. Bingo! Had my strategy. TSDN's schedule that night included *'Girlfriends Who Got Dumped'*, *'Women Who Hump'*, *'Cheaters Who About to Git Some'*, *'Judge Cranky's Courtroom Drama'*, and the midnight motel special, *'Who's Ya' Mama'?*

None of these shows had a thing to do with my tookus. I mean, my darling never got dumped. She didn't hump. Wasn't a cheater, and by the time Cranky hit the air, she'd be sound asleep. All this rivalry was for those who made their life the most it was ever going to be; none of my sugar plum's situation, but all of Reba's.

So, I checked in on Reba before fizzing back to the set, just to make sure she didn't have any out-of-pocket plans. She didn't. She was sunken in that special groove in the sofa, staring at a *hoochy* sitcom (on TSDN). Wasn't sure about the name of this one. Like I said. The channel never changed. Reba just laid there staring. This one apparently must've been a little to dry for her tastes. Not enough fists flying, or beeps to silence the vulgarity.

Her favorite shows was the nighttime lineup I saw beside Peaches's lunch. So I got busy, planning to bump the sponsored Ad...*the legal app commercial TSDN planned to slide in, (in lieu of another paid commercial),* for a clip more to Reba's tastes. All I had to do was inspect the low-grade hater-aid swanked up in the station, to figure out which hater would be best suited for my special project.

Chilling in a groove just above the *'h'* in Peaches Ludlow's nameplate I watched all of them strolling around talking trash and thinking they were cute, waiting for my cue. And trust me on this. I wasn't going to be bo-jangling around. This interruption had to be perfect... and swift. Couldn't be no mistakes...or fuddy-duddying around.

It got near the 4pm hour when I heard Peaches get up, just after telling someone *(on the phone)* called Bum, that she would be hooking up with him in a few minutes. This perked me up. Right away I decided Peaches wasn't going to work for this gig, since she and Bum were *hooking up* in a few minutes, and since I believed no one with the clout I saw engraved on them back nameplates would dare let someone with Peaches thick urban lisp get anywhere near the TV controls.

And that's when I saw her; about 10-minutes before Peaches left. She was a flat-faced wide mouth woman who smiled a lot, and whose neck was fully hidden by two pillows jutting out of her blouse. She was knock-kneed too, and had a pancake ass. I disliked her soon as I saw her, even before I heard that radio voice she leaned into, and listeners adored. To me, she sounded chugged full of word salad, mucus and S-H-I...you fill in the rest.

"Hey sweetie," pancake greeted Peaches. "What 'chu do-win in here so late," she asked.

"I had to print the rosters for tomorrow," Peaches said. And let me be first to tell you. This was the biggest commercial lie since Pinnochio pulled his first prank. Both hours I was there, listening to her yik-yakking to Bum and sucking on wing bones and inhaling fries she hadn't lifted one butt cheek to so much as expel some of that gas she expelled on Bum. In fact, she was supposed to have hooked up with him 45 minutes ago.

"Ump," replied pancake, who turned on her heels and twerked her pigeon-toed knocked kneed flat bA-hind self to the back where the big dawgs hung out. *She didn't believe Peaches either.*

So I hightailed it right behind pancake knowing she was going to be my go-to gal. Still didn't know how my game plan would play out, but felt I was on to something. *I'm saying... having my cake and eating it too!*

"Hey mamacita," someone in the back chirped, though I didn't catch who on account of the dude wearing the dreds appearing in a doorway. *'Oh yeah. This dude was going to figure in my plan too...'* I instantly surmised. I could tell by the way he leered at my pancake as she twerked by.

"Did you get the schedule from Peaches," asked the weeper with the big whopper shoulders. "We have to switch some of the commerks," she said, slipping an arm into her jacket Tim *(with the brass billboard hanging in his office)* helped her into. "Me and Tim are headed out for dinner. We should be back before the first one runs," she added.

"Oool...where y'all going," sang pancake, in what I'm sure was her natural nasally collapsed voice. "Bring me a medium boat of wings on ya'll way back."

Apparently pancake could care less about an app, or schedule. All on her mind was food, and by the zig-zag smile shifting her face, she was hoping the bosses were slow eaters. *'Oh yeah, I had my cast! I was cleared for take off!'*

64

5:22pm Tim and the weeping portrait strolled on out, and I rolled out too... to check on Ms. Reba.

It was too cute when I peeked in on her. Seeing that alarm clock, a relic from the turn of the 19th century, standing on one leg, held together by duct tape, and a prayer it kept ticking, made me smile. Obviously some of Teebok's handiwork.

Here this girl had no place of significance to be, but valued the importance of ensuring she didn't miss her favorite shows. Just too cute.

And still, for added protection, as this thing had to work, I had one of the older kids *(June-bug)* go back to the store to pick up a few treats for all the kids. *'Ain't you tired of sardines and that day old homemade food in the frig? Why don't you go on down to Stoffels Corner Mart and get you and the kids some of those pizzas,'* I egged him on.

Now, we all know how large frozen pizzas are right? Well, these pizzas June-bug picked up were bigger than him. Boy couldn't even see ahead of him, he had them pizzas stacked so high. He had to walk slowly, and carefully, looking like a cowboy from the back. Shoppers and the storeowners alike stood there and watched. Poor kid. I couldn't help but chuckle.

The Briggs didn't know it, but this family had such a reputation that each time one of them were caught shop-lifting, the store owner calculated the damage and sent the state the bill...with a cap. So long as they stole less than $1000, the goods taken were *(so to speak)* on the house.

So there was June-bug with three large pizzas up to his face, headed straight to the door thinking, *if he couldn't see the owners, then they probably couldn't see him.* In part he was right. The owners didn't know which one of the Briggs boys it was, but they knew it was one of them. All of them had the same kind of popcorn hair, and acorn shaped heads. Plus, not many were as bold, or dumb enough to head straight for the door with stolen goods rationalizing the way this kid did.

It was a Friday though, *1st of the month,* so there was still over nine hundred dollars left to use up. Usually when it got near to the end of the month, or if they were hungrier than other months, the owners would chase them away, rather than have the police pick them up. The police picking up them kids was a big waste of time and effort. And don't get all bunched up around the collar about any of this. No one lost in this deal. The Briggs weren't ever expected to rise above their circumstances, and they kept work nice and plentiful, and loads of people employed... from social services departments, to medicine and the medical system, all the way up to the judicial system.

6:19pm I joined Tim and the broad shouldered weeping portrait in Shaky's just starting on their salad. And so that I don't have to keep referring to the weeping portrait in this manner, I was glad to learn her name— Matroppolis. Wow. What an ugly name, huh? Now I don't feel so awful giving her them tags. It's rare I do someone like her a favor.

At anyrate there sat Matroppolis and Tim, forking green leaves into their mouths between discussing TV matters of the big-maafa quality.

"See, people like that really get beneath my skin talking all that bullshit about quality," said Tim. He was talking about grievances disgusted viewers had about his network. According to him, they were grouchy old farts, *'talking all that crap about bad TV, and what was wrong with the world.'* "'F' them," he said.

"This is business," he continued fuming. "Business isn't about what's moral. What viewers want to watch and what sells is BUSINESS!" —he damn near shouted across this low budget establishment. Looked like a drug deal going down in every other booth...but oh well...*who am I to judge?* Narcotics do sell. Druggies do love crack, coke and weed especially. To hell with morals. Long as it sells!

"I know that's right," Matroppolis agreed as well.

On this note I was glad we all agreed. Timmothee being the hard knuckled cruddy looking guy who rose up the ranks, acted like he really knew business. So I took off. I hightailed it back over to his business to give HIS viewers more of what they wanted.

Well, I did make a pit stop before entering THE BUSINESS.

I fizzed out West to check on my snookums and Iris. All the AOs had to be secured or else my next, and FINAL operation, would be pointless. And we do want a nice ending, right?

Check...my big girl Iris was good; just a singing her big heart out in church, thanking and praising the Lord for saving who turned out to be a cousin. MAN! I shook my noggin. I mean...Iris's voice was beautiful and all, but Man! That was her cousin!?! Stuck together with her sister like that!?! Was I about to tie my knot with this lot!?! Man!

But my snookums was good too. Still her same lil sweet self. And for that matter, June and Eric seemed content. All of them were in separate rooms; Eric inside his geek machine...June doing dishes...and my peach batting them pretty lashes gazing at whatever it was on her phone she wanted next. No one seemed ruffled about anything of consequence that required my immediate attention.

On the way out I fizzed by the Glovers place too. They weren't home, so I dashed around until I caught up with them; sitting in a crooked law office discussing compensation strategies against the Grille. I shook my noggin. Yeah, they were good too.

65

When I made it back East and slipped into TSDN it was 6:58pm–EST. The cow had head-phones on, and her arms folded across her extra huge torso. *Women Who Hump* was about to roll.

"This is gonna be the episode where Marcella whips that gold-digging tramp's tail for sleeping with her man," mooed the cow. "I can't wait," she smiled merrily.

Dreadlocks, in the box with her, didn't answer. He was busy working controls, I guess to make sure the theme music lined up with the opening credits. And the cow, I also assumed was in position for the first commerk that I further assumed was her job to line up as well.

Now, I had not a clue what this *Women Who Hump* show was about. I hadn't seen the show a day in any of my lives, though based on the title it's probably self evident what was about to air.

However, by 7:02pm no one was humping... yet. But, no sweat, since I can positively assure you this was forthcoming.

The main point here was, it was 7:02pm and the upscale important diners hadn't returned. They had NO idea that in two hours TOPS this worthless business was going to be defunct. This meant Reba was about to go off the cliff to see her favorite TV show she'd taken the time to set her 19th alarm clock for, interrupted—permanently.

And exactly how did all of this tie into uncovering the lockbox? Well, just hang on. We're ALL about to find out... Just How.

While the pancake cow and dreadlocks were busy at the controls, and also trying to catch the humping clips of *Women Who Hump*, I got busy humping the wireless lines the program ran on. I worked that line like I worked Iris the time she kicked out two more rails on her back deck. I wanted to put a dent in this one major line so that it would touch the line that was taping the activity in the sawed-off boxed room. Once I got the line just where I wanted it, and by the way, this is top secret stuff I'm laying out here, but once I got the lines humped together just right, I humped my way into Dreadlocks head.

'Dude, tell the truth...them knockers always did look like something you wanted to play with, didn't they?'

I hadn't met these two individuals a day before this day, but like you already know, I KNOW MEN! This is not a foreign thought for a dude like dreadlocks either, and the dude could have been gay as hell.

But before he could question what he was thinking, or second guess the question I laid on him, I humped my way in front of pancake's gut.

'Ooo darling, don't you just wish you were one of them women on Humpers? Just think, they're getting it, and you're not...though you could...especially since no one is here!'

I fizzed out of pancake and watched her do a little dance, sort of like twitching her legs to keep them closed, as if she had to use the bathroom, while Dreadlocks watching, tried to swallow the large lump in his throat.

'Go on dude! What you waiting on chump! No one is here...no one will know!'

Seconds ahead of lightening-speed I zipped back over to Shakeys. *Good!* Tim and Mat-weeper were just paying their tab. *Funny.* Those two *kind of* helped me out... downing a few suds. *Haha!*

I zipped back over to Reba's and found pizzas strewn from the front door to the parlor. Didn't make it by the sofa Reba laid on, frowning. Slowly I turned my lens on the TV and smiled big.

Whoa! Now this was some damn good reality TV! Them two fools were going hump freaking crazy. The cow was so happy from longing for so long that she was crying, "yes Lord! Yes Lord!" draped over dreadlocks like a limp ragdoll, as he with his pants wrapped around his ankles, humped her some kind of wicked, in a corner of the boxed in room. Cameras rolled meanwhile.

I'm going to guess... *'bet they assumed this was a safe location for humping.'*

"Whad' da'..." was all I heard behind me.

66

The station break never came. That app commerk some-one called to have switched never happened, despite dreadlocks and the cow having completed their humping session in time to move the dials in the right position.

"Shit! Fuck! I don't understand why it's not switch-ing!" dreadlocks panicked, frantically punching keys as if his entire career depended on it. *Which it did.*

At 7:24pm the keys were locked, and no ICON savior in sight. Guess I could've help, except why would I? My role in this situation was done...or rather almost done.

"Did you use the override key," panicked pancake.

"Yeah! Fuck! It's not turning though! It's stuck," fumed poor dreadlocks. He was absolutely correct, like his pants being up, but his fly still open.

I heard the main doors to the suite bang open, and two distinct bodies of movement barreling down the hall-way... towards...dun dun dunnn... the boxed in room.

Timmothee burst in first, "what the fuck is going on in here," he roared. And I do mean he roared. Sounded like the bossy brass nameplate looked, hanging over his woodgrain corporate desk.

"The FUCKIN' keys are stuck," dreadlocks cried. And I do mean the man cried. Tears literally streamed down his cheeks. These apps were serious business. But the stuck keys, messed up commerk and these apps were the least of his concerns. *Of course, and albeit, little did he know.* He still thought there was a snowball chance in hell all would end okay.

The weeping woman Matroppolis flew by tortured dreadlocks and incredulous Tim, over to the controls, as if her career lounged on getting those keys operating too.

"How did this—"

—and the phones started ringing. Tim had already retreated to his lavish office and taken two calls. The guy who ordered the app switch barked at him, but he hung up believing it was a matter of losing one sponsor, which was a big deal, just not as big a deal as what he was about to learn through these calls.

The four of them continued working the controls while trying to answer phones, intermittently checking the program, which was airing correctly. They just missed the clip. That was the key. They had no idea what the rest of the country had seen. No idea.

But they figured it out...when that producer Tim hung up on, called back. I really didn't give a hoot-ninny what was being said on that call, so long as my lens stayed on the prize. Because once the prize showed up, and I had no doubt without any prodding it would, that's when the real gala would be in the bag, and as they say on old time TV, *'it'd be a wrap!'* AKA—A Done Deal!

There was some yelling going on over the phone, behind Tim's closed door. The app producer was having a conniption...a fantastic meltdown he was so wired about what he saw. Normally he didn't even watch the show, and for this very reason. He hated, absolutely abhored smut TV, though had no distaste investing in this beastly medium, so his children attended schools of their choice, and his honey could buy anything money could purchase. And that's just the way he explained his ire; bloated by an unnecessary amount of expletives.

'What the FUCK was that SHIT !!! My fuckin' family had to see that SHIT...waiting on MY commercial that NEVER fuckin' aired!'

Better believe it. That fella was ticked the whuck off. He had his entire family gathered in the family room, waiting to see HIS AD, anticipated to set the family on a Rothschild path ...except that expectation was deferred because that shit never aired. Now Tim was getting an earful on what did air. Sad. And painful. *'Oh well...'*

Back to the trio; dreadlocks, Matroppolis, and the pancake cow, toiling feverishly trying to 'fix it'. Welp, as we all might already know; they figured it out alright, just much too late for damage control. The lever programmed to switch over to commerks hadn't been configured to redo time.

"I wonder if the glitch could've accidentially got mixed up with another broadcast," Matroppolis guessed. She scratched her wig on that one, not yet suspecting irate viewers had seen something far more controversial than anything they'd EVER seen coming out of TSDN studios. *'Oh man! Shit was about to hit the fan... and fly!'*

This was about when dreadlocks and pancake looked *really* worried. Dreadlocks answered one call that confirmed there was a far more serious problem at bay. His wife called and told him *'don't come the fuck home!'*

And pancake too. A girlfriend called clapping for her. "Giiiirrrrrrllllllllll..." was how the greeting began.

Then there was Tim, stepping out of his office, jaws locked...veins thumping around his temples...and eyes the color of *Bailey's Red Velvet.* All attention rotated his way. *'How bad is it,'* was the look on their faces.

"You guys are finished in the business," he hissed. "Finished," he quietly added, before turning on his heels to retreat back to the boss cave.

All three looked at each other. Did this mean they should collect their belongings and clock out? And never come back? Or should they be looking for cover...maybe diving beneath a rock, or perhaps be reaching for passports? Or how about shopping for coffins?

And exactly who was finished? Only Matroppolis wondered.

67

It was half past eight when the TV station broke into the regularly scheduled program to announce *Cheaters Who Gonna Git Caught* would not be showing that night, due to a special news bulletin.

All I heard after that, *and of course I was sitting on the ear of mad as hell, irate you-know-who Briggs,* was "Dooook-kkkky!!! Get me my scraper and go get me my tennis shoes!!!"

'Ha!' Perfect! I jetted back to the station where the mood was long, drawn, and somber.

Dreadlocks was in there walking into walls, and do take this description factually. He literally walked from one wall to the other, pounding it with his fists as he cried. It sure was a pitiful sight to see. I guess it could be said it was all my fault. But people really do have to be better reasoners, and not settle for listening to those voices in their heads. If it's any consolation, I did slide back inside his head and told him it would be okay and to calm down. It wasn't the end of the world. As a matter of fact I said to him, *'the world won't be ending no time soon anyway. The world is slated to turn many years after the last person gets off it. It's your choice dude...'*

After that mid-size deep lecture dreds picked up his beat up leather rucksack, slung it over his shoulder and walked out.

The pancake cow was different. She was in there streaming tears over Matroppolis's desk, begging forgive-ness, *and to keep her job.*

Now, y'all know I was pissed, right? Yeah, it was sad to watch and all. But dreadlocks took it *almost* like a man, and left. Yet this heffa, with her pancakes spread all over Matroppolis's desk, was going to try and insinuate dreadlocks raped her!?! OHTFN!

Hey, I'm a man. So you know what I was about to do. Yep, hump that rump right in front of Matroppolis. But I'm also a man *mostly* in love with one woman, and as well a father who has gone through extraordinary measures to ensure his darling daughter enjoys a good life. As much as my lions aroused me to do so, I couldn't fall off script. The weeping portrait troppolis tickled me though. She was friggin' pissed like me.

"Oh God! Oh, God!" pancake boo-hooed. "I tried to tell y'all a long time ago about Ronnie...*waaa...waa...waaaaaaa...*" she cried.

Now, see why we were so irked by the fake tears. *'Ho please!'* I dutifully inserted. *'We got the fucking tape, okay! If anything, you raped him with all that oh Lord! Yes Lord!'*

And guess what else? Eve's ass got away with eating that apple. Your ass won't!'

After this little meltdown I left. I didn't even bother checking in on Tim. His business act was a rainbow over a fallen crest too. He didn't know it yet, but I did... the best part to this whole saga on its way!

68

Got back to find Reba had made some progress getting off the sofa, but not a whole lot. She had her tennis shoes on and laced up, but she was still stuffing a scraper in her pocketbook.

"Bug, I'ma need you to ride me somewhere," she said, concentrating on positioning her scraper just right, situating the large metal object between welfare cards and prescription papers.

"Where to," June-bug asked, looking down on her with his hands on his hips.

"Boy! Don' be standing 'der lookin' stupit, askin' dees dumb ass questions! Go open da' car doors up so we can git go-win!"

"But how Reeb? You know I 'on't have no wheels like dat," he said backing up, leaning to his left, prepared to duck and run.

Poor kid, not long out of pampers, more concerned Reba would haul off and throw something at him, than the predicament he faced.

Whoosh! Ping! And a low *ssshing* sound followed. Reba had hurled a butter knife and hit a window. And no reason. She used the utensil to force open doors, or cash registers when no one was looking. But it was taking up too much space in her pocketbook. She didn't need it.

"Boy, didn't I jus' say don' be lookin' stupit at me! Now GO next door and git Spiderman's keys den'! Come on now, we gots to go!"

I got concerned. I'd forgotten about Reba's need for immediate transportation. And god help us all if I had to give that child directions.

Of course, too, I'd also forgotten how resourceful them Briggs were.

Minutes later a scrawny weathered looking guy came stumbling in the house on June-bug's heels, holding his head. "Reba, I can't let dis' here youngster drive my car," scrawny whined.

Reba hoisted herself up off the sofa, finally, using both fists to anchor her lift. She wasn't big, though she was seven months along, but moved like she'd been carrying her load for forty-two months, and was 100-years old.

"Shit, I ain't got time for all dis! You drive den!" she snapped at scrawny.

"But where you gone' Reeb?" said scrawny still rubbing his head. "Maybe you should stay here and jus' let me go git what 'chew need."

"Aww no babycakes, Reba's got to take care of this one herself! Dey done fucked with my show, and now I gotta personally deal wif 'da fuck up!"

Reba waddled by June-bug, popping him upside the head and hissing as she rolled her eyes. "You ain't had to hit him like dat," she said, waddling out the door to scrawny's car.

"Reeb, which TV show you want me to take you to?" scrawny asked when he got in the car.

"Just—"

—and before Reba could finish I was in scrawny's head giving him a pastorial speech. *Dude, just follow the lights like your ancestors did. Remember Harriet... the woman called Moses. She found the North Star and followed it.*

And that's what scrawny did.

69

Reba, bless her heart, found the station with no problem. She recognized the pip-smack hand logo, remembering the iconic symbol during times when it blocked her view from seeing what Dina was doing...or wearing. Dina was her favorite cheater, often stuffed in corners due to her rowdy shocking behavior producers tried to hide to curb the lawsuits. Of course Reba didn't agree with this tactic, hiding *her main girl* who had a good point. According to her, *'This was fucked up!'*

Reba hopped out of the car, no longer swaying, and I tagged behind her wide-legged gait. Scrawny stood watch by the car, like the typical *get away* driver—on edge but confused...waiting his cue to hop back in the car and take off.

BAM! Reba slammed her pocketbook against the glass door. Inside the building, closed hours ago, was dark inside, save for a faint light illuminating from a grave distance near where Peaches usually sat. "Open this fuckin' door," Reba yelled at the glass.

I had one better. I slipped inside Matroppolis and pressured her. *'It's about time you escort this one to the exit...'* I was talking about the pancake, still pleading for her job. *'You knew she was a slut to begin with...trying to pass herself off as a virgin! —the Slut!'*

"Rosie, I need you to leave now," Tropplis said. "It's out of my hands now," she softly added.

Y'all got to forgive me for this insertion, but I was like... *'Rosie?'* ...This wide mouth flat cake hardly looked like a Rose, or Rosie. She looked just like the name I gave her. A PANCAKE!

"Oh God, Mary! Please don't do me like this. We go way back," mooed the pancake cow *Rosie.* "You can't do this to me..."

That's when I remembered. *'Oh yeah, that's right. Rosie's got to go.'*

Oh, by the way, I probably should explain. For the most part the station was quiet, just how I wanted things. Several tekkies were called in, pulled out of their beds and away from their families to unbend those wires and fix the problem *I created.* So all the right people were in place; the perfect witnesses to pull off my final act.

'Hey guys,' I put in the tekkies head. *'Please stop what you're doing. Tropplis needs your help putting out a cow.'*

It was kind of funny because the tekkies knew just WHO I was referring to without further description.

They left the utility closet, not in a fantastic hurry, and entered *Tropplis's* office. "Come on Rosie *(and YUCK, I still couldn't get over that name),* it's time to go," one tekky calmly suggested.

"Let's go, NOW," barked Tim. He wasn't so gentle. He peeled Rosie's paws from around Matroppolis's shins and dragged her down the hall wailing about a shoe she lost along the way, and a purse she forgot. He hauled her pancake to the main glass doors where my *special* treat was still slamming her pocketbook against the glass doors.

"Who the hell is that," one of the tekkies asked.

Tim went for his phone... as did two tekkies and a building night watchman. That's where I intervened. The cops were the last people I wanted called. After I got what I wanted, they could call all the fuzz and whatever other law enforcement desired. As for now I didn't require that much help. I punched Rosie in an anger joint causing her knee a jerk reaction. She kicked the phone out of Tim's hand, pissing him off. Oh no. All stopped in their tracks, to assess the situation. *Forget this nonsense, one or all of them seemed to think.* Quickly the watchman unlocked and opened the door. A few moves later Rosie was pushed out ...and *our loyal reality viewer* inadvertently let inside.

Worked like a charm. *I'm smiling.*

"Who'da fuck turned my show off!?!" Reba wanted to know. "I wanna speak wif da manager!" she demanded, immediately upon her entrance.

I zipped right quick into Tim, laughing so hard I thought the man might puke up my voice. *'Mr. big boss man...isn't this you?'*

I fizzed out of Tim and flipped into the next one looking peculiarly aggressive. He was a short tekky but I picked up, with them red peppers stuffed inside those large green olive eyes, that he might try to hurt my prize. Like he nearly knocked me out! Man! This joker's head felt like I had cartwheeled into steel. I didn't pass out, but I had to woo this one.

'Isn't she cute,' I teased the steel head. *'But man! Doesn't she look kind of young to be carrying a life? She looks so harmless...'*

Jumped out of the steel olive eyes and cartwheeled back in Tim's head. *'Here's your listening audience boss! The audience your business caters to!'* The dude squinted. I could tell he heard me. *'Now aren't you ashamed of your big goofy self?'* I asked him. *'You're all dressed up in that over-priced suit, standing there in them cheap socks, talking to a kid who could be your daughter. You don't want to embarrass yourself any further do you?'*

Tim hesitated. I could tell he was doing some hard reasoning and thinking. But I didn't have time to wait around on those results.

Back to brass knuckles I made sure I kept his hands where I could see them. *'She's harmless dude...'* I reminded him, and then bit him, once on each knuckle. I saw each hand quiver. Told me he wouldn't be using them for a while. I had spit out some leftover bug juice I kept on me for times such as this. You know...when I needed someone to be still but didn't necessarily want to send them off with those scalped unusable tickets.

Not that this action was even needed with the way Reba was laying down her own tracks. I'm saying that little woman had a way with her point of views.

Still, I went back to the big brassy boss...you know him...Tim, and really let that big ugly suit have it. *"Shame on you,"* I yelled at him. *"How much your mama pay for your degree. Is this going to be a story you think she'll proudly tell her co-workers? Are you proud of your accomplishments?'* I plucked him in the head too. His big ego begged me to do it.

Meanwhile, Reba continued running her mouth. Both of us chopped on these dudes for ruining her night. And these chumps stood there looking at each other and staring, no one sure what next to do or say. None of this was on their minds a minute ago. There had been a major fuck-up and everyone was on edge.

Reba walked on right by them. Wide leg, pregnant and mad, thinking she was dealing with a complete bunch of imbeciles, which of course she was, she headed straight for the important people she presumed were in the back. And you can thank me later. *Hahaha!*

"Are you 'da manager," she asked the first person she encountered, which happened to be the big weeping portrait Matroppolis.

"Who are you," the weeping portrait snapped.

"Who'da fuck wanna know?" Reba clapped back. Are you 'da damn manager!?!"

"Yes I am," Matroppolis huffed. To the contrary this was not her first rodeo. She was raised in a hood too. Only difference, she joined the Army to see the world. So not only did she know a lot more hoods...just as rough and most times tougher, but she knew the language...and how to stop a bad ass.

Ahem, why Troppolis was my main selection.

"Well I wanna know why 'da fuck you turned off my show while I was watchin' it," Reba rowed, matching each word to poking the weeping portrait in the chest.

Matroppolis looked down, watching Reba's small fingers making tiny indents each time she poked her. Slowly she looked up, like Mona Lisa melting off a wall. *Note: I was in Matroppolis's head at this point,* ignoring the guys returning to the suite, all walking by like zombies.

'Isn't this something,' I told Matroppolis. *'This child somehow found the station to voice her passion for your wonderful program. And just look at her, with her little cute self. She's with child too. Now don't you feel just all energetic and great? Humping sure does bring out the best in people, huh?'*

Stepped out of Matroppolis just in time to hear her say, "little girl, if you don't get your hands off me—"

"—Aww bitch what!?! Get my hands off you and you gone' do what? I'll fuckin—"

—And that's when I jumped into Reba.

70

Don't tell me I didn't work it like a magician...or okay, maybe a surgeon. And here's the thing. As I've pointed out over and over and perhaps more repeatedly than probably appreciated, I'm one of the slow ones.

But before celebrating my success, you'd might want to know paramedics did have to be called for the weeping portrait. Emergency technicians came, scooped her up *(and yes, that was some heavy lifting)*, but they got to perform their miracle ER services, administering CPR, shocking her heart back to life before rushing the rest of her to the nearest hospital where she survived, returned home, and as of this ending is very much alive. Now, I don't know about how happy she is, but at the very least she isn't dead.

Reba, on the other hand, was taken away by the law. But she's fine. Sheriffs treated her well, as they knew her well. They released her back to the world she hailed from and... *more on her and her ilk to follow.*

As for the Glovers, the folks at Princeton, *to include my buddy Laticia,* and LOW-retta at Social Services, along with nosey ass Omega and the rest who tried *unsuccessfully, and perhaps unintentionally for some,* to screw up things for my peach, they're ALL out there well and very much alive too. With the exception of the Glovers, who didn't quite win that lawsuit against the restaurant, in fact they lost big time...thanks to their attorney who shared their values, my tookus name has not exited their mouths once. Of course the Glovers think of her often, as my tookus is their offspring. But they have no future plans to go near her, or that damn Eric, or June again.

Yeah, first the Supreme Court would have to over-turn their case, and then commute their sentences before that happened. I seriously doubt they will ever have the energy, not at their age, or in their current situation, which had/has nothing to do with me. Trust me. I did not start their dilemma, nor instigate their troubles. In fact, I did all I could to prevent their outcome. You may have heard it before. Sometimes we meet our match. And boy did they meet theirs, trying to rob people just like them! Man!

As for Pinecroft and TSDN, both businesses made substantial changes to its operations. Pinecroft liquidated its assets and dissolved. Mel was leaving anyway, which once he left that place was posed to fall. To that end TSDN merged with another operation running similar programs.

But guess who they rehired. Yep. Dreadlocks and the cow. *Moo-Who.* Oh, you might want to know the cow was warned upon returning to work; if she tried to press the issue about what went down at TSDN, a jury would get a copy of that famed sex-capade tape. Her peers would get to judge just how sexually harassed she'd been. Also, they stuffed her in a supply closet where few would see or deal with her.

And least I omit the one woman who moved me most. Granny! I really owed this woman, and made sure I repaid my debt to her and hers... in spades!

Yep. I got all up in Tim's head. You know those big politicians you only see around election and no other time, well I broke *my boss man* all the way down to run for office, and win his election, so that he could build a gated community for the Briggs family.

All things found outside this gated area were built inside it—schools, playgrounds, hospitals, stores, churches *(albeit small...to accomodate the few users),* and car lots *(all used),* plus a municipal building to handle welfare monies. Any and every type business or enterprise found in cities were erected inside this gated area; with the exception of one. A prison.

Incentives to live within this community were high for incorrigibles like the Briggs. Rent was negligible, home ownership possible for all who wanted one, and no bars—*jail cell bars that being.* That's what the gate surrounding the community was for.

Incentives for professionals to work within this community were great; especially for doctors, teachers and lawyers. Research grants were plentiful too, for those who enjoyed working with loud, combative residents who stole anything not bolted down or came with the earth.

This system worked. Everyone, except the Briggs, were free to move in the community, and leave at will. Granny's clan, Reba included, were instructed in explicit language; *'if any of you are caught with so much as one toe outside this gate, you'll be dropped in a black hole never to be seen or heard from again.'*

Officials meant it too. One of the Briggs boys' tested this. He stuck a toe across the line on a dare and was never seen or heard from since. And I know. This all sounds cruel. But you heard Granny, and you for darn sure know Reba, and how tired my BA-hind was keeping up with that clan. That is a difficult bunch to live with, which reminds me.

Guess who Reba married?

Tim! That's right. And they tied the knot right there in Rose Gardens where he not only gave his bride a ghetto fabulous wedding, he gave her, her own show. Now what can be a happier ending than that?

Trust me. This tired bA-hind daddy don't give a damn how happy...or disappointed others feel about this arrangement. What matters most is Granny and her brood aren't complaining, and nobody but them are required to live there.

But here's the real deal I just know everyone is hopping on pins and needles to learn. My ass is now chilling in eternity. After all the zipping around I've done, and getting my PhD in afterlife, I deserve it. In heaven it's chill. It's soft. I want for nothing. Need nothing. There is a lot of white, but there's also a lot of entertainment. All I have to do is look left and watch all that activity sprinting back and forth on that Causeway, which by the way, guess who I ran into...

Wait for it...wait for it... waaaaiit for it...

I ran into Rosie! Hahahahaha!

I was SHOCKED! "I thought you got a job at that TV station..." I said whittling my digits trying to remember the name of that network. *(Digits are the equivalent of fingers. When they are whittled it sounds like snapping them).* But you know what that hussy said to me?

"Do I know you!?!"

"No, you don't," I told her. "But everybody knows you," I laughed. I started to add more, except I was just trying to hit it and quit it. *You know, I started to hit it while she was spread all over Matroppolis desk.*

At any rate she told me some long sad story about how she got here, after I fed her a little *ish* about where I recognized her. The girl had major attitude though, but I don't blame myself one bit for her drama. I mean, driving off a bridge!?! Oh hell no! That's all on her.

"So I hear you selling one-way tickets back to the real world," she says all snotty.

"Aww, naw... you heard wrong," I replied.

"Hmmp, ain't what I heard," she smacked back.

See what I mean. Something was seriously wrong with this nome *(nobody).* Talking like this, up here, could get her on the Causeway, at the back of the line *for real.*

I turn and start moving the other way. You don't want to be anywhere near anyone (or thing) talking like this, least you could be found guilty by association. But you know what that hussy said as I moved on?

"You better watch your back!"

Alright. Laugh lines aside. First of all, that chick don't scare me. I have everything where I am, and I do mean e-v-e-r-y-t-h-i-n-g! Air, water, nourishment, safety, entertainment...all of this is free and plentiful. And you get to rest...in style and comfort. Also, there is no worry about the possibility of getting sick and dying. There's no reason to want for anything. Not even happiness.

Only drawback is my big girl Iris. It would've been nice to play around with her in heaven. We jelled so well. But that woman got involved with the church and had forgot all about me. But it's cool, since it was religion that swept her off her feet; and given I wouldn't trade being up here, for anything in the galaxy. Not even her. And not even my snookums... now that I have that eye I can keep on her, and if necessary, lend her some of my essence. *Wink.*

Other Books by the Author

About the Author

RYCJ is a book reviewer, blogger, publisher, and storyteller. Since 2009 she has written dozens of books in a mosaic of genres, and has read and reviewed hundreds of books. She is the ultimate book lover, passionate about reading and writing stories that educates, entertains and inspires.

www.ingramcontent.com/pod-product-compliance
Lightning Source LLC
Chambersburg PA
CBHW011553190726
48287CB00010B/2877